SOLACE
— *for a* —
SINNER

Caroline Roe

BERKLEY PRIME CRIME, NEW YORK

SOLACE FOR A SINNER

A Berkley Prime Crime Book / published by arrangement with the author

PRINTING HISTORY
Berkley Prime Crime edition / December 2000

The Penguin Putnam Inc. World Wide Web site address is
http://www.penguinputnam.com

ISBN: 0-425-17776-9

Berkley Prime Crime Books are published
by The Berkley Publishing Group,
a division of Penguin Putnam Inc.,
375 Hudson Street, New York, New York 10014.
The name BERKLEY PRIME CRIME and the BERKLEY PRIME CRIME
design are trademarks belonging to Penguin Putnam Inc.

PRINTED IN THE UNITED STATES OF AMERICA

10 9 8 7 6 5 4 3 2 1

*This little book is dedicated
to the memory of
that most learned and generous of scholars*

LEONARD BOYLE, O.P.

I would like to thank Professor J. Goering of the Department of Religious Studies at the University of Toronto. Not only did his researches in this area inspire me to create young Joaquim, but he offered generous assistance in sorting out the threads of the Grail legend in the Pyrenees in the twelfth and thirteenth centuries.

I would also like to express my deepest gratitude to the people of Aragon, Catalonia, and Valencia for their unfailing kindness, generosity, and helpfulness, and for answering all those questions.

And as always, any errors are all my own.

I could never have carried on without the help of my editor, my agent, my family, and friends—especially Harry, who clears my path of obstacles.

CAST OF CHARACTERS

Alicia, the placid wife of Master Vincens
Ana, wife of Rodrigue, innkeeper
Astruch, a wealthy and trusting banker
Baptista, a peddler of expensive goods
Bartolomeu, a fishmonger
Berenguer de Cruilles, Bishop of Girona
Bernat sa Frigola, Berenguer's secretary
Caterina, a sweetmeat seller
Daniel, nephew of Ephraim
Dolsa, wife of Ephraim the glovemaker
Ephraim, glovemaker, uncle and guardian of Daniel
Francesc Monterranes, a canon at the cathedral
Gualter Gutiérrez, merchant, dealer in fine leather
Ibrahim, porter and houseman in the house of Isaac
Isaac, a physician in Girona
Joaquim, a goatherd from Taüll, in the mountains
Judith, wife of Isaac
Laura, the young, pretty daughter of Master Vincens
Martí Gutiérrez, Gualter's son
Miriam and Nathan, Isaac and Judith's twins, eight years
   old
Nicholau, Rebecca's husband, Isaac's son-in-law, a scribe
Pedro of Aragon, King of Aragon
Ramon de Orta, canon of the cathedral at Girona
Raquel, daughter of Isaac and Judith
Rebecca, Isaac and Judith's eldest daughter, a Christian
   convert
Sebastià, a wealthy hypochondriac

Shaltiel, a learned rabbi and mystic
Sibilla, Gualter's wife
Vidal de Blanes, abbot of Sant Feliu, outside Girona
Vincens, a gullible and ambitious cloth merchant
Yusuf ibn Hasan, Isaac's apprentice, a ward of the king

PROLOGUE: THE SECRET

High in the Pyrenees, on the northwest edge of the kingdom of Aragon, the village of Taüll lay hidden from the world. The winding road that led up to it was steep and perilous; the meadows that fed its flocks were sparse and rocky. Hemmed in by towering mountain peaks, tumultuous rivers, and deep winter snows, Taüll had slumbered, protected from invasion as far back as the memory of man went.

In truth, most of the villagers believed there was little there to tempt invaders—neither gold, nor rich lands, nor objects of great beauty. The glory of the sun gilding the mountaintops and the dark majesty of the pines wreathed in clouds were no more counted treasures by the villagers than was the soft white of fresh ewe's milk in the pail. If you were to ask the inhabitants of Taüll, they would say that its greatest glory lay in its three churches. Should you climb one of those solid towers that rose high above their houses, they said, up to the bell chamber, you would be closer to heaven than any man or woman living anywhere else might hope to be in this life. Or so they believed, in the Year of Our Lord one thousand three hundred and fifty-three.

Although few would have denied that everyday life there was demanding and sometimes difficult, Taüll looked to be a peaceful place. But even in simple mountain villages, appearances deceive. The placid surface, like a mountain lake's, often concealed turbulent depths. Under its outward calm a momentous secret slumbered like a dragon on its cache of gold, hidden from the world. Now and then, the veil of silence that surrounded it flicked aside and a breath of rumor would escape from the village. Some foreigners from down below, valley dwellers who had made the trip up the mountain, whispered what they had learned on their visits, but few of their neighbors in the valley had been inclined to believe such fanciful tales or to pass them on. The rumors died. A jongleur traveled through once, and fashioned a spirited song about it, but it was generally reckoned to be too extravagant to be true, and the world took it for a poet's fancy.

Those who lived there knew that the simple tale was no poet's fancy. Thirteen hundred years earlier, Joseph of Arimathea—or perhaps his most trusted friend, or someone else entirely—sought safety in this hidden fortress, carrying with him the Holy Grail. The lonely shepherds who grazed their flocks in the vicinity built the Church of Sant Climent to house the holy vessel and do it honor, and in Taüll the Grail remained. Or so went the legend. And there were many who would swear to its truth; when rumors reached them that other villages, or churches, or distant monasteries claimed to have the precious relic, they sneered in confident disbelief.

For centuries it had been safely hidden. No one knew exactly where it was kept; only its guardians—priest and sacristan—were permitted to see it. One of the oldest women in the village insisted that the painting of Our Lady holding the Grail that graces the wall behind the altar had been done when her grandfather was a boy, and that one day he had slipped into the church, seen the flames shooting up from the sacred vessel, and had run, terrified, as far up the mountain as his young legs would carry him. Her grandfather also claimed, she was fond of adding, that the artist who had been allowed to see the Grail to paint it had been struck blind as soon as his painting was finished. But since the monk in question went on to paint many more altarpieces in villages not far away, that contention was difficult to prove.

But even such powerful protectors were not sufficient to safeguard the holy vessel from malice without and treachery within.

ONE

Girona

May 1354

The dinner hour was almost over; the day was unusually hot and Rodrigue's tavern by the river was empty, except for a single customer lingering over his wine. He raised his head at the sound of brisk footsteps coming up the stairway to the main room. A dusty hood appeared above floor level, then an even dustier tunic. With a clatter, the man inside them tossed a staff and a large bundle down on the floor, and drew a deep breath.

"Landlord," he called out, pushing back his hood.

The solitary drinker in the corner glanced at him, noted a head of curling light brown hair, a bright eye, and a handsome face. The newcomer grinned cheerfully at him.

"That smile won't do you much good here," said the customer. "It takes more than a smile to melt Mother Rodrigue's heart." He slumped back to consider his wine cup once again.

The newcomer nodded. "Is anyone stirring?"

Rodrigue's formidable wife appeared in the doorway on the opposite side of the room. "He's asleep," she said. "Can I get you something, or do you want me to wake him?"

"Wake him? Certainly not. Not when I have such a gracious hostess to serve me," he said. "I confess, mistress, that I have walked far today, starting at dawn. A great thirst and hunger came upon me as I passed by your establishment. And here in my hand I have a modest store of coin for the purpose of relieving them. What can you bring me?"

"Wine," she said, in a flat voice. Elegant speech was not prized at Rodrigue's either. "Other than that, there's not much left. Their Majesties are in the city, and a pack of their soldiers were in here. They ate me out of everything but the stewed mutton."

"Hot as it is outside," he said, "stewed mutton sounds like food for the gods, even if it's not dainty enough for His Majesty's troops. Bring me a jug of wine, a large plate of mutton, and half a loaf, if you have one."

"Join me in a cup of this excellent wine," said the stranger to his hostess as he pushed his plate aside.

"I have much to attend to," said the mistress of the establishment. "It's a busy time with all these strangers around. And with a useless lout for a husband, and a boy who's disappeared to God-knows-where, there's no one else to do it."

"He's off to see Don Pedro, that's what. You can't blame him for wanting to look at the King. Come, now," he said, with a wink, "I'm trying to decide if this is where I'd like to stay for the next few months. The fare is excellent as well as hearty, and I would like to know something of the town. You seem a shrewd woman, with a keener eye for those who live here than most. Am I right?"

"There's not many here I don't know a great deal about. More than they realize, if truth be told," she said. "I'll just fetch my cup."

The solitary drinker saw the landlady bring over a cup for herself, decided the world was indeed coming to an end, and left while he still could.

"That's better," said the stranger, filling Mother Rodrigue's cup. "Now sit down where I can see you and tell me about my new neighbors."

"I haven't that much time," said his new landlady.

"I've been everywhere, mistress, and done everything," said the stranger. "Including cooking. I'll help you in the kitchen if you'll sit here awhile and talk."

She gave him a narrow look and then suddenly relaxed. "What do you want to know?"

"I make my living buying and selling," he said briskly, "and it's easier to sell goods to a man if you know something about him. Also it's more profitable to sell to a man who can pay for your goods."

"What kinds of goods?" she asked.

He leaned toward her. "Expensive ones," he said. "You make more money selling gold cups than tin ones. My name is Baptista, and I have heard that there are many here who can afford my wares."

In a large house in the *call,* the Jewish Quarter of Girona, Judith, the physician's wife, was staring at her porter and houseman, Ibrahim. "Give me the message again, Ibrahim," she said. "Exactly as the man said it."

"His Majesty wants to see his ward before vespers, mistress," said Ibrahim.

"That was all?" said Judith.

"Oh. And he give me a letter."

Judith looked at it. "Raquel," she called, at the top of her voice.

"Yes, Mama," said her daughter, looking down into the courtyard.

"Come down here."

"What is it?" asked Raquel, and she quickly ran down the stairs.

"A priest brought a letter."

"Which priest, Mama?"

"I don't know," said her mother in exasperation. "And I don't know what he said. That fool Ibrahim—"

"Oh. Where's the letter?"

Judith handed it over. "What does it say?"

"It's addressed to Papa." Raquel looked carefully at the seal and broke it open. "It bears the royal seal," she said, "and it says, 'His Majesty, Pedro et cetera, et cetera, would be pleased to see his ward, Yusuf ibn Hasan, at the palace of the Bishop, Don Berenguer de Cruilles, before the hour of vespers.' And it is signed, I think, by one of his secretaries."

"Where is Yusuf?" said Judith.

"At his studies," said Raquel. "I was helping him."

"He must be made ready," said her mother, and the entire household, except for Isaac the physician, went into action.

It was well before vespers when the physician's apprentice, clean, in his finest clothes, and very much on his dignity, walked into the episcopal palace for an audience with His Majesty. He was whisked into a room where the King was sitting at a table with a small group of advisers, all of them obviously hard at work. Seated beside His Majesty was Don Vidal de Blanes, abbot of Sant Feliu, a skilled administrator and powerful ally— most of the time—of the Bishop of Girona. He had been recently appointed procurator of the province for the duration of Their Majesties' projected absence from the country. Next to him was the Bishop; the others were officials and functionaries from Barcelona and the court. Yusuf dropped to his knees and bowed until his head touched the stone floor.

Pedro of Aragon looked at him, frowning slightly. "Come now, Yusuf," he said. "To your feet. You must no longer pay your respects in this manner in a Christian court. Save them for your return to your own people."

"Yes, Your Majesty," said the boy, in a startled voice, rising nimbly to his feet.

Don Pedro studied him for a full half minute, as if he were a new problem in logistics. "We hear that you have a horse of your own now," said the King.

"Yes, Your Majesty," said Yusuf. "A bay mare, of excellent breeding, given me—"

"Indeed. We know of that," said Don Pedro. "And we are pleased. We also hear that you ride with great confidence, but in a wild and unschooled manner. It is time you learned the skills of a young man of your breeding. You must devote a substantial part of each day to acquiring them. Don Berenguer," he said, glancing over at the Bishop.

"It shall be done, Your Majesty," murmured the Bishop.

"This is a council of war that we have admitted you to, Yusuf," said Don Pedro. "A wise commander spends many hours listening to others and drawing up plans before he even thinks of picking up a sword."

"My father believed Your Majesty to be the wisest of commanders," said Yusuf.

"War is a complex undertaking, Yusuf," said Don Pedro. "Requiring thought as well as courage. Would you come and fight with us against the Sardinians?"

"Gladly, Your Majesty," said the boy hesitantly. "But I fear I would be of little use to Your Majesty. I cannot even handle a sword anymore. What I learned as a small child I have forgotten, and even that was only with a baby sword."

"That is disgraceful," said His Majesty, his face suddenly contorted with suppressed amusement. "And for one of your age. Is it not, Don Berenguer?"

"It is indeed," said Berenguer, winking at the appalled boy. "At thirteen!"

"And do you still learn much at your master's side?"

"I do, Your Majesty."

"Very well. We shall see," he murmured, half to himself, and returned to his papers. "We shall speak again, before we leave Girona," said Don Pedro. "And do not forget that we intend to include you in our battle plans one of these days."

Berenguer left the chamber a few minutes later and discovered the white-faced boy standing in the middle of the hallway. "Yusuf, Yusuf," he said, clapping him on the shoulder. "His Majesty is well pleased with you. You are growing into a handsome, well-formed young man, it is clear. And that is important to him."

"Then he was not serious about that training, Your Excellency?"

"He was perfectly serious," said the Bishop. "He intends to see that you are trained properly as a courtier. As you ought to be. Now—off you go, and tell your master that by the time Don Pedro and Doña Eleanora leave, I shall require his services without cease for at least month. They run me ragged. And tell him that Don Pedro is well pleased with you."

In addition to planning for war, the royal visitors had to hold court, pass judgments, and inquire with care into the affairs of the city before packing up and traveling on to Rosas, where they were to join their fleet. Finally, the day appointed for their departure came, and they duly left, with an army of mules, a host of guards, and a warehouse of supplies. The moment the last beast passed through the gate of the city, and the massive task of playing host to Their Majesties and their considerable train was over, an exhausted calm settled over Girona.

On the Sunday after their departure, Baptista emerged from the cathedral after Mass, having made up his mind, it would seem, in favor of staying in the city. He inspected the crowd, and then drifted over toward a group of priests—canons at the cathedral—who were standing together near the south portal. By the time the group had broken up, he was standing next to a sober-looking man with a handsome, intelligent face.

"I apologize for intruding on your leisure on a Sunday, Father," said Baptista. "But it was suggested to me—"

"By whom?" said the canon abruptly.

"By a man of some importance in the governing council of the city," said Baptista smoothly. "That gentleman told me that Don Ramon de Orta was the best person to approach in a matter that might be of interest to the cathedral."

"What sort of matter?" asked Orta.

"Let us walk to one side for a few moments and I will tell you something of it." And speaking earnestly in low tones all the while, he drew him farther from the cathedral, away from the gossiping clusters of humanity.

"We will stop here. I have little time today," said Orta impatiently, "and I do not wish to waste it on questions of buying and selling."

"I am fully aware of how busy your life is, Father," said Baptista, "and ordinarily I would not dare to approach you on a matter of this kind, especially on a Sunday. But with an object this rare and precious, and others so anxious to take possession of it, I thought that I must offer it first to someone at the cathedral. As I said, your name was mentioned to me as the most suitable person to discuss the matter with."

"Indeed," said Orta. "And what is this object?"

Baptista leaned forward and whispered its name.

"Come into the garden," said Orta abruptly. "I think it is empty at the moment."

"Thank you, Father," said Baptista.

Orta walked quickly into the garden and headed for a sheltered corner. "Now," he said, "ridiculous as it may seem, I am interested in knowing where this object comes from, how you came to be in possession of it, and what price you are planning to ask for it. We might buy it, if only to avoid the problems that would arise if you sold it to someone else."

"You doubt its authenticity?"

"Of course," said Orta coolly. "Anyone would. What are you asking for it?"

"One thousand gold *maravedís*," said Baptista. "I cannot charge less, and I would not charge more to the Church."

"Ridiculous," said Orta. "But come and see me in a week. By then I shall have been able to consult the Bishop, and can give you an answer."

"I am afraid that I cannot waste that many days while you go, cap in hand, to your bishop and seek permission to talk," said Baptista.

"You are an insolent thief, I have no doubt," said Orta. "And for that reason, I cannot see why I should go to extraordinary efforts to oblige you."

"There are three reasons," said Baptista.

"Three?"

"The other bidders for what I have to sell. Wait a week if you like, Father, but by then it may be gone."

Orta turned and left the garden.

Late the next morning, Baptista left the courtyard of a fine house built on the steepest part of the slope to the south of the *call*. With the air of one who considers himself at home, he let himself out, closed the gate behind him with great care, and walked jauntily down toward the river. It was near the dinner hour at Rodrigue's tavern.

His eye fell on a comfortable-looking merchant, dressed in a tunic of fine cloth, simply made, and belted fashionably very low at the waist. He did not appear to shift direction or to hurry toward the merchant, and yet, somehow, suddenly he was walking at his elbow. The day was fine and the merchant in a mellow frame of mind. They exchanged idle gossip on the weather, the varied attractions of the women passing by, and various other topics completely unimportant to either one.

"Who is that lad over there?" asked Baptista. "He has a rather foreign air for someone in these parts."

"As you would expect," said Gualter—for such was the merchant's name. "He is a foreigner. A Moor, they say."

"That's right," said another man, who had joined in.

"And he is apprenticed to Isaac the physician," said Gualter. "He has come far in the world, too. They say when Master Isaac took him in he was a street urchin. A beggar lad."

"I wonder the physician trusted him in his house," said Baptista.

"I've heard that tale as well. But it cannot be true," said the other man. "He is His Majesty's ward."

"It's because one day he wasn't there, and the next

he was," said Gualter. "People like a good story—and the worse it is, the better they like it. When I asked Master Isaac, he laughed and said only that he was his new apprentice."

"Is he really?" said Baptista. "His Majesty's ward? Why?"

"Who knows?" said Gualter cheerfully. "The world is full of strange occurrences."

"Everyone knows," said the other. "It is because the lad did some great service for His Majesty."

"What could a lad like that have done for His Majesty?" said Baptista.

"I heard," said a fourth man, "that it was his father who had done a great service for His Majesty, and had died in the performing of it. His Majesty is not one to forget those who aid him," he said loyally.

"Or those who attack him," said another man under his breath, drawing a finger across his throat for the benefit of a companion.

The first two shrugged their shoulders and took their leave of Baptista. Their dinner hour was approaching. Both of them had excellent cooks, and appreciated a well-prepared meal too much to arrive home late and out of breath from haste.

"I think I will go over and ask him," said Baptista. "He must be an interesting lad."

By now the street was filled with people heading home for dinner; the encounter between Baptista and the physician's apprentice was watched with great interest by many of them, each for his own reasons.

Not many days later, the bell at the gate awoke Isaac the physician from an uneasy sleep. It had been a long, hot day—even for May—and the bedchamber was still hot and airless. By the time Ibrahim, the houseman and doorkeeper, had started up the stairs to his master's chamber, Isaac was dressed. He needed only his supplies and his apprentice to be ready to leave. "Who is it, Ibrahim?" he asked.

"It is a message from Master Sebastià," said Ibrahim, yawning hugely. "He has been taken bad and wishes you to visit him. Shall I wake Yusuf, Master Isaac?"

"Yes—wake the lad while I fetch my basket. And send Sebastià's manservant in. I wish to speak to him."

"He left," said Ibrahim. "As soon as he gave me the message he just turned and left."

"Very well," said Isaac. "Go and get Yusuf."

There was no need for Isaac's apprentice to lead the blind man through the city on a dark night. The empty streets held no surprises for him, and he could walk through them as quickly as a man who could see—or on a very dark night, even more quickly. But it helped to have someone with him to describe the appearance of the sick man. Not that he thought for an instant that Master Sebastià was sick.

His patient was sitting up in bed, sipping delicately on a cup of watered wine and nibbling on a honey cake. "Oh, Master Isaac," he said, "I am relieved that you are here."

"And what is troubling you, Master Sebastià?"

"My head has been whirling with dizziness—"

"For how long?" asked the physician.

"Since just before the set of sun," he said impatiently. "And I can hardly hear for the ringing in my ears. I awoke in a terrible panic, scarcely able to breathe, and sent for you at once."

"Just a moment," said Isaac. "Say nothing more until I have made a little examination of you. Then I will know more."

When he had finished, he retired to a corner with his

apprentice. "Tell me how he looks, Yusuf."

"Extremely well, lord," said the boy.

"Be precise, Yusuf. Do what Raquel does."

"I beg your pardon, lord. His complexion is somewhat dark, and not too red, but he is not pale. His lips are reddish and healthy looking. His eyes are clear. He doesn't look sick," he added in a whisper.

"Take this down the kitchen, Yusuf," said Isaac. "And have it steeped in hot water. Lots of hot water."

"Yes, lord," said the boy.

"Your apprentice is a clever lad," said Sebastià as soon as Yusuf had left the room.

"He is," said Isaac. "I value him for that, although he is at the very beginning of his studies still."

"I have heard that he is much versed in Eastern lore," said Sebastià. "Is that true?"

"I am afraid that is one of those tales made up by people who seek to thrust more interest into their lives than they already have," said Isaac. "He knows no more than the average lad of his age. He was young when he quit his homeland."

"I liked the tale better the way I heard it from the gossips," said Sebastià.

"That is often the way of things, is it not?" said Isaac. "Now, Master Sebastià. I think there is nothing seriously wrong with you at the moment. Nonetheless, you should take care of yourself. Some people are much affected by the heat. I suspect that is what lies behind this feeling of panic and breathlessness."

"And some people can afford cool groves, fountains to cool themselves, and large houses built to offer shelter from the worst days of summer. What is a poor man like me to do?"

"Rise early, Master Sebastià, and do what must be done in the cool of the morning," said the physician briskly, choosing to take him at his word. "Drink liquids that do not heat the blood, and avoid rich dishes at dinner. I have left you a herbal preparation. It should be steeped in a pitcher of hot water until the liquid becomes dark in color. Let it cool before drinking it. You will find that it helps to keep your body calm and unheated. You may drink as much as you need of it."

"And where is your lovely daughter?" asked Sebastià. "I had hoped to catch a glimpse of her. Not that I don't agree with you about the boy—he does seem a quick sort of lad."

"Oh, he is," said Isaac cheerfully. "But like all boys, he's occasionally a trifle quick to disappear when you need him most."

"Ah, yes," said Sebastià. "Boys. Delightful creatures, but terribly unreliable, I agree."

"And since Raquel works so hard during the day, I prefer to let her sleep at night if I can use Yusuf instead."

"Ah, well, Master Isaac, soon I may no longer require the services of a physician," said Sebastià. "And you will no longer be troubled by me in the night."

"I am sure you will soon recover from this, Master Sebastià," said Isaac. "And live a long life."

"I certainly hope so," said his patient, sounding remarkably cheerful.

TWO

Monday, June 1, 1354

It was only a few nights later when Isaac was awakened from a sound and peaceful sleep at his wife's side by the heavy thump of someone pounding on his gate, and then the clanging of his bell. When the noises were replaced by the insistent voice of Ibrahim, pleading for him to come down, he sat up in his bed with great reluctance.

The heat of May had dissolved the evening before in a spate of cool winds coming down from the mountains. A warm and comfortable bed was a very pleasant place to be, and Isaac quitted his with some regrets.

"What is it, Isaac?" asked his wife, her voice sharp with worry.

"A summons from the palace, my love," he said. "I'm sorry you were disturbed. The Bishop is not well."

"Does the Bishop in his arrogance think nothing of your health, Isaac? Come back to bed. You can visit him in the morning. You, too, need to sleep."

"My dear, I am perfectly well. And the sooner you go back to sleep, the sooner I shall be able to leave and return." He took his long tunic from its peg and slipped it on. "Unless His Excellency is seriously ill, which I do not anticipate, I'm sure I will be home again soon."

As it turned out, Isaac was half right.

He set out with two of the Bishop's Guard and a very sleepy Yusuf to walk the short distance from the *call,* the Jewish Quarter of Girona, to the Bishop's palace, chatting with them of inconsequential matters. The full moon rode high over the city, casting her brilliant light on the cobbled pavements and creating impenetrable, velvety shadows. The three members of the party who could see made their way easily, keeping up with Isaac, who was striding confidently through streets whose slightest irregularities he knew as well as he knew his own house.

It was Yusuf, slowly coming awake, who caught sight of an unexpected black shape in the shadow cast by the palace steps. "What's that?" he asked.

"What do you see?" asked Isaac.

"It looks like a beggar asleep by the steps," said the junior of the guards. "I'll soon have him out of here."

"Let him sleep," said the sergeant, but before he could finish speaking, the guard had prodded the black shape with the butt of his pikestaff. It flopped over with a heavy thud.

"Wake up, you drunken sot," said the guard, giving the flaccid bundle a vigorous shake. Nothing happened. "I think he might be dead, Sergeant," he said at last.

"Well, find out, man," said the sergeant.

"Just a minute. I'll pull him into the light," said the guard.

"Ring for the porter," said the sergeant.

"Leave him," said Isaac, and everyone stopped for a

moment. "I can soon tell you if he's dead." He felt for the neck, and then for the man's chest. "He is. Not only is he dead," said the physician, "but the cause of his death is right under my hand, plunged to the hilt under his ribs."

"Murdered?" said the guard, crossing himself. "Right here on His Excellency's steps?"

"Why not here?" said the sergeant. "Do you think the one who bore the knife concerns himself with His Excellency's feelings? Porter!" he called impatiently.

"What do you want?" asked an ill-tempered voice from inside the door.

"Bring us a lantern," said the sergeant, "and hold it up so I can see."

"What do you have there?" asked the porter, emerging from his cubbyhole with a flickering lantern.

The sergeant bent over the body. "I should have thought you would know. What have you been doing all night, porter?" he asked.

"I sit there," said the porter. "And wait until someone rings the bell, that's what I do. That's what I'm paid to do. And weary work it is."

"And pay no heed to someone being stabbed on your doorstep?" asked the sergeant. "The captain will have something to say about that later, I have no doubt. But since you are wanted right away in the palace, Master Isaac," he added, "perhaps we may leave you and the lad to go in alone while we take care of this little problem."

"Certainly," said Isaac. "We know the way."

"And since His Excellency is not well," added the sergeant in a warning tone, "I do not wish to trouble him unnecessarily with this."

"Understood, Sergeant," said Isaac. "We leave you to your work."

• • •

Inside his austerely furnished yet comfortable sleeping chamber, Berenguer de Cruilles, Bishop of Girona, was sitting up in bed in a state of extreme irritation. "A dream, Isaac, that's what it was. A dream, and that fool Bernat panicked and sent them to drag you from your bed. He is supposed to be my secretary, not my nurse-maid."

"What sort of dream, Your Excellency?" asked Isaac.

"And what good does it do to speak of dreams?" said the Bishop impatiently.

"Sometimes it is helpful."

"Bernat, you may return to your bed. There is much to do in the morning, and I will not have you in a daze when you should be alert."

"I have slept well, Your Excellency," said the secretary, with calm persistence. "I shall stay for a while. The physician may need some assistance, Your Excellency."

"Compared to you, Bernat, a mule is a model of eager cooperation," said Berenguer. "Very well," he added with a sigh of resignation. "Stay if you like."

Isaac picked up Berenguer's wrist. Until the Bishop had spoken those words, the physician had not been concerned about his patient's state. Now he frowned in worry. His Excellency's usual reaction to helpful advice—especially from his underlings—was vigorous opposition. This acquiescence was alarming.

"I was dreaming of a huge mastiff in my father's house," said the Bishop suddenly. "A beast that terrified me when I was a small child. Any sorrow I had at leaving home for the cloister was greatly eased when I discovered that the dogs the monks kept were gentle creatures, and there were none as fierce as that."

"What happened in this dream?" asked Isaac. "Or was the appearance of the beast the substance of it?"

"Oh, no," said Berenguer. "There was more. The mastiff stepped onto my bed and sprawled over me, pinning me down and keeping me from moving." He took a deep breath. "It was no doubt some demonic fantasy," he said with a sigh, "that took that shape in order to distract me because I must be ready for a contentious meeting in the morning."

"I have no desire to instruct Your Excellency in matters of the spirit," said Isaac, "but I can think of other reasons for your dream than demons. If Your Excellency will permit, I would like to listen to your chest."

"But there is nothing wrong with my chest," muttered Berenguer, undoing the ties that held his shirt together.

Isaac applied his ear to the Bishop's chest and listened intently, first on one side of the body and then on the other. "Not true, Your Excellency," he said at last. "There is a congestion there—a great excess of phlegm. I can hear it very clearly. You must keep to your bed and forgo this morning's contentious meeting. I will leave a preparation of herbs for you. Drink a cupful now, and another when the bells ring for tierce. Much travel and too much work and worry on your return have weakened you. You must rest."

"How can I rest? I am somewhat weary, I admit, but I feel in full health. And although many appear to believe otherwise, the diocese does not administer itself."

"Call in your musicians; have someone with a pleasant voice and manner read to you. Forget the diocese and its troubles. And sleep." He turned to the servant, who waited unobtrusively in the farthest corner of the chamber. "Heap up more pillows on His Excellency's bed for ease of breathing until this little congestion clears, and see that he is not disturbed."

"Yes, Master Isaac."

"I will return before dinner to see how you fare, Your Excellency."

The door to the Bishop's chamber opened abruptly. The sergeant of the guard and Francesc Monterranes, the Bishop's most trusted canon, looked in. "Your Excellency," said the sergeant. "I apologize for this intrusion, but we have come across a dead man by the steps of the palace."

"Then he must be moved," said Berenguer wearily. "And measures taken to discover who he is."

"That has been done, Your Excellency."

"Then why do you trouble me—"

"It is Gualter Gutiérrez," said Francesc. "And he has died from a knife in the chest."

"Sweet music, you say, Isaac. And pleasant voices reading to me. Not very likely, I reply. Bloody murder right on my doorstep is what Fate has in store for me. And another disaster for the diocese."

"How can the murder of one man, even a wealthy, respected man like Master Gualter, possibly bring disaster to the diocese?" asked Bernat. "If his warehouse does not stay open, those who bought leather from him to carry on their trades will feel the loss, but surely other merchants can supply them."

"Oh, Bernat," said the Bishop, letting his head fall back onto the pillows now heaped behind him. "Master Gualter, it seems, was in the center of a different problem that is likely to bring us a great deal of trouble."

"You have not spoken of this to me," said the secretary reproachfully.

"Nor to me," said Francesc. "It might be best if Your Excellency were to tell us about it."

"His Excellency is too weary," said Isaac firmly.

"I may be weary, but I cannot sleep right now," said the Bishop. "I am too agitated. And if we tell Bernat and Francesc about it, Master Isaac, they can deal with the question of Master Gualter as well as I could, or better, while I am listening to soothing airs on the pipe or rebec. And I need not tell it all." He gestured in the direction of his physician. "Master Isaac knows part of the tale as well."

"I shall bear the burden of the story where I can," said Isaac.

THREE

Before the Bishop began his narrative, he paused to drink the warm preparation of herbs that had been brought to him from the palace kitchens, and then turned to his physician.

"The first part of the story belongs to Master Isaac. I shall allow him to tell it."

"Certainly, Your Excellency," said Isaac. "But you must say where you wish the story to begin."

"We will start from the moment you were called upon in great haste to go to the house of Gualter Gutiérrez."

"This being the time I was summoned because someone in the house was at the point of death?" asked Isaac.

"That time," said Berenguer, closing his eyes.

"Very good, Your Excellency. Master Gutiérrez lives, as you know, in a comfortable establishment located just beyond the south wall of the *call*. My daughter and I—and my apprentice, Yusuf—rushed off prepared for the worst. We assumed that we were to treat Gualter's wife, who had been in failing health since the summer, as many will remember, scarcely able to eat or sleep since her son had disappeared.

"When we reached the gate, there was considerable turmoil inside the house and it took some time for an answer to our repeated knocking. Raquel tried peering through the gate and saw nothing but the dark passageway leading to an empty courtyard.

"I may add that we were, by then, both very annoyed at the delay.

"We were about to depart when a hearty voice called out, 'Master Isaac. My deepest gratitude to you for coming so hastily,' and Master Gualter appeared in the passageway. 'It is Martí. My son. He has returned.'

"After expressing my delight, I inquired whether the young master was very ill. Master Gualter told us that his son was severely injured, and had only recovered enough to travel a few days before.

"There was a strong smell of barnyard muck in the chamber where Martí Gutiérrez had been placed. The young man volunteered the information that he had traveled to the city in a farm cart, the only conveyance that the monastery of the Holy Sepulcher at Palera possessed, and that he had just arrived. I was told that he was thin and weary looking, but that his lips had color and his eyes were bright. His left arm was heavily bandaged and he was wearing a monk's robe that concealed the rest of his body.

"I asked him what had happened, and I will tell you what he replied—as far as I can—in his own words.

" 'Strange to say, I do not know,' the young man began, in a very puzzled voice. 'I remember riding along the road from Montpellier with three companions. The next thing I remember, I was in a monastery, dressed like this. My arm was bound up, and my ribs, and my leg. Weeks had passed since I left Montpellier. The brothers had found me naked by a stream, and carried me up to their stronghold, where they looked after me.'

"I examined him, and assured his parents that the lad would do very well, but he had been seriously injured, and required rest and care. Would Your Excellency like me to continue?"

"You are doing so well," said Berenguer, opening his eyes again, "that I see no reason why you should not continue for a time, at least."

"Very good, Your Excellency. As soon as I had finished examining the lad, I said to Gualter Gutiérrez that he had every reason to be grateful to the brothers at the monastery.

" 'I have no doubt they are charitable enough,' Gualter said to me in very grudging tones.

" 'Your son suffered three broken bones,' I told him. 'Men have died from less. It is very fortunate that one of their number is an excellent bonesetter.' I pointed out that he had been tended with great care and had healed well, and that once he had regained his strength, he would be as good as new.

"And all that he had to say in reply was, 'I would have been better pleased if they had sent a message to us earlier, telling us that our son was alive. His mother was near dead from grief. And if they didn't think to do it, the lad himself should have insisted.' "

"Not a man of generous spirit," observed Francesc. "I would have expected more gratitude from him."

"Wait, Francesc," said the Bishop. "There will be gratitude enough later on."

"I pointed out that they cannot have known who young Master Martí was," said Isaac. "And that therefore they could not have sent word. I suspect that he didn't know himself for a long time. And those monks are far from the world. It is a long and perilous journey down the mountain.

"Gualter agreed finally that I was right. 'I still think they might have tried,' he said, 'but I shall see that they are suitably rewarded.'

" 'What do you mean by suitably?' asked his wife.

" 'I mean that I shall think of some suitable gift that expresses our gratitude for the return of our son,' snapped her husband.

"And there," said the Bishop, opening his eyes again, "lies the crux of our tale. And having noted that, I shall take up the narration. Thank you, Master Isaac."

"And now we reach last Friday," said Berenguer, after drinking another mouthful of the soothing herbal draft. "Near the end of May. And I don't have to remind you that May this year felt like August, with hot winds and burning sun, and the city was still gasping with the heat, praying for cool winds to come down from the mountains.

"Near the end of a day in which he had visited an almost endless stream of healthy patients, all demanding the same things—news of his recent trip to Tarragona, gossip about their bishop and his troubles, rumors of the war the King proposed against the Sardinians, Isaac sat comfortably in the study of Master Gualter Gutiérrez, chatting of local affairs, having greatly eased the discomfort of Master Gualter's wife, who was suffering from some minor ailment."

"A soreness in the throat," said Isaac, in interest of precision.

"Indeed," said Berenguer. "The physician mentioned a piece of news that he had heard several times that day, with no idea that it was to be a great secret."

"Shall I continue?" asked Isaac.

"For now," said Berenguer, "it being your conversation with him."

"Your Excellency," murmured Isaac. "I mentioned to him that I had heard that he was planning a great new business venture. 'Master Gualter,' I said, 'as your physician, I would suggest that you wait until the cooler weather of autumn before beginning something that will involve much labor and perhaps less sleep.'

" 'A new business venture?' said Gualter. 'Who spoke of that?'

" 'Three or four, at least,' I said, refraining from naming who they were. 'Is it not true?'

" 'It's not true at all. A man would have to be mad to start such a thing in all this heat—it is not even July. I wonder why that rumor began.'

" 'Easily enough. You have been calling in sums of money owing to you. Considerable sums. Therefore, or so the minds of neighbors go, you must be starting a new and expensive—therefore large—enterprise.'

" 'Can I not collect money owed to me without raising such ridiculous speculation?' grumbled Master Gualter.

"I laughed. 'That would be asking much of your neighbors. Too much.'

" 'In fact, Master Isaac, I have been thinking of speaking to you of this affair. To some extent you come into it.'

" 'I? Into your new business affairs?'

" 'No, no. It is not an affair of business. I have been thinking for some time of what I could offer to the brothers of the monastery of the Holy Sepulcher at Palera. And by a curious, and I think happy, chance, the perfect offering has come my way.'

" 'And what is that?'

" 'Not a word of this must pass your lips,' said Master Gualter. 'But I know you for a discreet man, and I am confident that you will not chatter to my neighbors. I have been fortunate enough to come across a man who has in his possession an object so holy—so extraordinary—that I myself have difficulty believing it is true.'

" 'And what is it?' I asked.

"He leaned forward until I could feel his breath in my ear. 'It is the Holy Grail,' he whispered. 'The very cup from which Christ drank at the Last Supper. No physical object could be holier.'

" 'And he's willing to sell it to you?' I asked.

" 'He is. He has heard that I am an honest man who can be trusted with it.'

" 'And will you keep such a holy object in your house?' I asked.

" 'Never. Not for more than an instant. I shall offer it.'

" 'To the cathedral, I suppose,' I said. 'That seems the logical thing to do.'

" 'Oh, no. After the inconveniences and irritations I suffered while the Bishop was away—and the delay there has been in dealing with my problems since his return? Why should I give anything to the cathedral? No. The Holy Chalice will go to the monastery of the Holy Sepulcher where my son was cured. He is in perfect health now, and you yourself said that I had much to thank them for.'

" 'So I did,' I said. 'And doubtless it was true.' And then I asked him, 'Are you sure of this man?'

" 'Even if I weren't,' said Gualter, 'he has documents that prove beyond a doubt that this is the true Grail.'

" 'Of course,' I said. 'He would have documents.' "

"And with that comment," said the Bishop, taking up the story, "good Master Isaac left Master Gualter's house and came here. This was to be his last visit of the day,

I believe, and it was for a nobler purpose than my foolish little health problems. We were to play a game of chess."

"And did you?" asked Bernat.

"We did," said Berenguer. "Finally. But first of all he told me of his visit to Master Gualter's house. And what the good merchant had said, including his flattering comments about me and my canons."

"And he told you that Master Gualter had the Holy Grail?" said Bernat.

"No," said Isaac. "I told His Excellency that Master Gualter asserted that he *would have* the Grail. He didn't have it, at that time. He had been offered it by 'some man.' I tried to discover who it was, but he was very secretive."

"I'm not surprised," said Berenguer wryly. "It is a somewhat contentious issue."

"It is commonly known that the Grail was carried to San Juan de la Peña to keep it safe from the Moors during the invasions," said Bernat. "If someone has stolen it . . ." he began, and then shook his head. "I'd be surprised," he said. "It is very closely guarded, they say."

"The monks at San Juan are not the only people to claim ownership of the Grail," pointed out Francesc. "Although most would allow that their claim is the strongest. Someone may have walked off with one of the other so-called Grails."

"That is quite possible," said the Bishop. "If it came from San Juan de la Peña, its theft could not have been kept so secret. Have you heard any murmur of such an event having happened, Bernat?"

"Not the faintest rumor, Your Excellency, and you would expect someone to have whispered of it at the General Council when we were there."

"He did ask me to be discreet," said Isaac, "but not in the manner of man who thinks he is about to take part in great crime. It was gossip he sought to avoid."

"Then it is more likely that he was being offered someone's grandmother's drinking cup. Why are people such fools, Isaac?" He turned to Bernat. "I then said very firmly that I would hasten to speak to Master Gualter before he did something very foolish. If I had been wise," he murmured, "I would have gone right away to find out what was going on. But I did not, and now this dishonest, fraudulent, and impious creature has murdered a good man."

"But why?" said Bernat.

"For all that money he had collected to pay him," said Isaac. "I doubt if there ever was a Grail, false or not."

FOUR

When Isaac and his apprentice had left the episcopal palace to return briefly to their beds, the moon was dropping below the hills and the sun was already considering rising. Berenguer de Cruilles had finally given in and taken the sleeping potion his frustrated physician had been pressing on him. He was asleep at last, reconciled to being confined to his chamber for the day, or perhaps longer.

When Isaac entered his own courtyard, he was almost as tired as his patient. He sent Yusuf to his bed, with instructions to sleep until he was called for, and headed directly toward the door to his study. There he had a comfortable couch where he could sleep for a few hours without disturbing the household or waking his wife. The room was on the courtyard level, away from the bedchambers of the rest of the family; he slept there whenever he suspected strongly that he would be called out in the night.

A soft growl stopped him at the door. He turned, and a furry object landed in the crook of his arm.

"Ah, you, too, have been working all night, have you?" he asked the cat. "Then we shall both sleep soundly," and went in.

Isaac awoke later that morning unsure of whether he had been asleep for hours or a few minutes, but with an odd sense that all about him life was in suspension. Muffled sounds came filtering through his stout wooden door, noises more distracting to his ears than the normal cheerful uproar of the household, of family and servants creeping about as if there were death or serious illness in the family. A slight chink of a plate on the table under the trees told him that the others were up, and attempting the almost impossible task of eating without a sound.

He rose, washed with his usual care, and said his prayers. Now ready for whatever the day might bring, he flung open the door. "I hope that you have left me a morsel to eat," he said. "I am famished."

"Why are out of your bed so early?" asked Judith. "You need to sleep."

"Oh, Papa," said Miriam, his eight-year-old daughter, who was sitting next to her twin brother, Nathan. "We tried so hard not to make noise, and we woke you up. I didn't mean to drop my spoon."

"I was awake before the spoon dropped, my dear," he said. "And out of bed," he added, almost truthfully. "Where is Yusuf?"

"Yusuf was awake before you were, Papa," said Raquel. "He snatched a piece of bread and some cheese off the table and rushed off to the stables. It seems he was promised a long lesson today in some particularly arcane area of horsemanship," she added airily. "I told him that

instead of learning anything, he would probably break
his neck from falling asleep and tumbling off the horse.
But you know he doesn't listen to me."

"He must be even more passionately fond of riding
than I thought," said Isaac, "if he allows it to come between him and his breakfast. Or his sleep."

"I think it's because he likes going off to the guards'
quarters," said Raquel. "They tell very crude stories to
pass the time off duty."

"It is very generous of His Excellency to stable the
beast and to provide Yusuf with lessons," said Isaac re-
provingly.

"He only does it because His Majesty has made a pet
of Yusuf," observed Judith.

"His Excellency is also fond of the boy," said Isaac.
"Now, what do we have this morning?"

And while his wife piled his plate with fresh-baked
bread, fruits, and a variety of cheeses, along with a slice
of cold cheese flan filled with savory herbs, Isaac and
his daughter carried on a spirited discussion over the
Bishop's condition. "Do you not think it likely that he
suffers more from worry and fatigue than from congestion of the lungs, Papa? Surely rest is what he needs."

"The initial cause may well have been worry and fatigue, my dear," he said. "It is certainly true that he
needs rest, but the congestion exists. You must remember always that the effect is as real as the underlying
cause, and in most cases must be treated first. Of course,
it didn't help that he received the news of Gualter Gutiérrez's death shortly after suffering the attack of
breathlessness."

"Master Gualter's death!" said his wife.

"Dead? What did he die from?" asked his daughter at
the same time.

Isaac sighed. Of that carefully thought-out little lesson, the only portion that stayed in his listeners' minds was the death of Master Gualter, and he was doomed to spend the rest of breakfast telling them about it.

An enormous pounding of the gate and clanging of the bell interrupted them again. "That must be someone from Master Gualter's household," said Raquel. "No one else attacks our door in quite that same way."

The urgent summons this time was for Master Gualter's wife. "The mistress is so overcome with sorrow," said the boy who had been sent with the message, "that she has not left off weeping and crying out, and now she cannot catch her breath. Master Martí is desperate worried."

"We will come at once," said Isaac, and in a moment, Raquel had the basket on her arm, her veil over her head, and was heading out the gate, closely followed by her father.

It took Isaac some time to calm the mounting hysteria that gripped Mistress Sibilla in the throat and chest. "Mistress," he said as her sobs eased and she drew her breath with less difficulty, "I cannot hope to take away your grief, but remember that you were ill before this terrible event happened. If you give way to your sorrow too much, you will quickly join your husband, leaving your doubly unfortunate son to grieve for both his parents. It is your duty to carry on, for his sake, if not for your own."

"But, Master Isaac, what use is there in my living on?" she said.

"There is much left for you in life, Mistress Sibilla," he said. "You cannot see it now, but—"

"You don't know what you're saying, Master Isaac," she said, clutching his arm with desperate intensity. "I

am ruined. My son and I. We are destroyed. Tell me—
they say you were there when his body was found—is
it true that there was no money at all found by him?"

"Neither the guards nor my apprentice saw anything
that would hold money."

"None hidden away on the body?"

"His purse strings were cut, they told me."

"And no priceless piece of silver either?"

"Priceless piece of silver?" Isaac shook his head. "Not
that I have heard," said the physician.

A faint moan escaped from Mistress Sibilla's lips.
"My husband was a good and kind man, Master Isaac,
although inclined to be choleric, and somewhat change-
able in temper. We all have our faults. But worse than
his occasional fits of ill temper, he was also as big a
fool as you'll find in this city. As far as I can tell, he
took every penny we had out with him last night—and
all that he would say to me was that he was going to
buy a priceless piece of silver. One of the servants tells
me that he overheard him talking about it, with someone,
and that the silver piece was supposed to be the Holy
Grail. Only my husband," she said bitterly, "is—was—
fool enough to believe that you could buy the Holy
Grail, just like that, as though it were a jar of spice or
length of silk."

"Surely he could not have paid everything you have
for this piece of silver that he planned to buy?" said
Isaac.

"Everything," said his wife. "I argued, I wept, I even
screamed at him. All he would say was that we had had
great luck this year, and that the warehouse is stacked
with the best of hides. The Grail brings prosperity, he
said, so that these goods should bring top prices. In a
month or two, by his calculations, he should have
amassed even more than he had last night starting out.

Precious little he'll be amassing for us now," she added bitterly.

"Does your son know of this?"

"I'm afraid he does," said Mistress Sibilla. "I was in no state to be discreet with my lamentations this morning. It is bad enough to be a widow at my age," she added sadly, "for I will sorely miss my husband's company. It is quite another to be reduced to begging in the streets. And my son is so enraged that I am afraid he will pursue this assassin back to whatever den of thieves and murderers he lives in. What would I do, Master Isaac, if both of them were dead?"

"How much money did he carry with him?" asked Isaac.

"Fifteen thousand gold *maravedís*," whispered the grieving widow.

"Fifteen *thousand*?" asked the physician. "How could he even carry that much?"

"He took two stout servants to help and protect him," said Mistress Sibilla. "But he sent the men away as soon as they reached the meeting place."

"And where was that?"

"Behind the cathedral. A holy place, do you not think, for such a noble act?" she added venomously.

Isaac administered what limited comfort soothing potions and a sleeping draft could give to the widow, promised to return, and greatly troubled by what he had heard, made his way home.

The rest of the long morning was too occupied with the demands of his patients for Isaac to think of the Bishop or the widow. When the bells rang for sext, he was bathing his face and arms in the cool water of his own fountain, considering what would be best to do next.

"Lord," said a quiet voice from behind him.

"Yes, Yusuf?" he said. "Have you finished your lessons so early?"

"No, lord," he said. "I haven't started them yet. I slept so late that I have just returned from the stables, but I thought that since the sun was high, you would wish to visit the Bishop again. As you promised him."

"You do well to remind me, lad," said Isaac. "Although the bells did recall me to my obligations as well."

"But, Papa," said Raquel, who was sorting dried herbs at the table under the tree, preparing to store and label them for later use, "have you forgotten our neighbor?"

"Which neighbor, my dear?"

"Mistress Dolsa. She has a thickness and soreness in the throat."

"I confess that I had forgotten for the moment. From the maid's description of her mistress's condition, I suspect it is the same complaint that many of our patients are suffering from. You know her well. Visit her in my place. If it is indeed as simple as that, you know what to do."

"Yes, Papa. I know. A few drops of liquor of bryony."

"Do not exceed that dose. And make sure that she understands that she must keep to her bed. If she seems very feverish, then treat the fever and tell her that I will visit her this afternoon. And remember—"

"Papa," she said, in slightly exasperated tones. "I know."

"Of course, my dear," said her father. "You know as well as I what is to be done in such a case."

Isaac and Yusuf walked up the steep hill leading to the south face of the cathedral through the ordinary midday crowd of women marketing and men going about their various businesses. In the midst of the everyday conversations swirling around them, two voices raised in angry shouts caught their attention. "Who is that, Yusuf?" said Isaac. "That voice sounds familiar."

"I only have glimpses of them in the crowd, lord. There are too many tall people between us. But I would swear that one of them is Baptista, lord. The man—the stranger—I told you of."

"The peddler," said Isaac. "And if I am not mistaken, the other voice belongs to a former patient of ours. That young monk who lost two of his toes. Joaquim."

As they drew closer, the words sprang out more clearly from the surrounding noise. "This must stop," said Baptista, his voice controlled and forceful. "You have done nothing but follow me about since I left. It will do you no good. No good at all."

"I tell you—you must do it," said Joaquim. His soft voice was pitched higher than usual and he sounded desperate. "You must."

"Can't you understand what I'm saying, you fool? It's nothing to do with you anymore," said Baptista. "But I want to be fair. Perhaps we can come to an agreement," he said in a much lower tone.

"No more agreements." The cry was despairing. "You must do it."

Then three men in Benedictine habits came swiftly up the hill, brushing against Isaac. "Excuse us," murmured the first. "Excuse us. Brother Joaquim," he called in the same breath. "Brother Joaquim."

"Yes, Brother?" said Joaquim in his soft voice.

"You must come back with us."

"Certainly, Brother," he said. "Is it dinner hour? I am sorry if I am late. Very sorry. Thank you for coming to get me."

"It seems that half of the people in the city are suffering from some complaint or other in the chest and throat," said Isaac. "But fortunately, not all of them have allowed their bodies to weaken from toil and worry as much as you have, Your Excellency."

"And how have you escaped it, my friend?" asked the Bishop. "Or are you, too, caught in its grip? Although you look well enough," he added.

"There are many oddities about illness that I do not pretend to understand—especially why one man should suffer and another escape, Your Excellency. These are not within my province. It would seem that today is not my time to fall ill," Isaac said, and bent his head to listen to the Bishop's chest once more. "But it is yours, I'm afraid. You must stay in your bed a few days more. And I am confident that Father Bernat and Father Francesc will do their best to prevent you from attempting to return to your duties."

"We have tried as hard as we can to avoid discussing diocesan business with His Excellency," said Bernat in exasperated tones. "It is not an easy task."

"No one seems to understand, Master Isaac," said Berenguer irritably, "that if I must lie here all day wondering what is going on, and what great problems are brewing while I am confined to this chamber, I cannot rest. I would rather know the worst, and then I will sleep, or listen to my musicians, knowing that someone else is dealing with refractory parish priests and conniving canons. Four times have I asked them about the death of Master Gualter, and they just look uncomfortable, mysterious, and completely alarming. Then they say that there is nothing to worry about."

"His Excellency may be right," said Isaac. "Perhaps you should let him know the worst if that is what will ease his mind. When he is too ill or weary to hear it, he will not be interested."

Bernat and Francesc looked at each other. Francesc

rose to his feet and, walking to and fro as he spoke, began. "We may be facing a rather difficult time, Your Excellency. I don't know how it happened, or through whom, but it seems—" He paused to choose his words.

"What seems, Francesc?" said Berenguer.

"Apparently word has spread that the Holy Grail is here in the city," he said abruptly.

"What?" said the Bishop.

"And that it has terrifying powers, and was the cause of Master Gualter's death."

"May Sant Narcís, who saved us from the French, intervene once more and protect us from ourselves," said Berenguer. "Who is saying this?"

"I heard it from the gardener," said Francesc.

"And I heard it from one of the guards," said Bernat. "And from one of the scribes who came to warn us. *He* heard it from a petitioner who had come to lodge a complaint in the ecclesiastical courts."

"Have you heard it, Master Isaac?" asked Berenguer.

"No," said the physician. "But this morning I have been very rushed. I scarcely took the time to greet my patients, and certainly gave them no chance to gossip. I was told something you should know," he added. "Although it did not concern those rumors."

"Let us hear what people are saying first," said the Bishop wearily. "Tell us the worst, as you promised."

"They are saying that it is death to look on it," said Francesc. "And instant death to touch it. And that unless someone can be found to take it into the cathedral and place it in some holy and hidden place, the city will be destroyed."

"And who is to perform this office?"

"That is their problem, is it not, Your Excellency? They worry about who is to find it, and then risk annihilation by carrying it into the cathedral."

"Someone will have to tell them that Master Gualter was killed by a physical dagger held in a human hand, and that his purse was stolen. It was a vicious act, but it was simply theft. Nothing more. Unless you have found out more that you are keeping from me."

"I have heard something," said Isaac. "Although I had no intention of keeping it from you, Your Excellency. I was summoned to visit Gualter's widow this morning. She was in a sad state, scarcely able to breathe for sorrow, but not for the reason you might think. It seems that, although she mourns the loss of her husband, she is even more distraught over the loss of their gold."

"Their gold? How?" asked Berenguer.

"I will simply tell you the story as she told it to me," said Isaac. "And I fear that it fits in well enough with these rumors. I suspect that they originate from her household." Isaac repeated, as accurately as possible, the conversation he had with Mistress Sibilla.

"Fifteen thousand *maravedís*!" said Bernat. "That is a considerable sum."

"Many a man would willingly commit murder for that amount, I'm afraid," said Isaac.

FIVE

While Raquel was listening to Mistress Dolsa's chest, looking carefully at her throat, and administering the drops that would, perhaps, clear the thickness in it, Dolsa's worried husband, Ephraim, was hovering solicitously nearby. Daniel, their nephew, had been left to look after the shop alone.

It was a quiet day, with few customers during the late morning. Daniel was bent over a pair of fine kidskin gloves he had just made, setting out beads in various colors and patterns, trying to make them form the design that at the moment existed only in his head. He was interrupted in his absorbing task by the sound of footsteps; he set the tiny beads down on the table and looked up. Two expensively dressed women, a mother and daughter, crowded through the doorway, followed by their servant.

He put away his work and smiled. "Good morning, Mistress Alicia," he said, rising from his stool and addressing himself to the elder of the two. "I trust you are well."

"Very well, Daniel, thank you," she said, with a languid but good-natured air.

Daniel concealed his slight irritation behind a mask of politeness. "And Master Vicens?" he asked, having been chided more than once by his uncle for not making exhaustive inquiries into the health and well-being of all their customers—whether they spent small fortunes on the finest kidskin or a penny or two on rough work gloves.

"My husband is well also," she said.

"May I show you anything, Mistress Alicia?" he said. "Or you, Mistress Laura?"

Instead of replying, Mistress Alicia smiled and began to examine some samples of work that had been set out on the counter.

The younger woman interrupted her musings. "Mama," she said, "look at these. Aren't they beautiful? I want a pair of gloves just like them. Only with that kind of beadwork," she added, pointing to another pair, "and in green."

"Those must be terribly expensive, Laura," said her mother. Then she gave them a careful look. "How much would they be, Daniel? The gloves my Laura would like?"

Daniel leaned forward and murmured a figure in Mistress Alicia's ear.

"I could buy a gown for that amount," said the woman, shocked. "A plain gown, perhaps, but still . . . That seems a great deal for a pair of gloves."

"But, Mama," said Laura, with a hint of tears in her voice, "gloves are always expensive."

"They would look charming on Mistress Laura," said Daniel. "But we have other styles, not quite so expensive, that her graceful hands would show off to advantage."

"But, Mama, I like the beadwork on those," said Laura stubbornly. "And besides, it doesn't matter anymore what they cost, does it?"

"Laura, what do you think you are saying?"

"Papa says we're going to be rich, Mama. So we can afford them."

"Shh, darling," said her mother, looking around in alarm. "Don't say things like that. And if we are, we'll wait until it happens before we start ordering the most expensive gloves in the shop." At that, she hustled her daughter out the door before anyone had a chance to speak.

"There goes a pretty armful," said the apprentice, who had been leaning in the doorway to the workroom, unobtrusively listening to the exchange. "You get all the luck, don't you?"

"Who?" asked Daniel, looking up from his new design once again.

"Mistress Laura," said the apprentice. "Although I wouldn't turn down the mother, either."

"No—I don't suppose you would," said Daniel, absentmindedly.

While Mistress Alicia and her daughter were dreaming over expensive gloves, the first word on the death of Gualter Gutiérrez reached their husband and father, Master Vicens. He had been seated in the back of his shop, leaving an apprentice to deal with customers. Over the years, by thrift, hard work, and shrewd bargaining, he had slowly turned a modest trade in cloth for the astute and penny-wise housewives of Girona into a grander operation, dealing more and more with sales to tradesmen, tailors, and other shopkeepers. Behind his little office was a room sufficiently stocked with goods to be referred to as the warehouse.

The lull in the day's work had given him time to start drafting some bold plans he had been mulling over for two or three weeks.

A squeal of surprise from his apprentice brought him to his feet and into the shop. "My dear Master Nicholau," said Vicens heartily. "How pleasant to see you. Is this a visit—a most welcome one, I can assure you—or can we show you anything? A length of pretty cloth for a summer gown for your good wife?"

"Master Nicholau was telling me of the murder of Master Gualter," said the apprentice. "And the terrible theft. And then my friend Pere, he came in for just a minute to ask if the new silk was in, because his mistress wants to see it, and he told us that Master Gualter was carrying the Holy Grail, the very one, in his hands to take it to the cathedral when he was struck down by the hand of God. That's what he said, isn't it, Master Nicholau?"

"Gualter with the Holy Grail?" said Vicens in a weak voice.

"That is a mere rumor, Master Vicens," said Nicholau Mallol. "All we know is that he was found near the Bishop's palace."

"But surely the physician—"

"I will ask my father-in-law when I next see him, Master Vicens. No doubt he will know more."

"Very true," said Vicens, and sat down heavily on a stool. "Isaac the physician hears everything there is to know around the city. Boy," he snapped at the apprentice. "I will stay in the shop. You have packages to deliver."

"Yes, Master Vicens," said the apprentice, picking up two small parcels with more than his usual enthusiasm and heading rapidly for the door. The street outside was clearly buzzing with the news, and he was hungry to be part of the excitement.

"Perhaps I should consult your father-in-law," said Vicens.

"Are you ill?" asked Nicholau. "You do look rather pale."

"No—I am not ill. I was grieved and startled to hear the news, that is all. Was he really carrying the Grail?"

"I don't see how he could have been," said Nicholau. "Where would he get it from?"

"I could tell you that," said Vicens in a whisper. "A man—a stranger—brought it with him into the city. Not long ago."

"I don't believe it," said Nicholau, startled. "Here?"

"Why not here? We have a beautiful cathedral—"

"It will be when it's finished," added the younger man. "But how did you hear about it?"

"He offered it to me," said Vicens. "For a lot of money."

"Dear God," said Nicholau. "He said he had the Grail?"

"Shh," murmured Vicens. "No one must know of it."

"Imagine if it were true," said Nicholau.

"Of course it's true," said Vicens. "He has papers to prove it. And can you imagine what having the Grail here—in the cathedral—would do for the city? We would have pilgrims here by the thousands. Every day of the year they would pour in, needing accommodation and food, with gold in their pockets and a great desire to spend it on trinkets and lengths of silk and such to show to their neighbors back home."

"It sounds noisy and uncomfortable," said Nicholau. "Where there are pilgrims there are thieves and cutthroats and all sorts of terrible people. No—I think it's best for it to remain hidden from the eyes of man."

Master Vicens stared at him incredulously, and shook his head.

The cloth merchant escorted Nicholau Mallol out and into the square. Nicholau stopped and murmured something under his breath.

"Pardon?" asked Vicens.

"My apologies, Master Vicens. I was looking at my father-in-law's apprentice deep in conversation with someone in the square, and thinking how much he has grown in a year."

"That's Baptista he's talking to," said Vicens. "Now, what business does Baptista have with the physician's apprentice? What is he up to?"

"Yusuf?"

"No. Baptista," said Vicens. "Excuse me, Master Nicholau. I have something to attend to." He hurried back into his shop.

"Is it possible that it's true, Nicholau?" asked his wife, Rebecca, as they sat down to dinner.

"No," said her husband. "I don't think so. But I must pay a visit to Martí. He loved his father very much, even though the man exasperated him a great deal, and he will be devastated at this."

"I will come with you and pay my respects to Mistress Sibilla."

"I want to come, too," said Carles, their son. "And pay my 'specks."

"Not this time, darling," said his mother. "Soon, but not now. I will bring the maid," she said to her husband, "and we will do some shopping on the way back while you talk to Martí."

• • •

"I cannot stand to be in this house for another moment, Nicholau," said Martí. They were seated in the courtyard, attempting to maintain an awkward exchange of polite banalities. "Let us walk by the river."

"The house must hold painful memories," murmured Nicholau.

"It won't do that much longer," said his friend bitterly.

"Why?" asked Nicholau. "Are you leaving?"

"You could say that," he said, rising to his feet. "I'm not exactly leaving. It's more that—" He stopped. "I might as well tell you the whole horrible story. You'll hear about it soon enough, I expect."

"If you don't wish to . . ." said Nicholau, following him out of the courtyard. Burning with curiosity mixed with embarrassment, he let his voice die away.

"The first time will be the most difficult," said Martí. "I shall practice the tale on you, like a fairground storyteller."

But it wasn't until they were away from the crowds, and seated on the riverbank, that Martí began with what he had gleaned from his mother in the morning.

"Fifteen thousand *maravedís*," said Nicholau. "I have trouble believing it."

"So do I," said Martí. "And so would any reasonable man." He picked up a small stone and tossed it into the water. "He might as well have done that with everything he earned and worked hard for—thrown it in the Onyar. Then at least he would not have been murdered for it."

"Did you know nothing of what was going on?"

"I knew that something was happening. I knew that he was raising money—going from family to family like a tax farmer, extracting everything everyone ever owed him. I thought he was going mad."

"Seriously?"

"Oh, yes." He tossed another pebble and watched it splash. "I had decided yesterday to suggest that he be locked in his room before he could do anything more."

"Did you ask him what he was doing?"

"I did. Several times. We had some terrible quarrels—shouting and saying things to each other that I could not—I cannot believe. The last words I said to him were to wish that he would rot in hell." Stricken, the young man covered his face and broke into tormented sobbing. At last, brushing away the tears, he said, "I was so angry at him. How can one love someone and be so angry?"

"It's easy," said Nicholau, grasping him by the shoulder. "Easier than being angry at someone you don't like."

"My mother is distraught. She fears starvation for the both of us. But there is the house, which is now mine. I shall sell it. There will be enough from that and her dowry to keep my mother in decency, if not in great comfort. She speaks of entering a convent; the money from the house would go there with her. It would be a sufficient sum, I think."

"And you?"

"I am young and strong," he said. "I can work. I am also sufficiently charming, I think, to attract some hard-working young woman with enough dowry to start us in a respectable trade. Yes—I think I can even sell myself to a prosperous father-in-law with an ugly daughter and a need for a son to enter his business," he added bitterly.

"I would not despair yet," said Nicholau. "Wait until you find out what the situation is. Now I must be on my way. Let us walk together back to your house."

"My house," said Martí. "It *is* my house, isn't it, if only for the moment?"

"It seems to be," said Nicholau.

• • •

Baptista entered Rodrigue's tavern with none of the caution he had shown the first time he walked in. He ran up the steps to the main room, nodded at a couple of regular customers, and went straight back, around the piece of hide that served as a door, and into the kitchen. Mother Rodrigue was chopping vegetables to throw into the soup.

Baptista was true to his word. He picked up a knife and with the speed born of long habit, peeled, diced, and chopped alongside his hostess.

"What's got into you?" she asked.

"Joaquim is in town, Ana," he said, with a particular vicious swipe downward of his knife.

"Joaquim. That's the one you told me of?"

"That one."

"What does he want?"

"For himself? Nothing," said Baptista. "That's the problem, Ana. I was every kind of a fool. It must have been the air up on the mountaintops. As soon as you begin to deal with people who aren't prompted by simple greed you run into problems. Big problems." He picked up a carrot and shook it, hard, as if he held Brother Joaquim by the shoulders. "I should have known better," he said ruefully.

"You may find some of those you are dealing with here as big a problem," observed Ana. "I would walk carefully, Baptista, if I were you."

"I had best move quickly as well, I think."

"Sit down. I'll bring you a cup and we'll think over what is best to do," she said.

SIX

Astruch des Mestre, businessman, banker, and astute, highly respected member of the council that
governed the *call* of Girona, was in Isaac's courtyard,
seated comfortably at the table under the tree with his
host. The heat of the day was slowly dissipating, and it
was pleasantly cool in their shady retreat. On the table
were jugs of wine, water, and a tart refreshing drink
made with mint and the sharp, sour juice of oranges.
Beside them were small dishes containing olives, nuts,
and fruits, both fresh and dried. The fountain splashed,
cooling the air still further; the birds, both wild and
caged, were beginning to sing as evening approached.

"It is a lovely evening," said Isaac. "I can feel it in
the air, and in my very bones."

"It is," said Astruch, pouring himself some wine and
adding a generous amount of water to it. "Let me give
you a cup of wine," he said, and poured another like the
first without waiting for a sign of assent.

"But I do not like the sound of your voice, Master

Astruch," said Isaac. "I think that something troubles you. I hope I am mistaken. Is all well in your household? Your wife? The children?"

"Well, very well, I thank the Lord," said Astruch. "And I have troubles, but they are small, especially when you remind me of what is important—my family, my community."

"Nonetheless, they must be great enough to cause your throat to tremble when you try to speak," said the physician. "Do you wish to talk of them? Or to forget them? I can recommend a game of chess—but you will need to give me a pawn, for you are a keener player than His Excellency the Bishop."

"It was to talk of my little difficulties that I came over, Isaac my friend. To trespass upon your good nature, and seek your advice. Then we will have a game and I will give you two pawns."

"Excellent," said Isaac. "Now, what are they?"

"I have been placed in a very awkward situation by the unfortunate death of Gualter Gutiérrez," said Astruch.

"You?" said Isaac. "In what way?"

"I recently advanced a considerable sum of money to the man," said Astruch, in his dry, precise manner. "I anticipated no problems with the loan. We had had dealings many times over the years. When he first started to expand his business, Master Gualter often borrowed small sums to tide him over until money came in—to pay his workmen or to buy hides of better quality. Soon he prospered sufficiently to build up his own reserves. He borrowed much less often, but in larger amounts for special projects—to build a larger warehouse, for example. One thing that never changed, however, was his attitude once he had borrowed money. He was scrupulous in meeting his obligations to the penny, with no complaints or difficulties or excuses."

"An admirable man to deal with, clearly," said Isaac.

"Indeed," said Astruch. "Four nights ago, he came to see me. He wanted to borrow a large sum for a very special project, he said. It would be for a month only, he thought. Perhaps two. I did not ask him the nature of the project. There was no need. He had never borrowed money from me for any but the soundest of reasons, and we trusted each other completely."

"Did he sign a note?" asked Isaac.

"Of course," said Astruch. "It was a loan, and he always signed a note. Once when he was in a great hurry, I offered to draft the note and send it to him for his signature. He pointed out that he could be killed on the way home and then where would I be?" He stopped for a mouthful of wine. "He was that sort of man."

"Then I do not quite see your difficulty."

"Isaac, Isaac—there is something you do not know yet. The problem is the size of the loan. I advanced him more than I could afford right now, because of who he was. And if a great sum was indeed stolen from him, as they say, I wonder what the chances are that I will be repaid. In the past four hours I have heard several figures—all differing wildly—on the amount of the theft. Do you know?"

Isaac paused. "I do," he said hesitantly. "You realize that I was told this figure in confidence, and it is not one that should be widely known."

Astruch made an impatient gesture. "Only tell me how much, Isaac, and I shall not breathe a word of it outside this courtyard."

"Fifteen thousand gold *maravedís*."

"Fifteen thousand," said Astruch. His voice was completely expressionless.

"How much did you lend him?"

"Five thousand." He drained his cup and filled it

again. "He must have converted everything he could into gold," said the banker. "There will be nothing left."

"Except the property and whatever goods remain in his warehouse."

"Do you think I relish the thought of trying to take a widow's house from her?" said Astruch. "And is it true what they are saying? That he was using my money to buy a—"

"A religious object?" said Isaac. "Yes, it is. Or rather, he thought he was using your money to buy it. I don't believe there is such an object in Girona, or that the person who offered it to Gualter had it."

"Do they know who he is?" asked Astruch. "Because if they do, I might be able to recover my debt from him."

"Not yet, but they will, I am sure."

"I wish I could be that sure. But you will let me know if you hear anything?"

"I will."

Francesc Monterranes finished a light supper and stepped outside to enjoy the cool air of evening. The sun had set long since, but in the western sky the ghost of its light still lingered palely on. The end of the day's heat and a few light breezes had drawn many into the plazas and onto the rooftops, but having no desire for company, Francesc strolled into the Bishop's garden.

"Father Francesc," said an all-too-familiar voice as soon as he entered. "It is pleasant in here, is it not?"

"It is, Father Ramon," said Francesc, resigning himself to conversation.

"And how is His Excellency?"

"Somewhat improved, I believe," he said. "He was in need of rest."

"No doubt," said Orta. "After this spring, we are all in need of rest, are we not?" He laughed, as a token of goodwill, and carried on as if he expected no answer. "It was a terrible thing that happened last night," he added.

"Yes, indeed," said Francesc. "My heartfelt prayers go with his family in their sorrow. It troubles me to think of such violence against an honest, upright citizen here in our peaceful city."

"But there is one very interesting aspect to it, don't you think?"

"Interesting, Father Ramon?"

"Yes," said Orta. "I have heard that he was killed while attempting to buy the Holy Grail to present to the cathedral."

"Not quite," said Francesc. "It seems he was intending to give it to the monastery of the Holy Sepulcher at Palera."

"Really?" said Orta. "How extraordinary. How very, very extraordinary." The canon paused. "But since he did not succeed in buying it, irrelevant," he added briskly. "Has it occurred to you how significant it would be for us—for all of us—if the Grail did come to be placed in the cathedral?"

"Significant?"

"Surely you must have thought of it, my dear Francesc," said Orta. "Consider how much importance the cathedral would gain if it enclosed such a holy object."

"Perhaps," said Francesc cautiously.

"Surely. And this importance would inevitably spread to all of us, from Bishop to canons and then to everyone else here. In my opinion we should be making an earnest effort to locate it, and install it here. Have you spoken to the Bishop about it?"

"I haven't," said Monterranes. "But you can be very sure that I will. And soon."

"Excellent. There are a few more scraps that I have gleaned today that His Excellency may wish to hear about," he added, and drew Francesc Monterranes into the deepest shade of the farthest corner of the garden.

SEVEN

Tuesday, June 3

E arly the next morning Martí Gutiérrez sat down
with his father's clerk and began, slowly and me-
thodically, to go through his papers and records. After
an hour or more he came across a notation that made
him stop.

"What is that?" he asked the clerk, pointing to a recent
entry.

"I do not know," said the clerk, looking up from the
papers he was sorting. "Those were his private financial
transactions. I never dealt with them."

Martí swore softly, tied up the bundle of papers he
had been working on, locked it away, and headed out
the door.

"Master Astruch," said Martí Gutiérrez, in a taut, nervous voice, "it is very kind of you to agree to see me."

"Not at all, Master Martí," said Astruch, moving away

from the window to greet his visitor. He gestured to a chair near the round table that dominated his study, and sat down at another across the table from it.

The study was a pleasant room, much pleasanter than the cluttered office belonging to Martí's father which he was used to. Each element in it was in quiet harmony with its owner, as if it had grown around him. The room smelled invitingly of leather, beeswax, and wood. The table at which they sat was dark in color, carved with an intricate design around the periphery, and well rubbed down. On its smooth surface sat a lectern holding an open book, pens, ink, a knife for mending pens, a curious rough stone vessel for sand, and the sheet of paper on which he had been writing before he was interrupted. Two polished wooden shelves near the table held an impressive collection of books—possibly as many as thirty, Martí estimated. The tapestry on the wall behind Astruch was Moorish in design, rich in color and yet unobtrusive. Before Martí had the time to finish his inspection of his surroundings, a manservant and a boy came in with trays laden with refreshments. Setting them down within easy reach of both men, they quietly withdrew.

"I could not help noticing that you have been examining my little retreat here from the world," said Astruch. "Do you look to criticize? Or to admire?"

"To admire, Master Astruch," said Martí. "It gives the air of being modestly furnished, and yet it is comfortable almost to the point of opulence."

"That is praise indeed, Master Martí," said Astruch. "It contains a collection of well-loved objects that span several generations. Even my great-grandfather's stone," he said, letting his hand rest affectionately on it. "The one he used to hold the sand that dried the parchment he wrote upon so long ago. He found it, with its curious shape, when he was a child, and kept it for that use. But please, will you take a little refreshment? The day is hot; it will do you good."

But the white-faced young man declined all offers of food and drink. "I am sorry," he said, "but I cannot think of such things until I have spoken to you."

"Then, if it will ease your mind," said Astruch, "please, speak freely."

"Today—this morning—I was going through the papers in my father's study. It is necessary for us to know exactly how things stand so that we may put his affairs in order."

"Of course," said Astruch. "I understand completely. A sad task, but a necessary one."

Martí waved his hand as if to brush away any attempt at sympathy. "In doing so, I came across a notation in my father's accounts, dated five days ago. It describes a debt—a note held by you, Master Astruch, for five thousand gold *maravedís*."

"Such a note does exist, I agree."

"And it is due in twenty-five days."

"I believe so," said Astruch. "If you will allow me—"

"Please. Let me say what I must say."

Astruch nodded gravely.

"I do not know how much you have heard of the circumstances of my father's death, but a large sum was stolen from him at the time—so large that it will be difficult for us to raise the five thousand within the twenty-five days. But we will raise it, I assure you. For today, I have brought an interim payment as an earnest of my intentions." He untied his purse strings and took out two *maravedís*. "It is not a great deal, I know, but it is all that I have at the moment."

"In that case," said Astruch, "it is too much." He pushed one of the gold coins back across the table. "Please, take it. Your father, unfortunate man, has already paid in blood for the gold. I will collect what is owed to me from the thieves, not from you and your mother, who are both blameless. But since you offer it, I will take the *maravedí* as interest on the debt. I shall return it when I succeed in recovering my loss from others."

Too astonished and confused to speak, Martí picked up the gold piece, bowed, and fled from the study.

"Now, what made me say that?" murmured Astruch to his retreating back. "I must ask the physician."

Berenguer de Cruilles was still in his bed that same morning when Francesc Monterranes and Bernat sa Frigola intruded on his reflections.

"Good morning, Francesc, Bernat," he said. "I was expecting my physician, who threatened to visit me this morning, not you two."

"Master Isaac is waiting to see you."

"Why does no one tell me these things? Ask him in," said the Bishop. "Unless you bring news of such importance and secrecy that he may not hear it."

"Not at all, Your Excellency," said Francesc. "My news is merely a trifle strange."

"Good. Fetch the physician and tell me what it is."

While Isaac listened once more to Berenguer's chest, Francesc described his encounter of the night before with Ramon de Orta. "In short, Your Excellency, Father Ramon seems to feel that it doesn't matter whether the Grail is real or fraudulent, or if, in fact, there is an actual cup, here or anywhere near, that could possibly be the Grail. His belief is that if the world is convinced that the Grail is here, it will be an excellent thing for all of us. I have rarely seen him so animated."

"I do not find that strange, Francesc," said the Bishop. "Ramon de Orta is an ambitious man. He sees an outlet for his ambition in this story of the Grail."

"He also said that he had heard that the Grail was still being offered for sale."

"When you consider what happened to the last would-be purchaser, only a very brave man would buy it now," said Isaac dryly. "Or one who possessed a strong personal guard. The terms of sale would not be attractive to most, I think."

"Losing your money and your life?" said the Bishop. "Perhaps not."

"But the man who stole those chests of gold from Gualter," said Francesc, "may not have the Grail."

"What do you mean?" asked Bernat.

"Gualter may have been deceived," said Francesc. "There is nothing to stop any one of us from offering to sell what we don't have."

"Of course," said Bernat. "And a man would feel free to sell something he didn't have if he were planning to kill the buyer as soon as he arrived with the purchase price."

"I cannot see that these speculations help us at all." The Bishop closed his eyes and turned his head away from the group by the bed. "I think I will resume the sleep you have interrupted," he said. "I bid you good day, Fathers, with this thought. Since we do not know who the seller is, we are no further ahead."

"Your chest is improving, Your Excellency," said Isaac.

Berenguer opened his eyes. "And is that all that you have to add to this discussion, Master Isaac?" said the Bishop. "I am disappointed."

"No. I have one thing to add," said Isaac. "And it concerns my friend Astruch des Mestre."

"What is it that concerns Astruch?" asked Berenguer.

"He advanced the sum of five thousand gold *mara-*

vedís to Master Gualter five days ago," said Isaac.

"And it was stolen?" said Bernat.

"It was stolen," said Isaac. "It would be an excellent thing for everyone if we were to discover who has that gold," he added.

"Indeed," said Bernat. "Gualter's widow and son can scarcely hope to repay so large a sum without recovering the gold that was taken."

"I have been thinking about this whole affair," said Berenguer. "The rumors about the Grail, the death of Gualter, and the theft of his money. And I have concluded, after much consideration and many prayers for guidance, that it would be most unwise for us to meddle in any of it. Therefore we shall turn it over to the city guards, and let them discover the whereabouts of the gold."

"But, Your Excellency!" said Bernat. "That will never happen. If you sent them out your door right now, they couldn't find that dog that's sleeping in your courtyard. Why do you believe they could find the widow's property?"

"I am very sleepy myself," said the Bishop, letting his head fall back on the pillows. "I will tell you later." He closed his eyes and gestured at them to leave.

"Your Excellency," said Francesc, "I beg of you. Just a few minutes more. Let us know something of your thoughts in this matter."

Berenguer opened an eye. "Very well," he said. "Help me to sit up." And propped up on additional pillows, with a cup of honeyed wine and water to soothe his throat, he began to explain. "I do not like this, Francesc. Not at all. There is hysteria enough in the city, if I am to believe your accounts, and if we are to begin to search for that gold, and to pursue the assassin of Gualter, we will give credence to the rumors. I strongly suspect this has nothing to do with the Church. It has to do with commonplace greed that exists in all men and the ingenuity of one evil and particularly avaricious one. Therefore let us leave it to the authorities who are best suited to dealing with it. Let them treat it as ordinary theft and murder. Fifteen thousand *maravedís* is a great deal of gold—even the city guards should be able to find it. And now, as I have said before, I am weary, and do not wish to discuss the matter further."

Nicholau Mallol, one of the cathedral scribes, and the Christian husband of Isaac the physician's convert daughter, Rebecca, had seen his friend Martí in the tavern by the cathedral as he walked by, and in a charitable moment, decided to join him. He was regretting his decision. Martí was slouched over the table, clearly having drunk more than was good for him.

"But what did he mean, Nicholau?" he was saying, for the fourth time.

"Yes, Martí?" asked his friend, tense with impatience, one ear trying to follow the conversation, the other listening for the first touch of the bells for vespers. He had several things to do before he could go home this evening, and he was already late.

"Whatever can he have meant?"

"Who are you talking about, Martí?"

"Astruch. Saying my father has already paid him in blood? And that he would collect from the thieves?"

"I think Master Astruch was saying that your family has suffered enough, and that he would try to get the money from the perpetrators when they were caught. It is a difficult thing to conceal that much gold. It will be found, and then he will have a claim on it." He did his best to keep his voice level and to hide his impatience.

Martí shook his head back and forth. "That's not what

he seemed to be saying. He as good as admitted to me that he hired those thieves, Nicholau. He intended to get his money back with interest—you lend a man five thousand, kill him, and take it back with another ten for your trouble. Why else would he reject my efforts to repay him?"

"I think you misjudge the man, Martí," said Nicholau, who by now had turned his full attention on his friend. "Your father trusted him—"

"And see what happened to him."

"My father-in-law thinks highly of him, and my Rebecca's father is not easily fooled. Astruch is a man of great standing in his community."

"You know perfectly well that he would not be the first man whose outward virtue and great standing concealed even greater depths of evil," said Martí, enunciating each word with care.

"That may be. You don't have to trust him," said Nicholau. "All I ask is that you not talk about this—this idea you have. Not to others. In minutes the rumors will be all over the city. And I truly think you may be wrong about him."

Martí picked up his wine cup and stared into it instead of responding.

"You already have, haven't you?" said Nicholau in exasperation. "You've been talking about this to everyone you've met, not just to me. Sometimes you can be a real fool. Don't you ever think, just for one moment, before you speak?"

"Not often, I'm afraid," said Martí, smiling apologetically.

On that hot afternoon, Rodrigue's tavern was beginning to quiet down. The potboy was collecting plates and bowls, and most of the customers were finished with their wine and grumbling at each other about work, and taxes, and the price of everything. Mother Rodrigue moved through the room with a jug, refilling cups for the more determined drinkers. Rodrigue assessed the room with a practiced eye and disappeared, leaving his wife to look after the stragglers.

Baptista sat by himself, staring into his wine. From time to time he raised his head, listened for a while to the complainers, and then returned to staring into his cup.

Rodrigue's wife came by Baptista's place as she went around the room and paused. "What are you looking for in there?" she asked.

"More answers," said Baptista. "I admit to being even more puzzled."

"What are you puzzled about?" she asked.

"Listen, Ana, my clever beauty. If you came into the kitchen all ready to cook a good dish of oxtail, and discovered a stew of mutton neck cooking on the stove, wouldn't you be puzzled?"

"I'd wonder which of the lazy louts around here had found his way into the kitchen," she said. "Yes. I'd be puzzled."

"Well, my love," he murmured, "someone's been messing about in my kitchen. I'd like to know who it is."

"Have you found any answers?"

"Not so far," he said. "Just a few more questions."

"What about?" she asked, seating herself across from him and causing a considerable stir among most of her clientele. "Aside from oxtail and mutton neck."

"The dead man up by the cathedral," he said.

"The one they say was killed by the Holy Grail?" she asked. "However that was supposed to be done."

Baptista shook his head. "It's not possible for the Grail to kill a man like that," he said.

"And who are you," asked Ana with a return of her old acerbity, "that you should know whether it's possible or not? A priest?"

"Who, me?" said Baptista. "Do I look like a priest?"

She leaned back and gave him a critical look. "Priests don't all look the same," she said, and laughed. "I've seen a lot of them in here at one time or another."

"Let's just say that without being a priest, I know that if he had that cup in his hand, it would not have killed him. And in fact I also know he didn't have it in his hand."

"How do you know that?"

"I'm an ordinary man, mistress, but I can tell the difference between a carrot and a pomegranate, for all that they're both red." He leaned forward confidingly. "It's just common sense. What would a man like that be doing with a holy vessel of that kind?"

"Then why are you worrying over it?"

"Am I?" he asked. "I suppose I am." He looked closely at her face and then laid a hand down on hers, as if to stay her from leaving. "Ana—you're a strange woman."

"No stranger than most," she said, leaving her hand where it was.

"Why do I have this powerful wish to tell you what it is—what is worrying me? Would you help me if I asked?"

"Likely," said Ana. She reflected for a moment. "Yes, I would."

Baptista stood up and pulled her to her feet. "There's something I want to show you—come up to my bed-chamber."

"Is there now?" she said sardonically. "I wonder what that could be?"

"God help me, Ana, I'm perfectly serious."

"If I leave this rabble for more than a minute, they'll rob me blind," said Rodrigue's wife.

"A minute is all it will take, I swear," said Baptista.

EIGHT

Wednesday, June 4

The next morning was clear and bright, with thin, high clouds that drifted lazily across the sky. By the time the cathedral bells rang for tierce, the clouds were gone, and the morning sun was dazzling to the eyes. Isaac and Yusuf had just entered the *call* on their way back from the Bishop's palace when they were stopped by a young man, scarcely older than Yusuf's thirteen years.

"Master Isaac," said the young man breathlessly, "I have run in search of you. I beg of you, for your kindness and charity, come to see my master. I fear he is ill, very ill."

"It is young Avi, is it not?" asked Isaac. "Who serves Shaltiel?"

"And learns great wisdom at his feet, Master Isaac."

"Certainly, we will come. And at once." Isaac turned toward the house of the philosopher, known by everyone in the *call* and for many miles beyond it for his great learning and his understanding of the mysteries of the Cabala. He quickened his pace. "Yusuf can run home for any of my poor medicines that might be needed to relieve your master."

"Yes, lord," said Yusuf.

Instead of being taken to the philosopher's bedchamber, Isaac was somewhat startled to be shown into his study. "Master Isaac," said Shaltiel. "I thank you for coming to visit me."

"I came the moment I heard you were ill, master," said Isaac. "But if you are ill, surely you should be in your bed, at rest."

"I prefer to see you here," said the Cabalist. "There are matters that we should speak of."

"Are there? It is always enlightening to speak to you, Master Shaltiel. Although by sending for me this way, you have frightened your pupil Avi, who seems to believe that Death has you in his clutches," observed Isaac. "But you have not the air of one who is near death. Not at the moment."

"I am ill, Master Isaac. A trifling digestive complaint, with a slight fever. Ordinarily I would not think of disturbing you for such a matter, but it provided a convenient excuse for seeing you, and a spur to move young Avi, who is something of a dreamer. Even though I tell him constantly that the greatest of minds and spirits are furnished with much dull learning and very hard work. But he is a good lad." He paused. "I wander from my topic," he said. "I beg of you, Isaac, sit down. There, beside you, is a chair."

Yusuf moved the chair closer to his master, and Isaac sat down. "Do you wish me to examine you, Master Shaltiel?"

"Not now, Isaac. That can wait." He drummed his

fingers on the tabletop for a moment, and then, in a changed voice, higher-pitched and no longer uncertain, he began to speak. "I see no evil in the fact that you devote much of your time to treating the Bishop. I have thought about it, and decided that there is nothing inherently wrong in it."

"Thank you, Master Shaltiel," said Isaac courteously.

"But I am profoundly disturbed to hear that you are assisting him in his search for this idolatrous symbol—this evil instrument—that he wishes to grace his temple."

"I have scarcely done that, Master Shaltiel," said Isaac.

"Please—allow me to present my case, and then you may answer it."

"Of course."

"And in addition, Master Isaac, you have dragged your innocent family into this quagmire, including this boy here."

"Where did you hear that?" asked Isaac. "It is not true."

"I have been told that your daughter Raquel and your wife have been called upon to assist you, as has your apprentice. You have put them, and us, in danger because of it. Much fury, they tell me, has been awakened in the city over this object. Your connection with it, Isaac, and your family's connection, means that the fury may well be unleashed against the community, with terrible results. If you cannot ignore a false god, Isaac, then you should strive to destroy it, not rescue it from oblivion."

Isaac sat still for the space of time needed to draw five deep breaths while he wrestled with his increasing anger. After the first moment, it was not anger against the scholar, who spent ten hours in meditation upon the paths to Wisdom for every minute he listened to idle gossip, but rage against those who had sought him out, and filled his ears with distortions and lies. It was not until he could control his voice and his words once more that he attempted a response. "Master Shaltiel," he said, "I do not doubt your wisdom or your learning. You have studied under great masters, some of whom had studied with Nahmanides himself. I do not doubt your wisdom, but I ask you to consider whether your information is correct."

"If there is anything that can be said in your favor in this matter, Master Isaac," said the scholar, his voice chilly with doubt, "I should be glad to discover what it is."

"Let me say what I believe myself to be doing, and if you find wrong in it, then I will listen, and—"

"And stop?"

"And consider," said Isaac.

"You were ever a stubborn man, Isaac. But I am willing to hear you."

"A man—one of my patients—has been murdered."

"By spells and sorcery, they tell me," said Shaltiel.

"No, Master Shaltiel. By a dagger thrust to the heart. There was no magic in it at all. In the course of the act, a vast sum of gold was stolen, one third of which belonged to a man of high repute and great importance in our community."

"The path to Wisdom is not laid with gold."

"It is not, master. I agree. But Astruch des Mestre uses his gold to provide for the poor. It would be a sad thing if he could no longer do that. An evil consequence of an evil act." Isaac paused. "You will no doubt tell me that others will provide for the poor, and I concede that you are right."

"You read my thoughts correctly, Master Isaac."

"More importantly I seek to prevent the most evil consequence of that act. The rumors arising from Gualter's death are stirring up a frenzy of fear and greed, cloaked in the name of religion, that could cause much havoc. Someone must locate the man whose hand planted the dagger, whether in his own person, or by proxy, and the gold that he committed the crime for. Someone must demonstrate to the frightened multitude that we do not have here a magical force, but a man. And that we do not deal with divine or fiendish retribution, but with simple, everyday greed."

"And do you believe that you can do that?"

"Do you doubt a blind man's ability to find the assassin?"

"I do not doubt that, Isaac. Everyone knows that you can find your way where a man with sight will not. I worry not about your physical blindness, Isaac, but your spiritual blindness. You are too headstrong to see the danger around you as you walk with perfect confidence through the maze."

"I see the danger, Shaltiel," said Isaac. "Sometimes it does not seem of great importance to me to heed its existence."

"Beware, Isaac. Those who transgress must suffer for their transgressions."

Isaac walked slowly away from the philosopher's house, considering Shaltiel's words with a worried frown.

"Isaac, my friend," said Astruch, "once more I seek your house to pour out my troubles. If losing all that gold were not an annoyance enough—"

"Annoyance?" asked Isaac.

"I try to convince myself that it is only that—that

many worse things could have happened to me and to my family in the last few days."

"Very true," said Isaac. "And it is a commendable point of view."

"But now," said Astruch, "something worse has happened. Young Martí has come to see me, to discuss the debt we spoke of. He brought with him two *maravedís,* to begin the repayment of the amount his father borrowed. Had it not been so heart-wrenching, Isaac, it would have been cause for laughter. At that rate of payment, our grandchildren—yours and mine, and even young Martí's—would all be dead before the debt was settled. It was all, he said, that he had. I believed him, Isaac. I still believe him. I took one coin and returned the other, saying that I intended to recover my loss when the gold was discovered and returned, not before. And now—so several people have told me—he goes about the city telling anyone who will listen that I killed his father."

"With your own hand?" asked Isaac, astonished.

"That I do not know—whether he believes I committed the act myself, or sent my agents to commit it, I cannot say. It is ridiculous. It is fantastical."

"It is very dangerous, as well," said Isaac. "I know a young man who is an acquaintance of young Master Martí," he added. "I will speak to him about it."

"Even if I were a bloodthirsty man—which the Lord knows, I am not, Isaac—why would I do something as foolish as that? Lend a man five thousand gold pieces and then kill him a few days later to redeem them?"

"For the other ten thousand pieces, Astruch. For the rest. That is why it is such a dangerous tale."

"I know, Isaac. And I also know that it is not a matter for the Albedín to settle. This matter would be tried in a Christian court. That is why it strikes fear into me."

• • •

And while Isaac and Astruch were in Isaac's garden, considering the problems raised by Gualter's death, Berenguer was donning his plainest black robe to meet his canons.

"Your Excellency," said Bernat, "you should not be leaving your bed. The physician said that tomorrow, if all were well, you could leave it briefly to walk around the palace, as long as you did not tire yourself unduly. That does not mean calling the canons together for what promises to be a difficult session."

"If Master Isaac wishes me to stay in my bed another day, he knows he must say that I am condemned to it for another week," said Berenguer. "I feel well. I am very tired of being in bed, and I must speak to the canons."

"They will not all be there."

"So much the worse for those who are not. Their voices will not be heard. Come along," he said, "and make sure that the scribe is there and that his pen is well mended."

"I will not keep you long this morning," said Berenguer to the assembled group. "I have only one thing to say. It is this. No one who answers to me is to talk about the Holy Grail. Not even among yourselves. Those who wish to speak to this prohibition may do so now."

"But why, Your Excellency?" asked one of the younger canons.

"The story has already roused too much fear—and greed—to allow unbridled gossip about it," said the Bishop.

"What do you suggest we say when we are asked about it? As happens constantly, for the subject is on everyone's lips," said Pere Vitalis.

"Gualter was carrying a large sum of money in order to buy silver dishes of rare and exquisite workmanship," said Berenguer. "He was set upon by thieves and murdered."

"It doesn't sound very convincing," said a doubting voice.

"If repeated often enough, it will be. Either convincing or too wearisome to continue to interest people."

"I object, Your Excellency." The loud voice, with its sudden pronouncement, caused every head to turn, except Berenguer's. "I wish to state that I object to your attempts to stifle debate on this question."

"Yes, Father Ramon?" said Berenguer, looking down the table at his infuriated canon. "Why?"

"It is much too late for secrecy," he said. "That is one reason. Everyone in town knows of the Grail being here, and we merely make ourselves foolish by denying it."

"And do you have another reason?" asked Berenguer. "For I do not know—nor do I believe—that the Grail is here."

"Another reason? Yes. Its presence in Girona can add greatly to the reputation and importance of the cathedral, which will in turn add to the glory of the Church everywhere."

"That might be true if we were not dealing with something that has been stolen, Orta," said Berenguer. "And the thief who has taken it. Under these circumstances, the tale will awaken emotions in people that can bring shame and disgrace to all of us. I will not have it," he added. "You will not speak of it again to anyone."

The meeting broke up in a spate of bitter wrangling, set off by Ramon de Orta's remark. Berenguer strode out of the room, buoyed up by his anger, but as soon as they were out of earshot, Bernat said, "I think he's right,

Your Excellency. It is too late to pretend it hasn't happened."

"Has the whole world gone mad?" said the Bishop. "Can you not see what you are letting loose in the city if we do not silence this talk? Think, man," he said, grasping Bernat's shoulder in his powerful grip.

"I agree with Father Bernat," said Francesc. "The time for silencing the issue was when it began, before we realized it was necessary. Now it is too late. I am quite sure that the physician is also seeking to find what or who lies behind it all. He fears an even greater force will be let loose in the city."

"How could he do this to me?" asked Berenguer of no one in particular. "Truly I am surrounded by madmen and fools."

NINE

Before the city roused itself from its after-dinner torpor, Isaac abandoned his meditations in the courtyard in order to seek his daughter. "Raquel," he said quietly, outside her chamber door, "we have a visit or two to make."

"To whom, Papa?" she asked, opening the door. "I didn't hear anyone call for us." It annoyed her that her father could sit anywhere in the house and, by listening, know exactly what everyone was doing, while she darted here and there, fully possessed of her eyesight, and seemed to miss so much.

"No, my dear. I received a message in the morning while you were visiting Mistress Dolsa. How is our neighbor?"

"Much improved, Papa," said Raquel, picking up her veil and hurrying out into the hallway. "I believe she is almost better. But I wish you would pay her a visit to make sure," she added.

"Is it your opinion that her malady is healing?" asked

Isaac as they clattered down the stone staircase.

"Yes, Papa. I am sure of it—almost sure."

"And when did you begin to doubt yourself, Raquel?" asked her father. "It is not like you."

"It is not that I doubt myself, Papa," said his daughter. "But she is a good friend to the family, and should something happen to her, I would—"

"You would suffer. And Daniel would suffer, as would my good friend Ephraim. Very true. Now fetch the basket, think no more of it, and let us be on our way."

Raquel threw the light veil over her head, went into the study for the basket, and headed for the gate.

"Where are we going, Papa?" she asked.

Isaac did not answer until they had passed through the open gate of the *call* and entered the city. "To Sant Feliu," he said. "To see your sister and brother-in-law. Nicholau stopped Yusuf on his way back from delivering some potions to the palace and gave him the message."

"I understand," said Raquel. For although her mother knew that her husband and daughter still visited her eldest and most beloved child, Rebecca, they hesitated to talk about it. When Rebecca abandoned her family and her people to marry a Christian, her disobedience and desertion caused such pain and anger in Judith that she felt it now as keenly as she had four years before. It did not help when neighbors murmured consolingly that it had happened in other families, or her husband pointed out that Rebecca had married a hardworking, learned, and upright man. Raquel and her father avoided mentioning Rebecca, even though she lived but a gentle ten minute stroll away, outside the city, in the shadow of the towering north wall.

Their visit had been timed to catch Nicholau after he had dined but before he returned to his labors at the diocesan courts. Little Carles, their son, was asleep, and Rebecca had set out cool drinks in the pleasantly shaded small courtyard of their house.

"I hope that I have not intruded too much on your kindness, Papa Isaac," said Nicholau, "in asking you to come to us, but I could think of no other way to deal with this situation."

"And which situation are we dealing with?" asked Isaac. "We have much to talk about, I think, and if you had not asked me to visit, I would have been here on another matter anyway—one on which I need your assistance. But tell me first what you wanted to speak to me about."

"Martí Gutiérrez," said Nicholau. "Doubtless you have heard of his father's death."

"Nicholau," said his wife, "Papa was there when his body was found outside the Bishop's palace."

"Of course," said Nicholau. "How could I have forgotten that? But there are complications, Papa Isaac. It seems that Martí's father owed money to Astruch des Mestre." And Nicholau, in his carefully precise way, told his father-in-law the whole story of Martí's anger and suspicions.

"Astruch has spoken to me," said Isaac, "and so I have heard much of this already, although not in so complete a form. I will admit that I find it alarming, and I assure you that Astruch himself is a worried man at the moment. It is not a matter of jest to be accused of the murder of a Christian, and to be brought into the Christian courts."

"Indeed not," said Nicholau. "And since it seemed to me that he was basing his accusations on the weakest of evidence, I became angry at him, and told him he was making false charges and acting maliciously, and that it was likely that the person who killed his father would go free because of his wild fabrications. He was drunk at the time, and I thought he had scarcely heard me, but this morning I saw him again. At the tomb of his father." He stopped.

"Yes?" said Isaac. "And had he changed his views?"

"It was clear that he was suffering from grief and remorse—for he and his father had quarreled as often as they had agreed," said Nicholas. "But his anger surpassed all other feelings. As his father's body was committed to its final resting place, he vowed eternal vengeance on those responsible for Gualter's death."

"Aloud?" asked Isaac.

"Yes. His mother was so distressed to hear him speak in that manner that I pulled him away before he could say more. He told me then that he still believed it was possible that Astruch had killed his father, but that there were others who could also have done so, and perhaps more readily. Then he said that rather than live a life of poverty and misery, he preferred to die in the cause of justice." Nicholau picked up his untouched wine and drained the cup. "I am worried for him, and for Master Astruch both. I do not know what I should do."

"It is possible that he might listen to the Bishop," said Isaac.

"Possible," said Nicholau. "But not likely. It was always difficult to make him listen to good advice until it was too late for it to help."

Baptista pulled aside the strip of leather that separated Rodrigue's kitchen from the public part of the establishment. "Ana," he said, "we must talk."

She looked up from the kettle of soup she was inspecting. "Sit," she said. "I'll bring you some wine in a moment."

True to her word, she finished what she was doing, gave some instructions to the potboy, and brought two cups and a pitcher of wine to the table. She sat down across from the trader, poured their wine, and looked up.

"Something has happened, my love," he whispered. "It is not safe for me to stay in the city any longer."

She blinked and took a mouthful of wine. "When do you go?" she asked stoically.

"I must leave before dawn. I'm sorry," he added, and set his hand over hers. "I'll miss you."

"It can't be helped," she said. "And I'll miss you more, as you well know. I'll be up early to get you some breakfast before you leave."

"Don't trouble yourself," he said. "I will slip quietly out without waking anyone." He glanced over, saw the frozen expression on her face, and shook his head. "Why was I fool enough to say that?" he said. "I would be grateful if you did. And here," he added. He slid a purse heavy with coins over to her. "This will cover my reckoning and maybe a new gown," he said. "Please. Take it."

"There's no need," she said in a dull voice.

"Yes, there is," he replied. "And if I thought there was some way to do it, I'd take you with me, clever Ana." He stood up. "I have messages to send. We will see each other later." He bowed gallantly and walked out of the tavern.

Raquel looked at her patient and nodded in satisfaction. "I think, Mistress Dolsa," she said, "that you are well enough to get up tomorrow."

"Tomorrow," said the glover's wife. "My dear Raquel, if I spend one more minute in this bed I shall be driven mad with boredom. The only reason I've stayed in it so far is that Daniel begged me to follow your instructions. But as soon as you leave this chamber, I intend to ring for my maid, dress, and go down to the courtyard."

"But you will send for me if you feel worse?" asked Raquel anxiously.

"If it makes you feel any better, Raquel, I will. I promise you. I will send for you if I think I am worse. And I thank you with all my heart for your attention. You might ring for the maid before you leave."

Raquel rang the bell close to Mistress Dolsa's bed and left the chamber. At the bend in the stairs, she gasped in surprise and stopped. Her way was blocked.

"Daniel," she said, red-faced and flustered. "I have just left your aunt. She seems to be much better. She's getting up."

"Good," he said. "She was happy to stay in bed for a day or two, but now she's a little impatient." He smiled at her. "I was on my way to her chamber to ask you to come down to the courtyard and sit for a while. Unless you have other visits you must make."

"No," she said. "Papa has taken Yusuf with him to visit the Bishop. Like your aunt, he is feeling much better and becoming difficult to deal with."

The table in the courtyard was spread with little delicacies. Daniel poured a cup of cooled mint tisane for Raquel and carried it over to a bench in the shade. The normally bustling house seemed deserted, and Raquel looked around for some sign of activity.

"My aunt will be down to join us in a moment," he said, divining her thoughts. "The maids are rushing about, getting piles of comfortable cushions and shawls for her. She won't be pleased," he added. "But they can't be stopped, either."

"She is so seldom ill," said Raquel, "that everyone worries when it happens."

At that moment Mistress Dolsa arrived in the midst of a flurry of attendants. She smiled with a helpless gesture at Daniel and Raquel, and allowed herself to be coddled. "They are trying to keep me in my bed," she said. "So they can run the house the way they like, but I've warned them that they have until tomorrow morning, and then we shall return to our usual ways." She looked around. "Esther," she said to her maid, "I would rather sit over there," pointing to the corner farthest away from Daniel and Raquel. "It is quieter and more peaceful. It will be better for me."

And with another great upheaval, they moved her chair, her cushions, her shawls, a table, and something for her to eat and drink to the other side of the courtyard.

"She's taking her revenge for all the nagging she's had to endure in these past few days," said Daniel.

"Pardon?" said Raquel. "Daniel, I'm sorry. I was thinking of something else and didn't even hear what you said. Papa is worried, very worried about what everyone is saying—he's gone off to talk to the Bishop about it, but the Bishop hasn't been very helpful, you know. He has his own worries about it all and doesn't much like what Papa wants to do."

"Raquel," said Daniel. "What are you talking about?"

"Master Astruch," said Raquel. "Haven't you heard?"

"Heard what?"

"About Martí Gutiérrez and Astruch des Mestre."

"What about them? I didn't realize they knew each other," said Daniel.

"Daniel," said Raquel in exasperation, "I think you've been spending too much time in the workroom. You must be the only person in this city who hasn't heard the foul rumors that Martí Gutiérrez is spreading about Astruch."

"I heard that Gualter's heirs thought that Astruch had hired assassins to kill Gualter, but it seemed so fantastical a tale that I didn't think that anyone would believe it."

"Many people do," said Raquel. "And it's all because of the money," she added, telling him the story as she knew it.

"And Martí is saying that Astruch killed his father?" said Daniel. "I cannot believe it. No one could believe it. A less likely assassin does not exist in the entire kingdom. How can Martí believe it?"

"As I heard it," said Raquel, "it is because of some remark Master Astruch made to Martí. Saying that he should not worry about trying to repay the loan, because he would recover the money from those who had it. And Martí thought he meant that he knew the men who had carried the gold off, and therefore he was part of a conspiracy to kill the merchant and steal his gold."

"There must be more to it than that," said Daniel. "That doesn't make sense. No one could think—"

"Nicholau said that Martí is very hasty in his judgments and inclined to stubbornness," said Raquel.

"I shall speak to him," said Daniel.

"Do you know him?"

"Of course I know him. Not only have I made him a pair of gloves that he prizes highly," said Daniel, "but we buy a great deal of leather from their warehouse. They bring in a particularly fine calfskin, excellent for riding gloves. I have had many pleasant conversations with him." He paused thoughtfully. "This one will not be so pleasant, I fear."

"I'm not sure that you should do this, Daniel," said Raquel.

"I am," he replied grimly.

• • •

The short summer night had finally darkened even the western sky. Above the mountains, the waning moon, just off the full, was struggling to make its appearance between flocks of racing clouds. When Baptista arrived at Master Vicens's gate, the city was alternating between being shrouded in shadows, illuminated by the flickering torches and pale lanterns of passersby, and brightly lit by the greenish-white glow of the moon.

The porter let him in, and accompanied him up the stairs to the family quarters. Baptista entered a good-sized sitting room where Master Vicens was poring over figures in the light of a four-branched candelabra, while his wife and daughter squabbled over the colors of their embroidery silks.

Vicens glanced up and then rose at once to his feet. "I'm sorry, my dears," he said, with perfect equanimity, "but this gentleman has come to see me on a matter of important business. I do apologize." Vicens went over to the door, had a word with the porter, and bowed Mistress Alicia from the room. She swept out in a rustle of the very best silk, leaving her daughter to gather up their work and carry it after her.

"Good evening, Master Vicens," said Baptista, not at all embarrassed by the disruption his visit had caused.

"What are you doing here, my good man?" said Vicens. "I thought we had agreed not to meet so openly."

"It is hardly openly," said Baptista easily. "The road outside your gate was as dark as pitch when I came in. I give you leave to explain me as you will to your porter and your family. I would imagine you can be a convincing man when it is to your advantage," he added with a sly smile.

"Very well," said Vicens grudgingly, settling his sizable frame back into his chair. "But if you visit here too often the whole world will know of it. Everyone's business is the food of common gossips. Sit down, man, for the love of heaven. The shutters are not closed."

"In a moment, perhaps," he said, wandering over to a shelf on which several silver dishes had been placed. "To say true, Master Vicens, I am very disturbed at what is going on around the city," he added, picking up one of the dishes and looking with great interest at it. "I believe I will pack up and go elsewhere. The climate here is not likely to be good for my health."

"But you—does that mean that you will not sell—"

"Like you, I am a merchant. I will always sell the goods that I have for sale, but if I cannot do it quickly, then I prefer to move on." As if to emphasize his point, he set down the silver dish and turned toward the merchant.

"Rather than have it go to another city, and be only of benefit to others, I will take it now," said Vicens. "It must stay here in Girona. Do you have it with you?"

"Certainly not," he said. "I am not so great a fool. I have no desire to join the corpse by the cathedral. Nor will I break my promise to the others by not allowing them an opportunity to buy," he declared piously, widening his soft brown eyes with a look of melting honesty. "Tell me what you are willing to pay, in gold, tonight, and if no one else matches it, then we will go together to where it is safely stowed and it is yours. You may bring a stout guard with you, if you are nervous."

"Will I have a chance to bid again after the others?" said Vicens.

"There is no time," said Baptista. "I intend to take its new owner to its place of concealment at first light and be gone at dawn. What is your offer?" he said.

Vicens turned away. He walked over to the door, opened it, and looked out. When he returned to his visitor, he whispered, "Eight thousand. But it must be brought to me here, in this house."

The next house the industrious trader visited was that of Sebastià. He was once more ushered into a sitting room. After a certain amount of scurrying back and forth in the background and some delay, the master of the house appeared.

"Well?" said Sebastià. "And what have you to offer me?"

"Nothing new," said Baptista, "except for the time. I must know your answer tonight."

"Why?"

Baptista repeated his tale almost exactly as he had told it to Vicens.

"What figures have already been bid?" asked Sebastià.

Baptista paused for a moment. "In all honesty, I'm not sure I should tell you."

"Why not? If I am not willing to surpass them, I will tell you. It will save both of us time and effort. If the figures already bid are too low, then I could well be outbid by the next contender. Unless I am the last?"

"No," said Baptista. "There is another."

"Excellent. Then tell me," he said.

"Eight thousand."

"In gold."

"Yes."

"Too much," said Sebastià. "As much as I would like to have it, I cannot gamble that much, knowing that it could well be false. But I am grateful that you have given me a chance to bid on it. Good evening, sir. I will see you to the door."

Baptista slipped out of Sebastià's gate without a sound and turned up the street toward the cathedral. The street was enshrouded in darkness and he had one more visit to make. He felt his way cautiously along the wall, listening for the slightest sound. A party carrying several lanterns and a blazing torch walked by, laughing and talking. He plastered himself against the irregular joint where two walls met, standing absolutely still and wrapped in thought. The amount that Vicens was offering had far exceeded even his greediest speculations. Perhaps he should have taken it then and there, but in his own way, he was honest in his dishonesty. As he had said, he had promised each of them a chance to bid, and he would fulfill his promise. The noisy crowd disappeared into a house and the street was quiet again. The clouds thinned, from time to time blowing off the face of the moon, lighting his way. He walked quickly northward, repressing the desire to sing as he went.

His heart and his step were light as he crossed the plaza toward the destined meeting place. The sky cleared. Moonlight flooded the area, showing up a couple of prowling cats. Something made a noise.

He stopped to listen. It sounded like the slight shuffle of leather on cobbles. With a lightning movement of his hand he drew his knife, still listening. He heard a slither and then a muffled curse, and relaxed. Somewhere not too far away some worthy citizen was making his way home after a night of revelry or devilry. But it was nothing to do with him, he thought, sheathing his knife again as he started up the hill toward the cathedral and the Bishop's palace. Let others enjoy the summer night in peace, for right now his luck was with him.

That was his first major mistake of the evening.

TEN

Thursday, June 5

A beggar who had elected to spend the alms that he
had wheedled out of the charitable on wine instead
of bread was the first person to catch sight of the body.
He had bedded down behind the cathedral, in a dark
corner soft with long grass, hidden from the probing rays
of the moon. It was a spot where experience had taught
him he would be able to sleep unmolested by anything
but the bells ringing the hours.

At prime, he had opened one eye. The bright light of
the new day hit it like a sharp knifepoint and he closed
it again, sleeping fitfully until tierce. This time when he
awakened, although he counted himself lucky to have
slept so long undisturbed, he was painfully aware that
he had a throbbing head and a powerful thirst. He struggled to his feet to go in search of cold water to quell
both.

He stretched, straightened his clothing, opened his

eyes wide, and screamed in terror. The log he had been lying against all night was a man—or had been a man— with a wicked deep gash in his throat.

"Had the man been there long?" asked the Bishop.

"When I saw it," said the captain of the guard, "the body was quite cold. And stiff. The unfortunate who had been sleeping next to him since some little time after matins was under the impression that he was a log of wood. He must have been cold by then."

"Why would the beggar seek out a log of wood?" asked Berenguer.

"In the hopes of avoiding the patrols, Your Excellency. The moon was very bright last night. Of course, where he was, in the shadows, he was also worried that someone would step on him in the dark," said the captain of the guard.

"Of course. And do we know who the dead man is?" asked the Bishop.

"He called himself a merchant, Your Excellency," said the captain. "He came into town during May, and took lodgings at Rodrigue's tavern."

"Not a particularly successful merchant, then," said Berenguer.

"He was more likely a peddler, Your Excellency, although perhaps in a grander way than some," observed the captain. "I was told to ask Mother Rodrigue about him. She appears to have known him as well as anyone, if the gossips can speak true."

"Then I will keep you no longer, Captain," said Berenguer. "I will leave you to pursue a further inquiry into the circumstances of this merchant's assassination. And, Captain, remember that I do not like all this murder and mayhem on the steps of the cathedral, or anywhere near it."

The captain bowed. "Certainly, Your Excellency," he murmured, wondering mutinously whether His Excellency believed that he was enjoying the disruption created by a couple of bloody corpses on the premises. As ever, though, his pleasant face remained impassive and unreadable.

Yusuf returned from his morning lesson in horsemanship to find the courtyard deserted except for Raquel, sitting at the long trestle table with a heavy volume opened in front of her. "You're late this morning," she said. "Papa has gone out already."

"Has he need of me?" asked the boy uneasily.

"He said not. He is visiting people nearby, and refused my help as well. None of them are ill, in my opinion," she said confidently. "They are after the most recent gossip."

"The basket was ready," said Yusuf, sounding defensive and anxious. "I packed it this morning."

"Stop worrying, Yusuf," said Raquel. "If he had needed someone, I was here."

"And you know more than I do," said the boy.

"That's a handsome admission, coming from you, Yusuf. And in return, I will confess that you know something very important that I do not. And that is your language," said Raquel. "I don't understand it at all. And I should. Many of the important texts in medicine are written in it." She pushed the thick, leather-bound manuscript toward him. "Like this one," she said. "You see? That's a treatise on herbs and plants. Many of them I can recognize from the paintings, but they probably have uses listed here that I've never heard of. And then there are pictures of plants that are completely strange to me."

"I will teach you my language. And how to read it," he said. "That way, you can study this book yourself."

"I would like to learn the speech," she said. "To begin with. And you can teach me some of that, if you would. But you can't read much more than the letters anymore. How can you teach someone else to read it?"

"A book like this will help me remember what I learned," he said. "I know more than you do, anyway. I know the common words, and perhaps there are scholars around who would help us with the difficult words."

"There are some," said Raquel doubtfully. "Papa knows it, if he could only see the letters."

Yusuf pulled the text closer to him and looked intensely at the page. "That is the word for 'harvest,' I think," he said. "But I am out of practice. Are you going to marry Daniel soon?" he added without a pause. "I only wondered because I have much to learn before I can assist my master as well as you do. And teach you to read my language."

"Marry Daniel?" she said, her face coloring. "Who told you that?"

"Well—any fool can see he is in love in with you," said Yusuf. "And the mistress is always trying to push you together when he is here. Are you in love with him?"

Raquel looked curiously at the boy. "It's none of your—well, I suppose it is your affair, isn't it? And in that case, the answer is no. I'm not in love with him."

"Why not?" asked Yusuf. It was clear from the look on his face that this was a very serious question. "He is handsome, isn't he?"

"I suppose he is," said Raquel. "I don't really notice. He's too—well, too everyday. Too commonplace. He's like a brother to me," she said irritably. "How can I be in love with him?"

"Don't you like him? I do, because he's clever. And amusing."

"Of course I like him. He's very comfortable to be with," she said. "But I wouldn't call that love. Do you remember Lady Isabel?"

"Of course I do," said Yusuf. "That was only a year ago."

"Love's more what Lady Isabel felt for her poor knight."

"And what is that?" asked Yusuf. "I ask you only because I think it is different for men, and here in Girona I have no sisters to ask."

"I suppose it is," said Raquel. "If what they say is true. Isabel said she felt strange and sick inside—which sounded very uncomfortable to me at the time—but—but it certainly isn't how I feel when I see Daniel." She pushed her hair back off her face. "It's hot today," she said.

"But you have known that feeling," observed Yusuf.

"You are a little devil," said Raquel. "Yes, I have, but not here, and not now. And that confidence is not to be passed on to Papa, either. It would only worry him, and there is nothing to worry about. Anyway, I suppose I shall marry Daniel someday, because one must marry, and he's better than many around here. Then everyone will be happy, won't they?"

"Will you?"

"I don't know."

It was midmorning before Daniel could find himself a reasonable pretext for going into town without arousing his uncle's curiosity. He had originally planned to explain that someone had to tackle Martí Gutiérrez about his reckless accusations, and since he knew him, he would do it. But now Raquel's uneasiness haunted him. If she thought it foolhardy to confront him, his uncle was going to feel it was complete madness. Delicate evasion of the topic seemed his best course. He left the shop, saying that he was going to fetch a few items and offering at the same time to deliver some messages. Of course, the items could well have been picked up by a servant, and the messages did not need great haste in their execution. His uncle concluded that the young man was restless and sent him off.

Daniel walked slowly along the crowded street, working out exactly what he would say to Martí. He marshaled his arguments with care, like so many pawns on the chessboard, ready to counter every attack, every justification the young man could possibly present in his own defense.

But his comfortably planned-out confrontation started badly. Martí himself came to the gate, looking bleary-eyed and somewhat pale. As soon as he saw who it was, he smiled gamely through his hangover at the sight of him.

"*Hola!* Daniel," said Martí. "It is kind of you to visit. Come in, come in. I have a head like the forger's fire and a mouth like a putrid swamp, but the sight of you cheers me up. Join me in a cup of wine."

"No, thank you, Martí," said Daniel, glowering at him. "I won't take anything. I merely wanted a few words with you."

If the cold tone of voice and stiff words had not alerted Martí Gutiérrez, Daniel's rigid back and hostile face would have. "What's wrong?" he asked.

"I have to speak to you on Astruch des Mestre's behalf," he said, starting out from his prepared script.

"Did he ask you to?" Martí's voice had developed a sharp edge to it.

"That has nothing to do with it," said Daniel, somewhat uncomfortably. That question hadn't figured on his list of arguments.

"It has everything to do with it. I would imagine that Astruch des Mestre is capable of fighting his own battles, Daniel."

"You have been trampling on his good name throughout the city," said Daniel, reverting to his lines. "Even a man well equipped to protect his body requires friends to protect his good name."

"And do you consider yourself to be his knight and protector?" he jeered.

A burst of anger swept Daniel's prepared speeches out the gate. "You are accusing him of murder on no evidence at all," he said, his voice shaking.

"I have evidence," said Martí, with an air of confidence that, under the circumstances, Daniel found maddening. "It's as good for him as it is for anyone else who might have done it." He sat down, sprawling, on a bench and looked up at his visitor. "Who pushed you into this, I'd like to know? Who sent you to see me? I'll warrant it wasn't Astruch."

"No one sent me."

"It was the physician's pretty daughter, wasn't it? And for her you'd accuse a friend of false witness, wouldn't you?"

"You lie!" said Daniel, maddened by the sheer unfairness of the blow.

"You say that to me once more and I'll take the flat of my sword to you," yelled Martí, jumping up.

"Would you attack an unarmed man? Give me the use of a weapon, and I'll prove the lie on you," roared Daniel. "Coward!"

"Now you go too far," said Martí. "You shall have a sword, and much good may it do you." He looked around the courtyard, as if he expected a sword to be thrust into his hand from nowhere. "Swords," he yelled.

Nothing happened. "Bring me swords, you lazy

louts," continued Martí, raising his arms in frustration.

"Martí," said a sharp female voice. "What are you doing?"

The spectacle of the younger man trying to conjure up a pair of swords in front of his mother, the formidable Mistress Sibilla, suddenly seemed comic to Daniel. "Even the servants pay no attention to us," he said, with a grin.

At that, Martí lunged at Daniel, who was older, taller, stronger, and longer in arm and leg, as if he meant to attack him with his bare hands.

By now the courtyard was filling up with servants. Mistress Sibilla stalked across the courtyard, heading for her son. "Your father is hardly in his tomb and already you are brawling in the courtyard like a drunken ruffian," she said in furious tones. "Get in the house. Go, you, take your master into the house," she said to a groom and the porter. "At once. I ask your pardon, Daniel, for my son's behavior. He is not himself. I must ask you to excuse me. I bid you good day." And she moved swiftly, with a rustle of silk, toward the door of the house.

The gate clanged shut behind Daniel. The front door slammed after the mistress and the young master. At once, a buzz of speculation rose among the servants. The porter and the groom returned, eager to add their uninformed observations to the slender store of fact. After several minutes of excited conversation, a kitchen lad slipped out to tell the fascinating tale to his friend who worked nearby; one of the grooms did the same; the maid picked up her shopping basket with much more than her usual enthusiasm and headed straight for the market.

The maid went first in search of fish. It was not that her mistress had particularly asked for fish—she had been too tormented with grief and worry to care what she ate—but that Bartolomeu's gossip was usually as abundant and accurate as his fish was fresh and expensive.

"You're late this morning," he remarked. "All the finest fat ones for baking are gone. But I have some lovely little sardines here. They'd make a tasty morsel to tempt your mistress's appetite—poor lady. And very fresh mackerel."

"It's no wonder I'm late, Bartolomeu," she said. "We had such a to-do this morning—"

"Nothing to what's going on here," said the fishmonger, lowering his voice to a whisper.

"Really?" she said, somewhat annoyed at having her moment of glory overshadowed. "My young master was in such a temper—"

"You haven't heard of the murder?"

"What murder? My master's? That's what the quarrel was about—"

"No—that's old news. I'm talking about the murder of the merchant who was staying at Rodrigue's," he said in a low voice as he filled up her basket with sardines.

She covered them with a linen cloth and then leaned forward. "He was murdered?" she said. "When?"

"Last night," said Bartolomeu. "Or this morning, early."

"What happened to him?" she asked, drawn in in spite of herself.

"Throat cut, and his body left beside the cathedral, right up against the holy walls themselves."

"Who was the cutthroat?"

"I expect that Rodrigue came out of his drunken stupor last night long enough to discover what everyone else knew," said the fishmonger. "For if the potboy can be believed, our friendly merchant found Mother Rodrigue particularly welcoming. It's only natural that Rodrigue would take the opportunity to assert his rights."

"Not at all," said Caterina the sweetmeat seller. "Rodrigue's still as innocent—and as stupid—as a newborn babe. I heard—and it came from good authority, mind you, straight from the cathedral itself—that Baptista had his hands on the Holy Grail when he had just climbed from an adulterous bed with his sin still fresh on him, along with plenty of other sins as well, I have no doubt—and that it is death for anyone but the purest of men to touch the sacred cup."

"Did they find the cup on his body?" asked the maid, wide-eyed with astonishment.

"Not at all," said Caterina, shaking her head ominously. "Not in any form."

"What do you mean?" asked the maid.

"They're saying that the holy vessel can change into anything it wants to save itself from being taken by wicked men, or being sold, or used for sacrilegious purposes—"

"There are those who would use it for witchcraft?" the maid whispered, in great excitement.

"For any foul purpose," asserted Caterina. "It could be anything in this market, you see, and if you touch it, and you're not completely free of sin, you, too, will die."

The maid stepped back in great alarm. "You mean it could be one of Bartolomeu's fish?" she asked, staring down at her basket as if it were about to attack her.

"Not that sort of thing, you foolish girl," said Caterina angrily. "A tin dish, an iron pot, even a wooden cup. It wouldn't hide itself in the form of something that could be killed and eaten."

All the while they had been speaking, a few women, and even a couple of curious men, drew near the knot of people in front of the fishmonger's stall. Each of Caterina's pronouncements drew a fascinated murmur from them. "So any dish in this market could be the Grail, ready to kill us?" asked a big, red-faced woman standing behind Mistress Sibilla's maid.

"How do we tell which one it is?" asked another.

"You touch it," said a wag, "and see how long it takes you to drop dead."

It was difficult to pinpoint the exact moment when this discussion turned from a tantalizing gossip into an hysterical rampage. It may have been when a young and very credulous kitchen maid, who had been sent to the market to fetch onions, reluctantly walked away from this fascinating conversation only to bump into a woman selling crockery and earthenware dishes.

"A lovely baking dish, my dear," she crooned, holding out a clay dish. "For your mistress or your dowry. Here, touch it—feel how smooth it is and how carefully made."

The little kitchen maid screamed in terror and thrust her arms out to defend herself. The dish fell on the ground and broke into a hundred pieces. "It is the Death come upon us again!" she shrieked. "Help me! O Mother of God, help me!"

ELEVEN

Everyone within earshot rushed over to see what was happening; seeing the maid screaming hysterically and the broken pot on the ground, each jumped to his own conclusion and took action. By the time two of the Bishop's guards arrived, some had already fled with tales of doom and destruction on their tongues, some stood and watched, and the two men who had turned over the table were occupied in smashing a quantity of clay dishes. The stall holder was nursing a cut thumb and voicing her indignation.

The two enthusiastic and destructive drunkards who had tipped the table were arrested; at that, most of the spectators melted away into the crowd. The sense of hysteria that was gathering over the city was not so easily stifled, however.

The captain of the Bishop's Guard rode down the short distance from the cathedral stables to the market-place with his sergeant and looked soberly at the groups of sobbing women.

"I can sort this out, Captain," said the sergeant. "It'll be easier now than later," he added. "Many of the witnesses have already disappeared, just looking at us."

The captain shook his head, looking grim. "His Excellency wants us to stay out of all this as much as possible. The city guards are on their way. Wait and tell them what you've seen, but purely in the spirit of friendship and cooperation. I'm going to report to him now."

"And without further authorization, Your Excellency, there is little more that we can do," said the captain, and bowed.

"Thank you," said Berenguer. "Keep me informed, Captain, but for now, proceed no further." The Bishop waited until the captain had withdrawn and then turned to his secretary and the canon. "What more have you heard?" he said.

"Rumors, Your Excellency," said Francesc. "And yet more rumors. Gossipmongers tell me they are being spread by Ramon de Orta."

"Orta," said the Bishop. "Are you sure that he is the source? And what are they?"

"He has said nothing to me, Your Excellency," said Francesc, "and therefore I cannot tell you if the rumors come from him. But I am told that they are spreading like fire through dry grass. The scene in the market was only the first of several flare-ups that we will see, I would guess."

"What are spreading, Francesc?"

"My apologies, Your Excellency. People are saying once more that the Holy Grail has been found. That it was on the body of the murdered man. And that it is highly dangerous to be near it, even inadvertently, unless you are a person of unspotted virtue."

"Anything else?" asked Berenguer wearily.

"And that because of its holy and magic powers, it can transform itself into any material it wishes, Your Excellency. Therefore you can touch it without knowing what you are doing, and suffer the direst consequences. That group of credulous idiots down there—"

"There's enough of them," muttered Berenguer.

"They panicked, thinking they could be slaughtered by a clay baking dish or a cup."

The Bishop straightened up and assumed a look of purposeful energy. "We must find out if these rumors are indeed being spread by Orta," he said. "And if they are, why? Why does he wish to terrify people?"

"Perhaps he feels it will prevent attempts at theft of sacred vessels in the treasury, Your Excellency," said Bernat tentatively. "Some might believe the Grail is there."

"Not if they are told it could be disguised as the poorest laborer's wooden cup," said Berenguer. He shook his head. "I am too weary to deal with the madness of the world right now. You may go, but please have the goodness to inform Orta that I wish to speak to him."

"Now, Your Excellency?" asked Bernat.

"No. Now I shall rest. I will see him at sext, here in my study."

"Shall I send for the physician, Your Excellency?" said Bernat in alarm.

"No," said Berenguer. "He is the like the rest of you. Convinced he knows what I should do. I need to be left alone to discover the best solution to this problem." He rose and headed toward his chamber. When he reached the small, heavy door that led into it, he turned back. "Yes. Inform him that I would like him to visit after Orta has left." He disappeared into his bedchamber, leaving the secretary and the canon looking at each other.

"I would not have expected him to regard this incident quite this way," said Bernat diplomatically.

"It could turn out to be a grave mistake, I fear," said Francesc. "We shall see."

"Often His Excellency has information he neglects to pass on to us," said Bernat, who was younger and more optimistic than his colleague. "If so, he may be pursuing the wisest course."

"Perhaps."

Ramon de Orta was punctual to the minute for his appointment. As soon as the first touch of the bell for sext shivered the air, he was ushered into Berenguer's study.

The Bishop awaited him, seated at his table, looking pale and rather weary. "Father Ramon," he said, "forgive this peremptory summons, but there are some matters of great importance to the diocese that I would talk over with you."

Ramon de Orta had not expected his bishop to look so tired, but he was suspicious of Berenguer's mild and conciliatory manner. He sat down in the proffered chair and narrowed his eyes, prepared for battle. "I would be delighted to give you any assistance in my power, Your Excellency," he said meekly.

The Bishop leaned back and attempted to consider his canon without the deadening influence of habit on his senses. What was Orta? he wondered. Ambitious, shrewd, intelligent, and impatient. He was all of those. Probably the most power-hungry of them all, and certainly the most competent. "Rumors abound in the city today, Father Ramon," he said. "Strange rumors. And the strangest of all of them concerns you."

"Me, Your Excellency?" said Orta. "I am astonished. Of course, the subject of rumors is customarily the last person to hear of them."

"So they say," said Berenguer.

"May I ask Your Excellency what they are, these rumors?"

"The most persistent one seems to be that those tales—the ones that are spreading in the market, and the corn exchange, and the wool exchange, and in the courts—have come from your lips, Father. Are you their author?"

"Is that what they say, Your Excellency?" asked Orta. He sat relaxed and yet upright in his chair, the very picture of a completely innocent man. "How extraordinary."

"You do not sound surprised, Father Ramon."

Ramon de Orta shook his head. "Does Your Excellency know what these tales are that I am reported to be spreading around the city?"

"I do. That the Holy Grail is in the city. That it was found on the body of the peddler Baptista. That it is death to come near it, and that it can take any form it wishes."

"That is not completely accurate," said Ramon easily. "Taking any form it wishes is a fanciful elaboration, and I did also say that it was no danger to a pious and holy man. Having in mind that Your Excellency could then rescue it should it be found without the general populace believing that the experience would destroy you."

"What?" said Berenguer, turning white with anger. "You have gone out to the markets and the exchanges and the courts and deliberately spread this tale? For what possible reason could you do this? Have you gone mad?"

"Not at all, Your Excellency. I was alarmed at the death of the peddler because I happened to know that he was claiming that he possessed the Grail. He wished to sell it. He approached me and several other people to see what price he could get. It seems that the first person he approached was Gualter, who died. Then he himself died the night he was to deliver it to someone else."

"You?"

"No, Your Excellency. I told him he was asking too much for something that was unlikely to be real. When I was in the court this morning, I was asked about the Grail by a respectable citizen who had already heard rumors, and I stressed the dangers of possessing it, hoping to head off further madness. It seemed a good idea, and so I did the same at the various exchanges and then in the market."

"And created hysteria in the city."

"I beg your forgiveness, Your Excellency, if my idea did not turn out as expected. I ought to have known that my tale would be elaborated in various strange ways."

"You might have spoken to me about it, Father Ramon, before you started. I would have predicted that easily enough for you."

"Your Excellency has not been well. I did not like to disturb you."

"I have found the consequences of your failure to do so much more disturbing."

Ramon de Orta rose, and bowed. "Again, I humbly beg Your Excellency's forgiveness. Of course," he added, almost nonchalantly, "if the Grail is in the city, it belongs in the cathedral, where it will be both an ornament and a bastion of strength."

Once he had left, Berenguer sat very still, his elbows on his desk, with his fingers forming a pyramid in front of him. "Well," he said to the empty room, "what did you think of it?"

"Extraordinary, Your Excellency," said Bernat, coming out of the bedchamber.

"What is he up to?"

"I find it difficult to believe that he could have done something so dangerous without realizing what its consequences could be," said Bernat. "But perhaps it is so."

"Oh, no," said Berenguer. "Orta is much too clever and knowledgeable in the ways of man not to know what he was doing. But why did he do it? What was he up to? And where is my physician?"

"Coming up the stairs, I believe, Your Excellency. I saw him crossing the plaza a few moments ago, and he walks at a speed that few can surpass."

"I am weary, Isaac, weary," said Berenguer. He was back in his chamber, stretched out on his bed, passively allowing the physician to examine him without any of his usual impatience. "Last night I was too weary to sleep, and now today the city is erupting into nightmares."

"Your Excellency has not recovered from the illness you were suffering from," said Isaac. "I warned you. You were to stay in bed, and you have done nothing since then but hold meetings and deal with difficult problems. Just because you have not left the palace does not mean you are resting."

"And now I have discovered that the unrest in the city was caused by one of my own canons. I cannot walk away from that and take to my bed, Isaac."

"If you do not, Your Excellency, you will not recover. I know that you are a strong man, but even strong men can fall ill, and die through neglect of their illnesses."

"If Orta is trying to kill me," said Berenguer, "he has chosen a very roundabout method of doing it."

"It is not one that could ever be brought home to him, is it, Your Excellency?"

Berenguer struggled halfway to a sitting position. "That is a sobering thought, my friend." He closed his eyes and dropped back again. "Well, Isaac, what do you think of this? I will rest until Sunday, when I must preach. Does that meet with your approval?"

"No, Your Excellency."

"No?"

"Your Excellency must postpone any further effort for another seven days," said Isaac.

"Seven days," said Berenguer. "Until Thursday next." There was a long pause. "I shall consider it," said the Bishop. "It may not be convenient, but it may be possible."

"I hope so, Your Excellency. Because if it is not convenient, nor possible, then your work may end up being done by your successor."

"But, Isaac, I do not feel ill enough to lie about in my bed."

"I do not care, Your Excellency. I shall speak to the head cook about your meals before leaving the palace. And you must eat what he prepares for you."

"Yes, Master Isaac," said the Bishop meekly.

"And I shall return later this afternoon."

TWELVE

Friday, June 6

The regular meeting of the council of the city of Girona had already dealt with the major issue of the day in the time-honored manner of governing bodies in a state of bafflement. Pons Manet, the wool merchant, in his capacity as temporary leader of the council, rose and delivered a concise and sober report on the disturbance in the marketplace, noting in a way that did not encourage further discussion that the guards had dealt with those responsible, and that the traders' losses had already been made good by those who had caused them. A general sigh of relief went 'round the chamber, and the gentlemen gathered there turned their attention to matters that were more to their liking.

They had just commenced a relatively heated debate over peddlers' licenses for the next fair when a completely unprecedented event shattered their normal calm. A shrill high-pitched voice echoed through the chamber, raising the dust of months—not to say years—and even waking some of the more somnolent members.

"I demand to be heard!" The words themselves were extraordinary enough, but that they should issue from the mouth of a young woman—a pretty young woman named Marta, dressed in her best gown, which was one of her young mistress's discards—was even more extraordinary. That she had managed to slip by the two guards at the door and thrust herself among them caused great consternation in the ranks of the grave merchants and lawyers of the city.

"Guards!" called one.

"Eject her!" said another, and then a whole chorus of voices arose.

"I have something of great importance to say," said Marta in her loudest voice, with no regard for proper procedure. "Something that I think you gentlemen ought to know about."

"And what is that?" said Pons, drowning out those who preferred to eject her at once, rather than listen to her. "But say it quickly. We have much to consider to-day."

"I discovered something yesterday," she said, with great self-possession. "My mistress sent me out to scrub the courtyard yesterday morning, even though it is not my work, and I found blood there—dried blood—on the stones under the lemon tree."

This caught their attention. In the silence, Pons asked, "And whose courtyard are we speaking of? Which household?"

"Oh," she said. "My master's. Master Vicens's court-yard."

A general uproar arose from the members of the council. "What did she say?" said a plaintive voice, rising above the rest. "Who is she?" asked another, looking bewildered and apparently addressing the stones of the vaulted ceiling.

"There is blood on the stones of Master Vicens's courtyard?" repeated Pons as soon as he could be heard. "I cannot believe it."

"This must be looked into," said another member, a grave man who rarely spoke. "As soon as possible. For is it not possible that one of the dead men by the cathedral was not killed there, but elsewhere?"

"Unlikely," said a firm voice.

"True," said another, "but it is important to look into it." A murmur of agreement ran through the council chamber.

"Shall we have him arrested?" asked a bright-eyed man known to all to be no friend of the cloth merchant.

"No," said Pons. "I will not request the arrest of an honorable man on the unsupported word of his housemaid. But certainly the allegation must be looked into."

Once more the murmur of agreement ran around the room, and Marta took the opportunity to dart out as she had come in—unseen and unexpected.

Isaac walked from the Bishop's palace to the *call* in a state of indecision. As he thought, his footsteps slowed, and the hand that customarily sat lightly on Yusuf's shoulder began to drag the boy back.

"Are you well, lord?" asked Yusuf, who could think of nothing else that would slow his master to this extent.

"What did you say, lad?" asked the physician.

"Are you well, lord?"

"Certainly. I am very well. I was deep in thought, and the world had disappeared for the moment. I am back in it once more, and shall stay for a while," he added with apparent good humor.

"His Excellency seemed somewhat improved," said Yusuf tentatively.

"He is," said Isaac. "If he keeps to his bed for a while longer he will recover his forces, I believe. And I think I shocked him into obedience yesterday. But that is not what my mind was engaged with. Today I would like to heal the breach with Master Shaltiel," he continued. "It grieves me that so good and wise a man should waste his strength and time in anger against me. Tonight the Sabbath begins, and I wish for peace and reconciliation before sundown."

As soon as they entered the *call,* Yusuf headed for Master Shaltiel's gate, but before they reached it, the boy paused. "What do we do if he refuses to admit us?" he asked uncertainly.

"We send him our very best wishes for his health and comfort and go away," said Isaac simply. "I will not force myself on a friend or a patient."

Shaltiel's pupil Avi opened the door, looked uneasily at the physician, and asked him to enter.

"And how is your master?" asked Isaac.

"I fear he is very ill," said Avi. "I wish you could do something for him."

"That is only possible if he will agree to be helped."

Heavy footsteps sounded on the stair. "Shh," said Avi. "He is going to his study. He must have heard you."

"Then let us follow him," said Isaac.

"Very good, Master Isaac," said the boy.

Isaac stood in the doorway to the philosopher's study. "Your pupil, young Avi, says that you are still unwell, Master Shaltiel," said Isaac. "I have come to see if there is anything that I can offer you to ease your pain and discomfort."

"There is nothing."

"I have with me simple remedies that will help your

condition. I ask only that you allow me to leave them here."

"To be honest, Master Isaac, it troubles me to take treatment at your hands," said Shaltiel.

"Why should that be? If you had a philosophical quarrel with the baker, would you refuse to eat his wholesome bread?"

"Isaac, you argue like the snake, twisting logic, making it sound fair and tempting."

"Have I twisted logic? I had not thought that I had done more than present a simple analogy to bolster my argument."

"It is an analogy that fails. A baker's philosophical convictions—should he have any—do not affect his baking."

"I assure you, Shaltiel, that a physician's grasp of logic does not affect the grinding of his herbs, or his power of smell or touch. For example, I can smell from across this room that you are still feverish, and that your body is starved for water. This is not good," he said, and gestured for Yusuf to bring him the basket. He reached in and took out a small vial, tightly corked. "I have here an opiate, a most efficacious one. A few drops in water will calm your gut. Not only will it allow you to drink, but also to eat and sleep." He laid the vial on the table between them and reached into the basket again. He took out a small bundle of dried herbs. "If you steep these herbs in hot water and drink the liquid, your fever will ease, and your body will be able to throw off the malady that it suffers from. These remedies do not come from magic or arcane lore. This is what I learned as a raw apprentice, and have done many, many times, as the baker has kneaded a loaf many, many times."

"If I take these preparations," said Shaltiel, "will you

give up your futile search? Will you stop disturbing the city and the community with your inquiries?"

"Do you threaten me with illness in order to quiet me?" asked Isaac.

"Master Isaac, by your blundering about, you are bringing disgrace upon yourself and our community. I beg you, think of your fair name."

"What is more important?" asked Isaac. "Truth and Justice? Or Reputation?"

"If you were a laborer, I would answer Truth and Justice, Isaac."

"Why?"

"Because few would be swayed by your actions. But since you are what you are, men see what you do, and hear what you say. They believe you must be right. They are convinced of your virtue, and model their actions upon yours, knowing nothing of your motives. Since they do not ask themselves why you do what you do, then the outer perception becomes as important as the inner reality." Shaltiel said. "For example, if a fool sits on a stone in the heat of the July sun wrapped in a warm cloak, men will remark that only a fool would do that, and pass by. If a man of wisdom and virtue does the same thing, they will conclude that there is wisdom and virtue in such behavior, and never wonder why the wise man does it. And some of them may imitate him."

"There is much in what you say," said Isaac. "I do not promise to change my approach, but I will remember that."

"Do you do this at the behest of your friend the Bishop?" asked Shaltiel.

"No, Master Shaltiel, I do not. What little I have done is for the sake of Astruch des Mestre, no one else. His Excellency is as angry as you are that I am stirring up mud that he wishes would remain at the bottom of the pond."

"I am not angry, Master Isaac," said Shaltiel. "I am saddened by your actions."

"The air is thick with your anger, Master Shaltiel," said Isaac. "Even your lad can feel it, and trembles at the sound of your feet in the passageway. I can feel it like a heavy blanket that must be choking you, and it grieves me that I am its cause."

"And are you free of anger yourself, Master Isaac, that you chide others for it?"

"Not at all. Anger lies coiled in my belly constantly. Usually it sleeps, but without a moment's warning it rises and strikes and then I am doubly blinded, for it smothers my other senses and my reason as well. I know its dangers, and its smell, Master Shaltiel. I shall leave these preparations for you. You may take them or not, as you will." And the physician turned and headed for the door.

" 'Ware the door, lord," murmured Yusuf. And Isaac ducked to pass his tall frame under the lintel.

"Is anger so evil, lord?" asked Yusuf, once they were on the street again. "I thought that anger in a good cause was a noble thing."

"You could see its dangers yourself, Yusuf."

"That the philosopher refuses to take medicine?"

"No—that my anger at his stubbornness made me forget how wretchedly small the doorways are in his house. Had it not been for your timely warning, I would have been suffering now from a fine crack on the head. Do not speak of this to your mistress, lad," he added. "I would not worry her."

"No, lord."

"You have eaten almost nothing, Isaac," said Judith, her voice sharp with worry. "What is wrong? Are you ill?"

"No, my dear. I am quite well. The heat has blunted the edge of my appetite, I admit, but nothing else ails me."

"You are worried," pronounced his wife.

"I am in excellent health and spirits," said Isaac grimly. "Or I was until a moment ago."

"Are you worried, Papa?" asked Miriam. "Why?"

"I am not worried, my love," said Isaac sharply, "except that you will spend too much of your life listening to other people's conversations instead of attending to your own affairs."

Chastened, Miriam bent her head to her plate and played unhappily with her piece of bread, breaking it into crumbs and throwing it to the birds.

"Miriam," said her mother, "that bread is for you to eat, and not—"

They were rescued by the clanging of the bell. Yusuf slid from his place on the bench and ran to open the gate, admitting a tall, heavily veiled woman, dressed in respectable dark clothing. "May I speak to the physician?" she asked in a low voice and then remained standing where she was, by the gate.

"Raquel, Miriam, help Naomi to clear the board," said Judith, rising to her feet and admitting that dinner was over, in spite of the food left untouched. "There is much yet to be done for tonight, and Naomi cannot possibly finish it all. Hurry!"

And with incredible speed the table was cleared and moved to the edge of the courtyard. Judith followed her two daughters into the kitchen to lend a hand with preparations for the Sabbath.

"Is someone ill, mistress?" asked Isaac. "It will be the matter of a moment for me to fetch my basket and—"

"No, Master Isaac, no one is ill," she replied uneasily.

"I would like to speak to you, that is all."

"Then come over by the fountain and we shall speak. Will you take something to drink after your walk? The day is warm."

"I would be grateful for a cup of water," she said, "if you please, Master Isaac. Nothing else."

Yusuf hastened over to fetch her cool water from the fountain.

"Thank you," she murmured, and removed her long veil in order to drink.

The fine dark cloth that obscured her hair, features, and the upper half of her gown had concealed a handsome woman, broad-shouldered and strong, with dark eyes and a ruddy complexion. At the sight of her unveiled face, Yusuf took an involuntary step backward.

He knew her well—probably much better than she knew him. In his poverty and rags, when he had first scratched out an existence in the streets of Girona, he had more than once helped himself to a piece or two of bread from the kitchen of her establishment. "Mother Rodrigue," he said, with trembling voice, convinced that she had come at last to call him to account for his crimes.

"That is what they call me," she said. "My husband is Rodrigue who keeps the tavern down by the river, Master Isaac. But my name is Ana."

"Well, Mistress Ana, is it about your husband that you wish to speak?" There was a pause that lasted slightly too long. "Yusuf," said the physician, "the basket must be refilled and made ready as soon as possible. Don't forget to replace what we used this morning."

"Yes, lord," said the boy nervously, still waiting for the blow to strike. From his knowledge of Mother Rodrigue, he doubted that his presence would deter her from complaining about him to his master. But she appeared to have lost all interest in him; instead her eyes were fixed on the interior of the courtyard and then on the walls of the house as if she were planning to build herself a copy of the physician's dwelling. With a flash of relief, it occurred to him that he had changed so much since he, too, had first entered this courtyard—from a filthy street urchin to the polite, clean, and properly dressed apprentice of an important man—that Mother Rodrigue had not recognized him. He ran off to his master's workroom, buoyed up with confidence.

"That is a clever lad you have there," she said. "I have seen him about."

"He is frequently out on errands for me, Mistress Ana. A most trustworthy boy," said Isaac firmly.

"I don't doubt you, Master Isaac," said the publican's wife. "But I have made bold to visit you because I must speak to you about Baptista, the man who was found dead near the cathedral. On Wednesday, if you remember."

"You knew him, Mistress Ana?"

"I did. He lodged at our house, and we became— friends, shall we say. He may not have been entirely honest, but he was a pleasant man. And in many ways, a good man." She stopped again. "He made me laugh, when I thought I had forgotten how."

"You will miss him, then," said Isaac. "I am sorry."

"He was leaving anyway," she said, dismissing any grief she might be suffering. "Early yesterday morning. He settled his account the night before. I had packed food for him for the road, and rose early to prepare him some breakfast, but when I went to wake him, he wasn't in his bed. And he never came back. Then I heard that he was dead, and I thought it must have something to do with what he was selling."

"And what was that?" asked Isaac.

But she ignored him, and continued on with her tale in her own way. "He had a list of men he was trying to sell it to—"

"A long list?" asked the physician.

"No, not long," she said. "Three or four, I think."

"Forgive my interruptions," murmured Isaac.

"It is nothing," she said. "Then that last night he went to visit them all, to ask them what their final offer was. The one willing to pay the most would get to buy it, of course. He didn't leave to talk to them until well after compline."

"And he never came back?"

"I think I heard him come into the house later and go out again, but it might have been a dream I was having," she said. "I never saw him again."

"What was he selling?"

"A cup. It was a silver cup. He was selling it as the Holy Grail," she added flatly.

"And was it?" asked Isaac curiously.

"He didn't know," she said. "He told me that the person who gave it to him believed it was. And then he said that for all he knew, maybe it was the Grail. Master Isaac, one of those people he went to see last night wanted it very badly, and had no gold to pay for it, and took it by cutting Baptista's throat."

"Did you ever see it?" he asked.

"Yes," she said. "Before he decided it wasn't safe to keep it at the inn. It was just a cup made of silver—old and in poor condition, too. It was very plain, and badly dented. Tarnished. He wouldn't let me polish it because he said he wanted it to look old, and it mightn't if it were all cleaned and shining."

"And you touched it?"

"I did. I even gave it a little polish with my sleeve, it looked so sad. What they're saying just isn't true, Master

Isaac. It doesn't hurt anyone. I'm fine, except I'm angry about Baptista."

"Then why have you come to me, Mistress Ana? Since I cannot help your anger."

"I heard that you were trying to find the Grail for the Bishop, Master Isaac, and I thought it might help you if you knew about Baptista. It bothered me that everyone was saying that Master Astruch took it, and I know that he wasn't on Baptista's list of people."

"Who was on the list?" asked Isaac.

"I cannot say, Master Isaac. I never saw it. Nor would it have helped me if I had, since I never learned to read or write, except to keep a tally of money owed. I know enough to chalk up a reckoning, but this list was all writing, and he never read it out to me."

"Then how do you know Master Astruch was not on it?"

"Because he is a Jew," she said simply. "Baptista said that a Jew or a Moor would only pay what the cup was worth as a drinking cup. He wanted more than that. So there were no Jews on Baptista's list."

"That does not surprise me," said Isaac dryly.

Again she carried on, as if again she could hear no voice but her own. "There were only rich Christians—rich and gullible, he hoped."

"I am still puzzled, Mistress Ana. Why do you come to me?"

"I do not know Master Astruch. He is not a drinking man, and Rodrigue and I have had no need of bankers. But still, from all I have seen and heard, I think him an honest man. It would anger me to see him suffer wrongfully just to satisfy some of his enemies."

"Your feelings do you credit, Mistress Ana," murmured the physician.

"They are no better nor worse than most people's,"

she said. "Master Isaac, Baptista made me laugh. I want the man who killed him to be taken up for his murder." She stood up and wrapped herself in her veil again. "And I believe what people say—that you can make sure that it happens. That was all that I wanted to say, Master Isaac," she added. "Except that if I knew who killed him, I might slip a sharp knife between *his* ribs," she said bitterly. "And I would not need your help to do it."

"Will you come with me and tell your story to the Bishop's secretary?" asked Isaac.

"I don't know about that," said Mistress Ana doubtfully.

"You continue to improve, Your Excellency," said Isaac, lifting his head from listening to his patient's chest. "How do you feel?"

"Still weary, but able to sleep," said Berenguer. "I have done little else since I last saw you but sleep and eat. I am recovering my strength at a rapid rate, I believe."

"Excellent. I have brought with me the woman who gave lodgings to the murdered man. She will tell her story to Father Bernat and he can read it to you when you are well enough. But I wished to let you know that she saw the cup that is being called the Grail. She handled it and even gave it a little polish. I can assure you that she is strong and well in spite of the experience."

"Let her tell her tale to the council. This has nothing to do with the diocese. It is a matter of civic order, not religion." Berenguer rolled over on his side. "I wish to sleep now," he said.

"A very good idea, Your Excellency."

"And, Isaac," said the Bishop. "Don't tell anyone out there that I'm getting better. I am enjoying the quiet."

"Certainly not, Your Excellency. Not even Father Bernat or Father Francesc?"

"They may visit me and I shall tell them—what they ought to know."

THIRTEEN

Saturday, June 7

At least an hour before the bells of the city rang out prime, Yusuf ran the short distance from Isaac's house to the guards' quarters. It was there that his riding gear was kept in readiness for him; in the doorway stood the captain of the guard, waiting. "You'll have something new to learn this morning, Master Yusuf," he said.

"And what is that?" asked the boy cautiously.

"His Majesty suggested that before you grow any older you should learn to hold a sword in your hand—and discover what it's for. And so His Excellency has arranged for lessons in swordsmanship."

"But who is to teach me?" asked Yusuf, looking around, as if he expected to find a fencing master hidden under the stool.

"His Excellency entrusts me to start your education in the basics, and then a master will be engaged. We'll begin this morning, while you are fresh, and when we finish, you can take your mare out."

"But I have no sword or—"

"Do not concern yourself." The captain went back into his quarters and returned with a long package. "This is for you. It seems that His Majesty promised you a sword. It is now ready."

Yusuf set the package carefully on a bench and untied the rope that secured the canvas covering around it. Inside was a long wooden box containing a sword with its scabbard, baldric, and gloves.

"The boots and hat are in there," said the captain, jerking his head in the direction of the guardhouse. "His Majesty always does things as they should be done. But dressing up is unimportant right now. What is of concern to us first is whether you can hold a sword."

"When do we start?"

"Right now, of course," said the captain.

The cathedral bell rang for sext. The June sun blazed high in the heavens; out in the meadows and on the flatland on the other side of the river Onyar men sweated and hurried to finish their weekly labors, cursing the sun, the heat, and the flies that tormented their beasts. The shops were crammed with ill-tempered housewives, filling their baskets.

Inside the high walls of the *call,* only the faint murmur of commerce could be heard from the other side, and the ever-present cry of the bells by which everyone, Christian or Jew, reckoned the hours. Small groups of men chatted in the cool and shady streets; in Isaac's courtyard, the fountain played, creating its own light breezes. It was shady, quiet, and pleasant out there, and the household had disposed itself under the trees or in the shadows cast by the south wall.

Only Yusuf was missing. Judith had firmly decreed that no one in the household was to expect the boy to work on the Sabbath. When Raquel had rashly pointed out the undisputed fact that Muslim slaves worked hard enough on the Sabbath in some of their neighbors' houses, her mother was unmoved. If no one—man, woman, or beast—was to work on the Sabbath, then surely that should include a Muslim boy, whatever his status. And thus the day was Yusuf's to spend as he pleased.

It was market day in Girona, and as he often did, he passed his free time wandering about the market and the rest of the city until sundown. That morning, as soon as his lessons at the palace were over, he had returned to the house—his right arm aching from its unaccustomed exercise—only long enough to eat and help himself to a packet of bread and cold meats for his dinner.

A cold meal was set out on the trestle table; those who were hungry helped themselves to what they wished whenever they wanted it. As long as relative peace and good order prevailed, Judith allowed herself to relax her surveillance over her family's meals from dawn to sundown.

Raquel sat by the fountain, listening to the birds' lazy chirping until the clangor of the bells throughout the city drowned out their song. "I think this is my favorite time of the week," she said as soon as the noise of the bells had died away.

"Do you mean the midday hour?" asked Isaac.

"No, Papa. I mean now, on the Sabbath."

"Why now in particular?" asked her father. "Surely last night—whether you speak of the excellence of the dinner or the beauty of its ceremonies—surpasses this?"

"Of course it does, Papa," she said. "And when I think

of family, that is what I think of. But also this. Mama
is sitting over there, calm and happy. She has nothing
she feels she must do. In a little while she will have
something to eat—and on the Sabbath she only nibbles
on things she particularly likes, I've noticed—and then
she'll sleep away the whole afternoon. It's the only time
she permits herself to rest. And unless it is too cold or
wet, we sit out here. I love this courtyard, and the birds.
I love talking to you like this, not about sick people, or
problems—just idly talking. I think I must be very lazy
at heart," she confessed.

"For a lazy woman, Raquel," remarked her father affectionately, "you work very hard."

"Papa," she said, "why was Yusuf so disturbed when
that woman—Mistress Ana—came to see you?"

"Was he disturbed?"

"Surely you noticed. Even I noticed that his voice
sounded strange. And he went pale as soon as she unveiled herself."

"I suspect it has to do with his life before he came
here, my dear," said Isaac. "Since he does not wish to
speak of it, I have never inquired too closely how he
managed to live. I only know that from time to time he
earned a penny or two by working. And that when we
first met him, he was very hungry."

"I suppose he must have begged for his bread," said
Raquel uneasily. It seemed impossible to her that the
poised and lively lad who lived with them, a member of
their own household, should have been forced to beg in
order to eat.

"When he first arrived, your mother expressed the
opinion that he would rob us of everything we had, and
his denials of theft were both loud and indignant. He
roundly declared that—except for the occasional piece
of bread, as he put it—he had never stolen anything in

his life. Now that we have come to know him, I am
convinced that he was speaking the truth that morning.
But some of that bread—and he did admit to bread—
may very well have come from—"

"Mother Rodrigue," said Raquel, laughing. "Poor Yusuf. Perhaps he thought that she was coming to have
him taken up for theft after all this time. I don't suppose
she even recognized him."

"She recognized him," said Isaac. "And probably remembered the bread, too, but didn't seem to begrudge
him whatever he escaped with. It's odd how much some
people worry over a piece of bread—something that our
Miriam crumbles and gives to the birds."

"She'd rather feed them than herself sometimes," said
Raquel, yawning.

"Like that poor monk who lost his toes. Joaquim. So
conscience-stricken over stealing a piece of bread. Remember that?"

"No, Papa. He never said it was a piece of bread. He
just said he stole something."

"Are you sure?" asked her father intently. "I remember it as bread."

"You suggested that such a simple lad could well have
taken an extra piece of bread at dinner, and thought it a
crime as dreadful as murder."

"So I did," said her father.

"But it was more than that," said Raquel. "Joaquim
was feverish and restless. He kept moving back and
forth, trying to get up, and saying over and over, 'I have
done a terrible thing.'

" 'We will cure you of it,' you said to him, Papa, very
gently."

"Did I say that?" asked the physician. "How curious."

"Then he talked to me later, when you were discussing him with the surgeon."

"Did he? I would not have thought him capable of reasoned speech by then."

"He wasn't, Papa. He repeated what he had said before, except that he was raving more by then," said Raquel. "And his words made even less sense. But at one point he grasped me by the hand and pulled me down close to his face. 'I had to do it,' he said, or something very like that. Then he asked me if I understood, and kept saying, 'They made me.' He dropped his head back onto the pillow and said, 'They forced me to do it, and I'm damned. I don't want to burn in hell. Tell Our Lady I don't want to burn in hell.' He looked at me as if he knew me well, as people do when they rave from fever, you know?"

"Yes," said her father. "I remember that look."

"I wish he had told me who he thought I was. But he didn't. Then he said that he would never do something like that, and I think I said, 'Of course not,' just to ease his mind."

"They made me?" repeated Isaac. "I wonder who he was talking about?"

"I didn't think to ask him that," said Raquel. "But I did ask him what he was talking about, and he repeated that it was bad to steal a holy thing. And that he hadn't wanted to do it, but that they made him. And he begged me again to tell Our Lady that he hadn't meant to do it and he didn't want to burn in hell."

"A 'holy thing.' Are you sure that was what he called it?" asked her father.

"Yes, Papa," said Raquel. "He called it a holy thing. I asked him again what it was," said Raquel. "And he looked at me very strangely. All this time he was clutching my arm—it was covered with bruises for days after, Papa—and he said over and over again that *he* was the one who made him steal it. And the voices. Then he started muttering that it was *his* voice, but they weren't the same, and that he didn't understand. And by that time I didn't understand much, either. Then he fell asleep. That was all. But now that—"

"How very interesting, my child," said Isaac, interrupting her. "And it illustrates the errors one may fall into through incomplete knowledge."

"But, Papa, no one can possess complete knowledge, can he?" asked Raquel, ready to settle into a long dispute over an interesting question.

"Only over a few things. At the moment I am completely aware of the fact that I am hungry. I think I shall explore what has been set out for us. We will talk of this another time."

A hushed expectancy fell over the Bishop's palace that Saturday. His Excellency did not leave his chamber— or if he did, it was to retreat to his study. Either way, he received no one, turning over control of the diocesan matters to Francesc Monterranes. Rumors of his failing health abounded in the city, and when no sign of his physician going back and forth between the *call* and the palace appeared, it was quickly concluded that Isaac had moved into the Bishop's quarters to be with him at all times.

In truth, Berenguer had been content to keep to his bed for much of Friday and Saturday, dozing lightly off and on, seeing only his attendants and his secretary and leaving the usual crowd of importunate clergy and members of the public to be dealt with by others. He had dutifully eaten the light but nourishing meals that had been prescribed for him, and listened with amusement to reports of the palace gossip.

Inevitably, when a bishop is ill, every person in the palace begins to measure him for a shroud. They size up the contenders on the ground to replace him, always forgetting the possibility of an outsider—always just as likely as someone currently at the palace. The contenders agonize; the rest worry about the disastrous effect on their own ambitions of this man or that one picking up the reins of power. By sundown on Saturday, the palace was seething with excitement, fear, and greed for power.

Sunday, June 8: Trinity Sunday

The Bishop preached on major feast days. That was as fixed a principle as the sun rising in the east. For that reason, when Francesc Monterranes climbed to the pulpit on Trinity Sunday and began to read the careful sermon that he had drafted in close consultation with Berenguer and Bernat, a shiver went through the congregation. By the time Mass was over, everyone had concluded that Berenguer's end was near. An hour later, most of the city had consigned the Bishop to his tomb, planned the funeral rites, and decided on his probable successor.

Raquel was sitting in the courtyard, staring in frustration at the open book in the Arabic tongue and alphabet in front of her when Yusuf came in. "Come over here, Yusuf," she said firmly. "I want to talk to you."

She turned to look at him as he walked slowly over. "Sit down," she said, "you're pale as a ghost. What is wrong?"

"I don't know," he said. "I suddenly thought I could see my mother by the fountain—but it wasn't anything." He sat down and she could see that his hand was trembling. "I thought she must be dead and her spirit had come to sit here by the fountain."

"You mustn't think that, Yusuf. You're just upset. I'll get you some mint and lemon."

"Will the scent of mint chase away ghosts?" he asked, half-curious and half-sorrowful.

"No," said Raquel. "But—"

"Scent! That's what it is," he said. "The courtyard smells of jasmine. And so did ours."

"Did your mother smooth her skin with jasmine oil?" asked Raquel.

"I don't know. She always smelled of jasmine."

"I'm sorry," said Raquel.

"It's not your fault."

"Yes it is. Jasmine oil is so pretty I put some on my hair. But I'll wash it out if you like," she said.

"No, I like it," said Yusuf. "And now that I know what it is it won't bother me." He stared off in the distance and then turned to the book in front of Raquel. "There's no use starting with a hard book like this," he said, pointing to the open treatise.

"What do you mean?"

"My papa," said Yusuf awkwardly, for he still had difficulty talking about his father, an emissary from the Emir, who had been killed in the uprising in Valencia in 1348. "Papa always made me draw the letters in the dust of the earth before we started. He said that way your hands learned as much as your head."

"Mama is going to think it very odd if I crouch down and start drawing in the earth. It's all right if you're a little boy," she said. "People think you're playing."

"We can sprinkle dry earth on this table," he said, pointing to the low table on which Raquel's needlework was resting. With the air of conspirators plotting the commission of a grave crime, they moved a bench near the garden wall, set the small table on the far side of it so that their bodies would shield them from any curious glances, and hastily scooped up dry soil from the top of the flower beds.

"There," said Raquel, spreading it out evenly on the table. "A few too many stones, but very usable."

Yusuf picked up a small stick and began to draw.

"Raquel, what are you doing over there?" asked her mother, appearing from the kitchen. "Naomi could well use some help."

Instead of sharply pointing out that Naomi had a kitchen boy and Leah to help her, Raquel turned and smiled. "We're looking for something in this book that Papa requires," she said innocently. "But if you need me, we can do it tomorrow."

"No, no," said Judith, retreating at once. "Leah can help just as well as you can."

After drawing, correcting, and redrawing what felt like an endless number of letters in the dirt, Raquel finally set down her twig. "My head is whirling," she said, "and my fingers are numb. We'll do some more tomorrow."

They began to tidy up their little corner of the courtyard, clearing away the fine dirt and returning everything to its place before anyone chanced to notice what they were doing. "You rode a long time yesterday," said Raquel as they were finishing.

"I wasn't riding."

"Then whatever were you doing?"

"His Majesty has sent me a sword, and the things that go with it. Yesterday I began lessons in swordsmanship."

"Swordsmanship?" said Raquel. "What are you being trained for, Yusuf? All these lessons every day—first in riding and now in fighting."

"And what I learn here," he said, "which is great deal also." He looked unhappily over at her. "I don't know."

"So while Papa is teaching you medicine, His Majesty wishes you to become a courtier. It seems odd."

It was Sunday evening before Isaac and Raquel returned to the question of the unfortunate young monk, Joaquim. The whole family had been in the courtyard, when Daniel and his aunt, Mistress Dolsa, came to the gate. "We cannot stay," said Mistress Dolsa. "We only stopped by to ask a small favor."

"You are most welcome, Mistress Dolsa," said Judith. "We would be delighted to help in any way," she added, with more sincerity than usually accompanies such an offer.

"We were about to take our evening walk," she said, "and we hoped that you might join us. If you can wait for a few moments."

"Wait?"

"We were ready to leave—my husband was already outside the door—when one of his customers appeared," said Mistress Dolsa, "a good customer, swearing that he was unable to wait another moment before ordering several pairs of gloves," she added comfortably. "He could just as well have ordered them tomorrow morning," she said, "because he won't get them a minute earlier. I was about to tell him so, when Daniel suggested that we wait for Ephraim here. It seemed a pleasant idea."

"I am glad he suggested it, Mistress Dolsa," said Judith, and the two women fell into easy conversation over domestic affairs and the weather—very hot, they agreed, although not surprisingly so for the time of year. Daniel wandered over to join Raquel and her father, hoping to entice them both to join them in their walk.

"It seems clear to me," Raquel was saying, "since poor Joaquim was tormented by the thought of having stolen a holy object, that he must have been the one who brought the Grail here."

"How did he carry it here?" asked Isaac. "I understood that he arrived in Figueres with nothing. Certainly not with a pack large enough to conceal a silver cup. If he had, he could scarcely have hidden it from the monks, could he?"

"Then someone took it from him in order to sell it," said Raquel stubbornly.

"Stole it, you mean? Who?"

"Baptista," said Raquel, "if what that woman from the tavern said was the truth."

"Mistress Ana?" asked her father. "I expect it was the truth, my dear. As far as she knows it. And Baptista could well have taken it from him," said Isaac. "Although there are other possible explanations."

"But did you not say that Joaquim was still nearby?" asked Raquel. "With the brothers at Sant Pere de Galligants?"

"I believe so," said Isaac. "Or he was only a few days ago. It would be interesting to talk to him."

"Surely the Bishop can speak to any monk in the diocese if he wishes it," said Daniel, breaking in.

"Good evening, Daniel," said the physician. "You are most welcome. And you are also correct. He could, if he wished, but he does not wish. He does not wish to do anything about this whole problem. He claims it is something for the city to look after, not the diocese."

"But, Papa—" said Raquel.

"I will be speaking to the abbot tomorrow," said Daniel.

"You?" said Raquel. "Why?"

"Why should I not speak to an abbot?" said Daniel. "I have to go to Sant Pere to deliver a pair of gloves to him. I can at least ask about the young monk on your behalf. After all, you must be interested in his present health, are you not?"

"We are," said the physician. "And in his present state of mind and conscience, which is a related question."

"They may have sent him back to his own monastery, Papa," said Raquel.

"That, too, would be interesting to know. I hear the footsteps of my good friend Ephraim coming toward the gate," said Isaac. "Shall we join him in an evening walk?"

FOURTEEN

Early Tuesday morning, Don Vidal de Blanes, abbot of Sant Feliu, paid a visit to the Bishop's palace, where he was received by Francesc Monterranes with grave courtesy, and taken up to Berenguer's study. After a murmured conversation at the door, too low-pitched to be heard by a passing clerk and two female servants who were lingering nearby, the canon opened the study door.

"Those documents that His Excellency had prepared for you are in his study," said Francesc. "If you would be gracious enough to look at them, Don Vidal, I will endeavor to answer any questions I can. Those that are beyond my competence can be referred to His Excellency as soon as he is well enough."

The abbot's reply was not loud enough to be heard by curious ears, but an imaginative clerk reported that his face was like a thunder cloud. "He was not pleased," said the clerk. "Not at all pleased to be slighted like that.

It would have been better if His Excellency had risen from his bed."

"If he can," remarked Ramon de Orta, who had paused to hear an account of the meeting between the abbot and the canon vicar. "It is uncharitable to chide a man for those things he cannot help."

"Yes, Father," murmured the clerk, excusing himself as rapidly as possible.

As soon as the door to the Bishop's study closed behind Don Vidal, the door to Berenguer's chamber opened, and the Bishop came out to greet him.

"I apologize for this little deception, Don Vidal," said Berenguer. "I have been suffering from a trifling illness, I admit, and my physician insisted that I have a few days' peace and quiet."

A servant slipped in from the bedchamber with a tray of tempting food and drink, set it down, and left them to their own devices.

The abbot of Sant Feliu was a shrewd man and a skilled administrator—his skills had brought him the position of procurator of the province for the time that Their Majesties were at war with the Sardinians—and no stranger to useful deceptions. "I would have suggested a week or two in the country, Don Berenguer," said the abbot, seating himself across from the Bishop. "It is more convincing."

"I am reluctant to leave the city at the moment," said Berenguer.

"That is understandable, Your Excellency. And I think we have much to talk about concerning what is happening."

"I agree. Was there something in particular that brings you here today?"

"Your physician seems to have caused a flurry

amongst my charges, Don Berenguer," said the abbot.

"My physician?"

"Yesterday morning a pleasant young man, very skilled in glove making, delivered a new pair of gloves that I had ordered. I am told that he is betrothed—or close to it—to the physician's daughter."

"Young Daniel, Ephraim's nephew."

"Precisely. Having gained access to the abbey, he spent a great deal of time talking to—questioning, even—one of my monks. And that disturbed the others, causing much speculation. A nuisance more than anything else, but it worried me. Did he come from you, Don Berenguer?"

"Certainly not, Don Vidal. Had I wished to speak to someone at the abbey, I would have gone to you. Between us it is a simple thing to arrange, openly and amicably. I will look into it."

"Thank you. I am rather concerned about young Brother Joaquim. He needs, perhaps, to be sheltered from the world more than most."

"Concerned?"

"After you brought him to me, he recovered quickly enough in body, but we could see that his soul was much troubled. He seemed very confused about many things, including where he came from. After patient questioning, we deduced that he might be from the monastery at Sant Llorenç, near Baga. The name seemed to mean something to him—none of the other houses we spoke of did—and it was clear that he came from the mountains.

"I wrote to the abbot at once, inquiring about him. It was some time before I received a reply."

"That is understandable," said Berenguer. "It is some distance away."

"Before their reply came, Joaquim told something of

his story to one of the brothers whom he had grown to trust, and then, at last, to me."

"I would be most interested to hear it," said the Bishop.

"I will be as accurate as I can," said Don Vidal, "but I beg you to understand that he is a young man of few words, and many of those are not to the point. Some of what I say will be what I think must have happened. His story began in early November of last year, at Taüll, in the high mountains. One morning, long before the sun was due to rise over the eastern peaks, he was standing in front of the little Church of Sant Climent and staring at the door, greatly troubled in his mind. I have no doubt that he looked like a hunted deer who hears the baying of the hounds as they close in on him. He does, whenever he's confused or frightened. When he grasped the latch the iron burned his palm as if it had been new-forged in the fires of hell and he was convinced that the whole village was watching his odd behavior. I expect that the villagers were still in their beds. No one was going to rise before dawn to see poor Joaquim set to work. Out of the charity, Father Xavier paid him a penny now and then—likely when there was a small surplus in the church's money box—to sweep the church every day, for the sacristan was old and too bent with pain for all but the lightest of labors.

"Sweeping the church, by the way, was the only work he had, except for watching his mother's goats, who could well look after themselves. He told one of the brothers that he often spent the rest of the day in the high meadows, lying in the grass, staring up at the clouds that swirled in patterns around the mountain peaks, or simply wandering about on the slopes and in the forest.

"He lived in this way for several years, poor and despised by his neighbors. He had a fine patch of flowers that he tended; he brought the loveliest of them to the church to place in front of the wall painting of Our Lady, but only during the week, when few but Our Lady Herself and the priest would know they were there. It seems that for him this was their church—his and Father Xavier's and Our Lady's. I have noticed that he cares nothing for and understands little about the complexities of our faith. He only knew the painting, and the well-swept stones. They were his.

"Then a voice in his head said to him that he must go in, as he always did, early, before Father Xavier arrived.

"He grasped the latch again, realizing this time that the metal was not hot, but icy with the chill of dawn. He stepped inside, and the familiar darkness enveloped him. 'Now do what I told you,' said the voice. 'Nothing will happen to you if you remember what I told you.'

"He stared up at the brilliantly colored and elaborate piece behind the altar. The saintly faces painted onto the wall, who were his strength, his friends, and his consolation, looked down sternly. Our Lady, on whose veiled hand the holy cup rested, no longer smiled gently at him. As the light grew stronger, he thought he glimpsed her head moving in admonition. Then the voice in his own head drowned his thoughts. 'You must do it today,' said the voice, 'or you will live miserable and despised forever.'

"He covered his eyes with his hands and turned away from the painting, thinking it would be easier if he couldn't see their faces. He crossed over to a wooden cupboard that was hidden behind a piece of tapestry, and taking a file from his tunic, he attacked the soft iron fastenings that held the lock in place. As soon as the metal clasps were weakened, he used the file to wrench open the cupboard door.

"This small cupboard contained a few miscellaneous pieces of altar plate that were seldom used. Joaquim took a tarnished and battered silver cup, very plain in design—or so he told me, for I have not seen it—from behind the rest and thrust it into his tunic. He threw down the file and turned toward the door. The metal clattered as it struck the stone floor. I tell you this because of what he told me happened next.

"A chorus of voices rang out in the empty church, crying aloud in pain. 'Stop,' they said. 'Stop, Joaquim.' These voices, he was certain, did not come from his head. They emanated from the walls behind him; they were the voices of his saints, calling out to him, telling him he had done something inexpressibly evil.

"He flung open the door. Once outside, he began to run."

"He told you all this?" asked Berenguer.

"He did. Not all at once, nor in those exact words, but what I tell you I heard from Joaquim himself." Don Vidal paused for a little wine before continuing. "When he reached the meeting place the sun was already halfway up in the heavens. There the man with the voice—that was what he called him—was waiting for him in a little hollow, stretched out in the sun, a smile on his face.

"Joaquim reached into his tunic and pulled out the cup. 'Here,' he said, hurled it at him, and continued on his way.

"The man called out to him to wait, saying, 'This is yours,' and tossed a small leather purse at him. It hit him on the back and fell to the ground. 'For taking the risk. We'll divide the profits once it's sold.'

" 'I don't want your money,' said Joaquim. He let the purse lie where it had fallen and kept going." The abbot stopped.

"Then it was a chalice from Taüll that was stolen," said Berenguer.

"He has suffered greatly from what he has done," said Don Vidal.

"He should not have done it," said the Bishop. "And having done it, he should have returned it, not given it to a confederate. He told you no more?"

"He said that was all that he remembered. I wondered if perhaps his confederate had hit him on the head."

"Possibly. Did you hear anything of interest from Sant Llorenç?"

"I did. The abbot wrote that they had lost a monk by the name of Brother Vitalis, of some forty years, of middle height, with gray hair. Blue-eyed and round of face. Clearly not our Brother Joaquim."

"Clearly not."

"They feared that Vitalis had been murdered by a young sacristan from Taüll, who had fled the village after stealing silver from the church. They reasoned that someone who could commit such a sacrilegious act could well murder a passing monk for the bread in his bundle."

"Joaquim."

"They inquired into the circumstances and wrote me what they had been told about Joaquim—that he had stolen an old chalice from a locked cupboard in the church or, at least, that the cupboard was broken open the same day the young man disappeared. And that fits with his own account.

"It seems that the pursuit after Joaquim was cut short by a sudden shift in the weather, bringing pelting rain and blowing snow in its wake. The pursuers hurried home; but Joaquim, it seemed, had learned as much from the fox and the weasel as he ever had from Father Xavier. He found himself a rocky burrow, curled up, and went to sleep. His pursuers found traces of that first burrow. What happened after that can only be guessed at," added Don Vidal.

"Is it your belief, Don Vidal, that our young monk is not a monk at all?"

"That's possible," said the abbot. "But, as you know, in the diocese of Ripoll, for example, there are numberless small foundations up in the mountains. Most of them would accept a healthy and willing young man into their ranks without much further inquiry. The brevity of his stay with them would explain his lack of knowledge and general confusion."

"Very true. It would be difficult to inquire at all of them."

"There was something else that I discovered," said the abbot. "Although you may not consider it to be evidence, it fits in well enough with what I have seen of his character. This, you will remember, was a winter of two memorable storms, one well before Christmas, and one in the spring. Father Xavier told the abbot of Sant Llorenç that even Joaquim's mother condemned him for an idle thief and a stupid lout, not worth anyone's prayers or tears. He and the baker were young Joaquim's only supporters. Between them, they said many prayers for his safety out in the fine driving snow that whipped across the face of the land.

"The baker claimed Joaquim hadn't the wit to steal something like that. He might steal a cake, if it sat in front of his eyes and he was hungry, but he would no more steal something from the church than their cat would. Father Xavier agreed, although he felt it was awe and esteem that would have held him back."

"As you say, it is not evidence, but it is important."

"How did Brother Joaquim come to you, Your Excellency, in the guise of a monk?"

"It was thanks to the charity of unfortunate Gualter Gutiérrez. It was near the end of winter," said the Bishop. "February, I think. Gualter told me he was sheltering from a ferocious storm at a tavern in Figueres, when a young monk staggered in. His feet were wrapped in rags, his habit muddy and torn, he was soaked with water up to the knees, and trembling with cold or fever.

"The miserable young monk stood by the door looking like a drowned rat, Gualter told me. He suggested that the lad come in and sit near the fire to warm himself. Next," said Berenguer, "he ordered a bowl of good soup for the unfortunate brother, and a cup of wine. When the monk protested that he could not pay, Gualter told the landlady to add it to his own reckoning and to find the monk a bed with warm coverings. You will remember how openhanded he was," added the Bishop.

"He was, indeed," said Don Vidal.

"Gualter had just settled in to find out from this young man where he was from and why he was there—" Berenguer paused for a sip of wine to moisten his throat.

"Gualter also suffered from great curiosity," said Don Vidal dryly.

"He did," said the Bishop. "But at that very moment the landlady set a bowl of soup and a large portion from her sturdy loaf before the young man. He lost all interest in Gualter and ate like a starving man.

"Gualter tried to get him to stop eating for a moment—'before he did himself harm,' as he said—and tell them where he'd come from. Whether he did this out of kindness or his never-ending inquisitiveness, I do not know," said Berenguer, "but apparently he was frustrated again in his search for knowledge.

"The monk crammed another morsel into his mouth, swallowed and then turned to his benefactor. 'From the mountains,' he said, telling the simple truth.

"Then you've had a hard journey,' said another, seated nearby. 'The storm is hardly over.'

" 'I was caught in it,' said the brother, who had taken the chance to grab another mouthful. 'It was bad, but I stayed in the woods.'

" 'Then you've been lost,' said a third. 'That explains it.'

"The young man shook his head. 'No. I followed the stream down. But I slipped and fell in and lost my shoes.'

" 'So it's not your faith that counsels you to go barefoot in this weather?' said Gualter.

"Apparently that remark only confused the young man, Gualter told me," said Berenguer, "instead of revealing more about him."

"Likely he had no notion of what Gualter was talking about," said the abbot.

"I think you are right, Don Vidal. Having not discovered where the poor young monk came from, he asked him his name and offered to bring him here, assuring him that you would be glad to take him in."

"Of course," murmured the abbot.

"Gualter decided that the young man—feverish and with injured feet—was in no condition to walk any farther, and offered him the use of a pack mule. In return for such kindness, the young monk admitted that his name was Joaquim, all the while looking down at his feet as if he had never seen them before. The landlady made him a warm bed by the fire, assuming, I suppose, that the icy air in her attics might kill him off before morning.

"But in the end," said Berenguer, "it was to his own house that Gualter Gutiérrez brought the unfortunate Joaquim. They placed him in a small chamber by the kitchen, good and warm, where the boy who tended the fires slept. When the merchant's wife objected to having a stranger in the house, her husband pointed out that he could be from the same monastery that had rescued their Martí from certain death. In addition, they sent for the physician to tend to him.

"As soon as Isaac entered the sickroom, he told me, the sadly familiar smell of decayed flesh struck his nostrils, and he sent for the surgeon at once, pointing out to Gualter that Joaquim had an injury that had festered.

" 'His feet, I think,' murmured the merchant. 'He has been roaming about the woods for I don't know how long, with old rags tied to his feet instead of boots.'

" 'Frozen, no doubt. We must see how far it has gone, then. I can treat him for his fever and other ills, but he will need the surgeon.'

"It only required one look for his daughter to find the putrid toes on his left foot, the fourth and fifth. Fortunately no other flesh was yet affected.

"The surgeon's knives were sharp," said the Bishop, "his eye keen, and his hand very quick. The toes were gone and the wound sealed and bound up almost before the young man, already groggy from the physician's pain-dulling compounds, had a chance to feel the agony of the knife.

"The surgeon and the physician went off to report the results of their efforts to the charitable merchant who was paying their fees. As soon as the physician judged it proper, he contacted me, and I had the young man moved to the abbey. It was, I believe, while you were in Barcelona, Don Vidal."

"I believe so. And the young man has never claimed to you that he belonged to the Church?" asked the abbot.

"Not in so many words. If he did kill Brother Vitalis—"

"We have no shadow of proof of that," said Don Vidal. "But nonetheless, if he is not one of ours, it is not our problem. Still, if ever someone needed our protection, this unfortunate young man does. I will speak to him again, more closely this time. I have been much distracted from my duties by affairs of state, and too much travel. As have you, Don Berenguer. I shall leave you to enjoy repose and tranquillity even for the few days you have allotted yourself."

Later that morning the physician was summoned to Berenguer's bedside for the first time since Friday afternoon. He walked up to the palace with his accustomed quick stride. He said little on his way to His Excellency's chamber, but those in attendance—and those who hovered in doorways, listening—reported that he seemed concerned, or even preoccupied. "Not his usual self," said the porter. "Usually he has a friendly word for me. This time—nothing. He's very worried."

Isaac was ushered into Berenguer's chamber with more haste than ceremony. By the time the door was shut behind him, a remarkable number of people in the palace had discovered urgent tasks that needed doing not far from the Bishop's apartments. "With all them people in there," said a man wielding a broom in the corridor, referring to Bernat, Francesc, and the attendant, as well as Isaac and Yusuf, "we know His Excellency is awake anyway. I haven't liked to sweep this part since he fell ill."

For the most part, all they heard for their efforts was a buzz of voices through the solid wooden door.

FIFTEEN

"How is Your Excellency this morning?"

"Puzzled, Master Isaac."

"Puzzled, Your Excellency?" asked the physician.

"Why should young Daniel be lurking about the abbey, spying on the brothers? Brother Joaquim in particular. That is what is puzzling me," he said. "I would appreciate some enlightenment on the question," he added, his voice sharp with sarcasm.

"Joaquim?"

"For a man who does not carry a sword, Isaac, you are adept at fencing," said Berenguer. "You know which Joaquim I mean. That young monk who lost a pair of toes in last winter's storms. You treated him, Isaac. He was your patient."

"Ah, yes," said Isaac mildly. "I remember him well."

"Well? Why was Daniel at the abbey?"

"To deliver a pair of gloves, I believe," said Isaac. "But before Your Excellency loses your temper, which would not be good for you, I will admit that when I heard he was to be there, I asked him to inquire into the young lad's state of health. I was interested."

"Aside from pure charity, why would you be interested, Isaac?"

"The case had many interesting aspects," the physician said, and then fell silent.

"A frozen toe in winter? A simple case for the surgeon. Interesting? I don't believe you. Come, now—confess."

"That in itself was not interesting, I agree, Your Excellency. But it had proceeded far—the putrefaction, I mean—causing a high fever. He raved. He was out of his wits with the fever when I left him with my daughter while I discussed matters with the surgeon and with Master Gualter."

"You are making the telling of this longer than the illness," said Berenguer impatiently.

"Pardon me, Your Excellency. I will be briefer. He repeated many times that stealing was wrong, and that stealing a holy object was even worse. But I beg you to remember, Your Excellency, that when a man raves he is not responsible for his words. Often they refer to something in the distant past."

"He is too young to have a distant past, Isaac," said Berenguer coldly.

"Someone he revered may have stolen a holy object."

"Very true," said Berenguer. "That would upset him. He is not a clever lad, but he seems to feel things. What are you trying to say to me, Isaac? That you would not hang a dog on what young Joaquim said in his ravings?"

"Precisely, Your Excellency. But I wondered if he knew something about the appearance—or the rumor of the appearance—of that wretched cup in Girona."

"Whether he does or does not," said Berenguer angrily, "it is not your affair. You are my physician, Isaac, and not my archbishop, nor the archdeacon, nor the captain of my guard. You are here to look after my health, not the spiritual health of the diocese. Why do you continue to pursue this?"

"Because it is important, Your Excellency."

"It is so important, Isaac, that it is best left to others. Because of your meddling, Don Vidal spent the morning here. One of his monks found young Daniel in the monastery garden talking to Joaquim earnestly and at great length, and now he thinks that I might be sending spies into his abbey to find out what his monks are up to."

"I would not have had that happen for the world, Your Excellency."

"We speak of Don Vidal, Isaac. Do you know what that means? Although we have had our differences from time to time, Don Vidal has always been a powerful ally—and until His Majesty heaped extra responsibility on him, one of the few men to whom I could trust the affairs of the diocese. Don Vidal and I owe each other much, Isaac. I have no desire to cause a breach between us."

"I understand, Your Excellency. I had not intended to annoy him."

"Whether you desired it or not, he is annoyed." Berenguer fell back on his pillows with a weary sigh. "As it is, Joaquim is a problem for him."

"If someone can discover which monastery he comes from, he should be sent back there," said Isaac. "Because if Daniel can find his way to him in the garden, so can anyone."

"No doubt that is true, Isaac, but you have not answered my question."

"Which question, Your Excellency?"

"By now, I do not know."

"I feared that by repeating myself I would anger you

more, and that would not be very good for you."

"Isaac. That is not what I want to hear."

"Your Excellency. My apologies. Master Gualter was my patient. He was sometimes a fool, but he was basically a good man, whose wife and son are both in their way excellent creatures. By allowing himself to be stripped of almost everything he possessed, Master Gualter left those two good people in a terrible situation. His wife's only recourse may be to sell her property and use the money to enter a convent."

"Then let her do it. It is a good life for a woman. From my own observation I would say that it is a better life than many—perhaps most—marriages."

"It may be the happiest of lives for her. I do not know. But one would prefer her to embrace it of her own free will. Gualter's son has been left nothing but an enormous debt that he is determined to repay. Someone in this city has their money. The possession of it would not bring back a husband and father, but it would give them a reasonable life."

"Of course. All this is true, and I have never disputed it. But the matter should be left to the civil courts," he said with emphasis.

"And what are they doing?" asked Isaac stubbornly.

"Isaac—this thing, this object, is undoubtedly just one more false relic, like a fingernail wrenched from a beggar's corpse, proclaimed to be from a nonexistent saint, and used by a traveling preacher to dazzle his audience before passing around the bag for offerings," he said contemptuously. "But it is far more dangerous. I cannot tell you how profoundly disturbed I am by the supposed appearance of the Grail in Girona." As if to illustrate his disturbance, Berenguer sat up abruptly in bed. His attendant hurried over to drape a shawl over his master's shoulders.

"The Grail is probably false," continued the Bishop, irritably throwing off the shawl, "in which case it is a travesty, an abomination—in fact, a true instrument of the devil."

"There are many in my community who agree with you in this, Your Excellency, and who are as angry at me as Your Excellency is for trying to locate it. Including the philosopher Shaltiel."

"I am glad to hear that," said Berenguer sourly. "The other slight possibility is that it is real. If this is so, then it is an object so holy that I am unworthy to handle it."

"Why do you not turn the problem over to your archbishop, or your pope?" asked Isaac.

"I have," said Berenguer impatiently. "I referred it at once to the Archbishop. I received his reply today. He wants the whole business taken care of before it leads to chaos."

"Chaos," said Isaac. "That is a strong word, Your Excellency."

"That is the word he used," said Berenguer. "And I cannot help but agree with him."

"And is peace more important, Your Excellency, than truth? Or even justice?"

"Are you questioning my obedience to the Church, Master Isaac? On a matter of faith and morals?" asked Berenguer. "By Our Lady, you have gone too far this time. You overstep the freedom I allow you."

"I do not question, Your Excellency," said Isaac steadily. "I only ask which is more important."

"I can tolerate being surrounded by fools, who do not understand what they are doing, Master Isaac, but you are not a stupid man. Now I see that you have crawled behind my back to act. And by God in heaven, I call that treachery."

"Your Excellency knows well that I am no traitor," said Isaac.

"And what else am I to call it," he said, his voice rising, "if not treason? You may speak of justice, but you are interested in one thing only, and that is finding Astruch's money and returning it to him. And why?" he said, thumping the bed beside him with his closed fist. "It has nothing to do with notions of justice. It is because he is a Jew and you will break any vow to protect him." As he spoke the words, Berenguer saw the white face of his physician and drew his breath in sharply. "Leave us," he said, with a wave of his hand to the others in the room. "Wait outside until you are summoned."

And with incoherent mumblings that went for leave-taking, Bernat ducked into the study, the attendant disappeared toward the kitchens, and Francesc Monterranes headed for the corridor, taking Yusuf with him. Francesc closed the door firmly as he left and stood immovable in front of it.

The Bishop rose from his bed. He laid a hand gently on his physician's shoulder. "I would give much not to have spoken those words, Isaac. And I would give more if you could forget them."

"Do not concern yourself, Your Excellency," said Isaac, his voice shaken.

"You see, Isaac," said Berenguer quietly, "that cup is indeed the devil's instrument. It is a false relic and sows discord in its path. I tremble to think that I was within moments of consigning you to the palace prison." He sat down on the edge of his bed.

The physician walked over to the window, taking a deep breath, and then moved back toward the bed. "I am greatly to blame, Your Excellency," he said at last, in a murmur. "You have cause for genuine anger. I allowed my concern for others to catch me up. I became immersed in a whirlpool of interests that conflicted with yours. It would be inexcusable at any time, but to do so when Your Excellency was ill was very wrong."

"Let us not battle over apportioning the blame, Isaac," said Berenguer softly. "But we are left with a problem."

"I believe that Your Excellency is right in saying that the cup, whatever it may be, is surrounded by evil. But in itself, it is only a metal object. Made of silver taken from the Lord's good earth. It is innocent."

"Very true," said the Bishop. "It is men who make it good or evil. We are in ultimate agreement over that. The question is, what are we attempting to do?"

"Someone," said Isaac, "should find Mistress Sibilla's and Master Martí's gold and return it to them. Stealing it was a very great crime against them."

"And with the finding of the gold, the assassin will be taken. And I would also like the false Grail to be found and destroyed in the silversmith's hottest flames."

"Must it be found and destroyed?"

"Yes. Or it will continue to be a source of infection to the city."

"To find it," said Isaac softly, "several things must be done first."

"There you go, Isaac," said Berenguer, in his normal voice. "telling me how to run my diocese again."

"My apologies, Your Excellency, but since by now everyone in the palace must know that we have quarreled, it occurred to me that we might use the quarrel to help trap the assassin."

"How would that help?"

"I have the beginnings of several ideas, Your Excellency. One of them might flush him out."

"Let us hear them," said Berenguer.

The two men retired to the farthest corner of the chamber, away from any one of its three doors—to the study, to the corridor, or to kitchens. There they sat, engaged in a long, murmured conversation.

"We will try it," said Berenguer finally, rising. "But first I think you should not be found here. Can you find your way out the back way?"

"Certainly, Your Excellency. If I might ask only that Yusuf be told not to wait in the corridor for me." And Isaac opened the narrow door to the kitchens and walked silently down. After twenty steps, another stair branched off to the left, leading into the Bishop's garden.

Yusuf caught up to the physician as he was walking across the plaza toward the gate of the *call*. "Lord," he said softly, "I cannot believe what happened."

"Good. In certain kinds of disbelief lie the beginnings of wisdom," said Isaac.

"But what about my horse?" he asked, in a voice frantic with worry. "How will I be able to visit my horse, and ride?"

"The Bishop is not angry with you, Yusuf. You should behave as you always have."

"How can I, lord? After what I heard?"

"Believe me, Yusuf. You must behave with His Excellency exactly as if nothing at all had happened this morning. Do you understand? Tomorrow morning you will go to the palace and do whatever it is you do just as always."

"No, lord. I do not understand. But if you say I must, then that is what I will do."

SIXTEEN

The rumors of the Bishop's imminent demise had been growing apace since Sunday morning. On Monday, another physician had been sent for, only to be dismissed when His Excellency refused to be examined by him. It was also being said in the city that Master Isaac's clever daughter had been seen going in and out of the palace, seeing to His Excellency's health.

Meanwhile, Baptista had been buried, unmourned except by Mistress Ana from Rodrigue's; and the city guard had been asking everyone they met on the street whether they knew of anyone who had suddenly acquired large amounts of gold. But no one had been seen wandering around the market with a purse heavy with gold coins recently, nor had anyone noticed strongboxes filled with gold lying about in a neighbor's house.

"What do the fools expect?" Bernat had said. "That the thief will scatter gold coins over the cathedral steps in full view of the congregation? Whoever stole Gualter's money will have it safely hidden away until he can plausibly bring it out again."

"Don't complain about the guards, Bernat," the Bishop had replied. "They are performing a worthwhile function."

"And what is that, Your Excellency?"

"They are convincing the populace that something useful is being done."

The guards had not failed to visit Master Vicens's courtyard. When the merchant came out to speak to them, they were staring unhappily at the washed cobbles. "I beg your pardon, sir," said their leader. "But can you account for that stain? We heard—"

"I know what you heard," said Vicens irritably. "And my wife tells me the porter knows all about it."

"May we speak—"

"Of course," said Vicens. "I was told that he has taken to his bed, but I don't suppose he's too ill to talk to you." He clapped his hands together and the lad from the kitchen came slouching out.

A young member of the city guard patrol was sent off to question the porter. He returned red-faced and whispered something in his officer's ear.

"What?" roared the officer.

"He swears it," said the miserable youth. "The dog caught a rat, and in worrying it scattered blood on the stones. The porter chased off the dog and dispatched the rat with a blow. He says he might be able to find the corpse if it's important."

They exited with apologies and started back. "It doesn't make any difference," said the officer. "He's too rich and important to be thrown into prison anyway."

• • •

But on Tuesday, right after Isaac's quarrel with the Bishop, the physician sat down with Yusuf and Raquel. "If anyone asks you what transpired today between His Excellency and me, you will—"

"We shall say that we know nothing of it," said Raquel firmly.

"You will do nothing of the kind," replied her father. "You will raise your shoulders, shake your head a little in sorrow, and say that it pains you too much to speak of such a rift between physician and patient."

"We will, lord?" said Yusuf, shocked.

"Yes. And on my own part, I shall do my best to assist you, with evasions and half-truths. That is one thing."

"But why?" asked Raquel.

"You will see soon enough, my dear," said her father. "And then I have specific tasks for each of you as well. Listen carefully."

Raquel and Yusuf went out the eastern door of the *call,* with Leah, the maid, in attendance. She, at least, was looking quite pleased with herself, since she considered carrying the physician's basket for her young mistress to be a large step up from her usual run of tasks around the house. She had hoped for a stately entry through the main door of the palace. To her disappointment, they skirted the plaza, approaching the episcopal palace from the rear, and went into the kitchen.

"*Hola*, young Yusuf," said the head cook, "and Mistress Raquel, as well. We are pleased to see you, in spite of all this trouble we're having." And even the first assistant cook shed his habitual gloomy expression for a moment to greet them, for they both had become general favorites in the Bishop's household during their recent long trek to Tarragona and back.

"I have brought a basket of remedies. Papa did not

wish His Excellency to run out of anything he might need," said Raquel.

"That was thoughtful of you, mistress," said the cook. "They had best be placed in the stillroom with the others. And tell Brother Whatshisname in there how they are to be used." While Raquel and Leah were occupied in this task, Yusuf went off to chat with anyone who might be temporarily unoccupied. He settled down at a table at the farther end of the kitchens with a likely group.

"My master is distressed," admitted Yusuf, after some coaxing. "Very distressed. It is all this Grail thing. That is what has come between them."

"I don't see how," said a servant who had dropped by for something to sustain himself until the dinner hour. "My master says that the Grail is clearly false, and that no one should take any account of it."

"That is not what my master thinks," said Yusuf. He leaned forward and spoke in a soft whisper. "It is killing the Bishop. That's what he thinks."

"How?" asked one of the grooms, fascinated. "His Excellency doesn't have it, does he?"

"Not His Excellency," said Yusuf. "But one of his enemies does, and is conjuring with it. If he succeeds, no doubt he will kill the Bishop."

"My master said nothing about that," said the servant, "and he will likely be next Bishop—so he understands these things."

"Or so he believes," said a second groom contemptuously.

"Who else but Don Ramon?" said his servant. "The others are all too old, or too insignificant." There was a pause for silent agreement. Ramon de Orta was definitely the fastest horse in the Bishop's race, in the view of the small army of servants in the palace. "But does your master really think that His Excellency is dying?"

"Why else would he be behaving in such a strange manner?" asked Yusuf. Again he lowered his voice to a whisper. "This business of turning away his physician when he is ill—that is a sure sign. Even I have seen it in the gravest cases."

"And that is not all," said the other groom, and they settled in for a long and detailed gossip about palace business.

"Yes, lord," said Yusuf. "I had a long conversation with the canon's personal servant. He seems to be ambitious to rise to power with his master. The interesting information I brought to him will be passed on to Father Ramon well before nightfall, I would guess. And should be common property around the palace by tomorrow morning, if not sooner."

"I am pleased," said Isaac.

"I always enjoy the palace kitchens, lord," said Yusuf. "But now I will see if I can find Master Martí."

While Yusuf was attempting to track down Master Martí, Raquel and Leah were trying to combine the ordinary business of the physician's practice with pursuing citizens in the town.

Their first visit was to the house of Master Pons, wool merchant, leader of the council for the time being, and one of Master Isaac's most grateful patients. His wife had sent for some remedies that she needed, and she received Raquel with her usual calm friendliness.

"What do you think of this business with the Grail, mistress?" asked Raquel as she slowly searched for two packets in her basket.

"Rumors, that's all it is," said Pons's wife briskly.

"There are many who believe them," said Raquel. "They say one of our wealthy citizens has it now," she added, intensifying her search through the basket to avoid looking up. "One of my father's patients swears it is Master Pons."

"The Lord spare us from that!" said his wife. "Pons buying such a thing? And from a cheat—a fraud! I can assure you, mistress, it is not true. As if we have not had enough trouble in our lives without being dragged into a scheme like that."

"I didn't believe it could be true, mistress," said Raquel. "It did not sound like Master Pons."

"Let me tell you, Mistress Raquel, my husband is a good man, and very clearheaded. He does not chase such fleeting fantasies, nor waste his gold on thieves and tricksters." Her cheeks were pink with indignation.

"I would never have thought so," said Raquel. "But I wonder who in this city would be foolish enough to waste his gold on a trickster?"

"Does it matter?" asked Pons's wife. It was quite a serious question.

"It seems to matter," said Raquel. "It is causing great harm in the city, isn't it? Two deaths have been attributed to its presence here."

"Or rumors of its presence. After all, no one has actually seen it, have they?" asked Pons's wife.

"One person—and only one that I know of—says that she has seen it," said Raquel. "Or rather, saw something that she was told was it. It was silver; a plain cup, battered and tarnished. She touched it and it did her no harm."

"Then she saw no magic in it," said Pons's wife. "Was she shown this by the man who claimed to own it?"

"Yes," said Raquel uneasily, unsure how far her father wanted her to go.

"Only a child, or one who still believed like a child, would think such a holy object could be found here, in this city," said Pons's wife. "And now, in these modern times. There are many such fools in the city, though," she added.

"Wealthy enough to tempt a greedy trickster?"

"Oh, yes. Certainly wealthy enough to tempt any greedy man." She thought for a while. "The most credulous man I know is Master Joan, the corn merchant. But he has had a bad year, and I doubt that he has enough wealth on hand—or even enough credit—to tempt anyone right now."

"Was Master Gualter easily deceived?"

"Poor man—he was indeed. But his wife is not. Mistress Sibilla knows the value of a penny, and she always kept a shrewd eye on him and all his dealings. I don't know how she missed this one."

"She is certainly suffering greatly."

"But if the man who stole poor Master Gualter's gold is the one who has the Grail, then surely he is the one the guards should be looking for."

"He must be," said Raquel.

"In that case, you seek a greedy man, Mistress Raquel, and there are so many of them about," she said bitterly, "that I would be hard-pressed to list them all. But surely His Excellency the Bishop must know more of these things than the rest of us? Can Master Isaac not ask him . . ." Her voice trailed off.

"Unfortunately," said Raquel, and paused to think how to say it. "Unfortunately, Papa and the Bishop . . ."

"So it is true, what they are saying," said Master Pons's wife. "I am truly sorry, my dear. And I hope the rift can be healed. And with His Excellency so ill, as they say."

Raquel nodded, in some confusion, and decided she was not adept at this sort of delicate deception. She liked the wool merchant and his family, and her attempts to manipulate Pons's wife distressed her. She took her leave, sent for Leah, who was gossiping in the kitchen, and set out again, having learned nothing more, but with another name for her list.

Raquel had one more legitimate call to make, and that was to the house of Master Sebastià. She was not looking forward to it. She suddenly remembered that she had promised Master Ephraim that she would take a flask of strengthening tonic to Mistress Dolsa, to prevent a recurrence of her illness. She sent Leah for the flask, and wandered slowly in the direction of the glover's shop.

The sun was high enough in the sky to penetrate to street level. When she opened the door of the shop, her eyes were dazzled still from facing its bright June light. At the far end of the room, near the door to the workroom, she saw a blur of pale blue and heard Daniel's familiar voice. "Mistress Laura," he said, in tones that she had never heard from him.

She blinked and her vision cleared. There, not five paces away from her, was Daniel, holding Laura Vicens in his arms. Her head had fallen back, and her blond curls spread out over a small counter. Daniel was leaning over her, his back to the door.

Raquel turned and walked out, her cheeks burning.

Leah came 'round the corner, panting with the effort of walking so quickly. "Mistress, I have the flask."

"Good," said Raquel. "Take it in and give it to Master Daniel, if he has a moment."

Leah darted into the shop and returned in a moment. "Master Daniel says 'thank you' and asks if you will stop in for a few moments after he has looked after his customer."

"I would think he has enough to do without worrying about us," said Raquel coldly. "We have other calls to make."

"I told him we had to go to Master Sebastià's," said Leah sadly.

Raquel had little time to think about the scene in the glover's shop. At Sebastià's, even with Leah in close attendance, she needed to keep her wits about her when dealing with the master of the house, whose bright, hot eyes on her made her distinctly uncomfortable.

Master Sebastià lived in constant fear of illness and imminent death. Pale and rather plump, he looked like someone who took too little exercise. But, as she knew to her discomfort, there was strength in those flabby arms. He had once caught her by the wrist when her father had stepped outside the room to give some orders to the housekeeper regarding his patient's diet, and strong and healthy as she was, she had not been able to release herself.

On that occasion, after a silent struggle, she had called out, "Papa!" Sebastià had favored her with a knowing grin and loosened his grip.

And so today she went directly around to the kitchen to seek out the housekeeper in hopes of avoiding the master. She had with her in the basket a new sleeping preparation for Master Sebastià, as well as a different herbal mixture to ease his digestion.

She had no need to raise the subject of the Grail in that kitchen. She barely had time to issue instructions on the preparation of the remedies, when she found herself seated at the table with refreshments and the latest gossip. The cook and the housekeeper—along with the kitchen maid and the lad, a pair of thin, unhealthy-looking children—all ceased their labors to join her.

They favored her with the latest sightings of the Grail, including a vivid description of it, and a long recitation of the terrifying wonders it had performed.

"Maria saw it in the marketplace," said the kitchen maid, "and went stone-blind all at once. But she fell on her knees and prayed to Santa Tecla and her sight was instantly restored."

"Why Santa Tecla?" asked the lad.

"I don't know," said the kitchen maid, and the two children squabbled over saints for the rest of the visit, unhampered by any knowledge of the subject. No one paid them the slightest amount of attention.

"I wonder," said Raquel, "who in this city would be foolish enough to waste his gold on a trickster? For they say that is all that he is—the one who is trying to sell the Grail."

"Anyone with no sense and gold to waste," said the cook, suddenly descending from the realms of airy speculation to everyday reality. "Our master for one, who's too cheap to pay for good meat."

A chorus of agreement interrupted her, with each person dragging forth instances of his niggling economies.

The cook glared them into silence. "Yet everyone knows that he has enough gold for ten households. He gives it away to charlatans and false healers."

This was clearly a sore point with his servants, who must have considered themselves poorly rewarded for their hard work. It brought another chorus of agreement, another—and much longer—round of examples.

"Begging your pardon, mistress," said the cook finally. "We weren't including your father or yourself as false healers. The whole world knows your skill. And that syrup your father mixed for my throat last winter kept me from dying with not being able to eat or drink."

"I'm glad it helped you," murmured Raquel.

A bell at the gate made the lad and the kitchen maid give up their uninformed theological squabble. He went out to see who it was, returning almost at once with a creature in a grubby apron who was even younger than himself, but who looked somewhat better nourished. She curtsied. "Are you Mistress Raquel?" she asked.

"I am," said Raquel.

"The mistress asked me to fetch you, because the young mistress is not feeling well. And having heard you were here, she said I might as well just run over and see if you could drop by to see her."

"Thank you. And where am I to drop by?"

She received a blank look in reply.

"Whose house is your mistress the mistress of?" said Raquel, managing with great difficulty to keep herself from laughing.

"Oh. The house of Master Vicens, Mistress Raquel. Mistress Alicia asked me fetch you for Mistress Laura."

Raquel could feel the blood rush up to her cheeks again. The last house in Girona she wished to visit right now was that one and the very last patient she wanted to see was little Mistress Laura. Just as she was about to dismiss the maid, she remembered that Master Vicens was on her father's list of householders to visit. She took a deep breath and forced a smile. "Tell your mistress I will come as soon as I have finished here."

"Does Master Isaac believe that the Grail is in the city?" asked the cook, as soon as Master Vicens's young maid had left.

"He does," said Raquel hesitantly. "Or he thinks it may be."

"And what does His Excellency think? Does he agree with Master Isaac?"

"I'm afraid that His Excellency and my father have had rather a disagreement over that," said Raquel.

"So it's true that they quarreled?" asked the cook. "We heard something of a quarrel."

"They did," said Raquel.

"And is it also true that Master Isaac is no longer the Bishop's physician?"

"Yes," said Raquel.

"We had heard it," said the housekeeper, "but no one could believe it. Tell me," she added, avid for news, "was it just the Grail they quarreled over, for I heard that—"

The cook poked her in the ribs and she was silenced.

Raquel stood up to take her leave. It had occurred to her that although everyone in the kitchen was willing to repeat gossip all day, and to abuse their master for a fool and a tightwad, she had said all she wanted to, and they seemed to have little useful to add to it.

Mistress Laura was lying on her side on her bed, with her knees drawn up, looking, as far as Raquel could see, rather pale in the face—almost green, in fact. Her hair, the color of honey, had been unbound and tumbled over her pillow; her blue eyes had dark shadows under them. She was wearing a loose gown over her shift.

Raquel pulled up a chair and picked up her hand. It was cold. "Tell me what is wrong, Mistress Laura," she said.

She shook her head. "It is nothing, Mistress Raquel. It is just the usual time. But I felt so sick and with such pains that Mama went into a panic and sent for you. So you see, there is nothing to be done for me."

"Of course there is," said Raquel. She rang for the maid, and handed her a small packet sewn up in linen. "Put that in a cup and pour very hot water over it," she said. "Then bring it back to us." As soon as the maid had gone, Raquel poured some water, added one drop of liquid from a vial, and gave it to her. "This will stop the pain. Drink it."

"I'll be sick," said the girl.

"Nonsense," said Raquel firmly. "Drink it."

She struggled to a sitting position and drank the liquid, grimacing at the taste.

"Now lie down and roll over on your belly," said Raquel.

Laura gave her a startled look and did as she was told. With strong, capable fingers, Raquel massaged her lower back. The maid returned; Raquel nodded at her to put the cup down and carried on.

"That feels better," said Laura, her voice rising and falling with the rhythm of the movement of Raquel's hands. "How do you know what to do? I think you're wonderfully clever. My mama says the only cure is to marry and have a baby. I am glad there are other cures."

"How old are you?" asked Raquel, continuing the massage.

"Fourteen. Papa says I am too young to marry yet."

"He may be right," said Raquel. "It is all right for some, but most do well to wait a few years." She stopped. "You can roll over now. Your maid can do that for you, too, you know. If you prefer, you can have her use sweet oils on your bare skin."

Laura rolled over and sat up. Raquel poured the liquid in the cup off into another one and gave it to her to drink. "She's Mama's maid," said Laura. "She won't do it for me. She won't dress my hair or help me with my gowns, either. She's too busy fussing over Mama. Mama likes to look her best, always," she added, a little resentfully.

"Then get the kitchen maid to do it. She's young, but she looks as if she has good strong hands—that's what's needed. Give her an extra penny for it and she'll be glad to learn and help."

"I knew you were what I needed," said Laura, looking pleased.

"Me?"

"Yes. I went with Mama to Ephraim the glover the other day to see what they had, and there was the handsomest young man there—tall, and with such a charming smile and voice. Well—I went back again this morning, because I hadn't been able to make up my mind, and Papa said I could only have one pair of gloves, not three, and while I was there I felt faint, and he told me how skilled you were, and how clever, and said that I should get my mama to summon you. Your maid said you would be at Master Sebastià's." She finished with a look of almost gloating triumph on her face. "His name is Daniel."

"Yes," said Raquel. Her words were slightly distorted by being spoken through tightly clenched teeth. "He is very charming, isn't he?"

"I don't feel sick and dizzy anymore at all," said Laura. And, indeed, her ghostly pallor had disappeared, and she seemed prepared to leap out of bed.

"Those drops I gave you may make you sleepy," warned Raquel. "You had best lie down for a while. Then you should be fine."

Raquel left three more packets of antispasmodic herbs with her, with instructions, and headed down to have a little talk with Mistress Alicia.

She was stopped on the staircase by a familiar voice floating up. It was Daniel, inquiring most solicitously for Mistress Laura, and delivering a sketch of a glove pattern that he seemed to feel would meet her requirements.

She was not the only one to hear his voice. Upstairs there was a flurry of urgent preparations, and in less time than she would have believed possible, Mistress Laura, buoyed up with the smallest possible dose of Master Isaac's strongest pain remedy, pushed past her and floated down the staircase in a blue silk dress, all pale blond and lovely, smiling sweetly at Daniel's upturned face.

"*Hola*, Daniel," said Raquel. "I hadn't expected to see you here."

"Raquel," said Daniel, with a bow. "I am not surprised to see you. I urged Mistress Laura to send for you. And you have accomplished a great cure, as anyone can see," he added gallantly.

"Thank you," she said coldly. "Mistress Alicia, may I have a word with you?" And she took the lady of the house aside to explain what she had done. "I have left some of the preparation. If she takes it when the discomfort begins, she will not need stronger remedies. And I suggest that one of the maids be shown how to massage her back, since it seems to give her great relief. In all likelihood, the problem will ease in a year or so— it is her youth that makes her feel it so keenly."

"I never had such trouble," said Mistress Alicia. "Nor did my mother, so I have little experience in dealing with it."

"You are fortunate, then. I will return tomorrow to make sure that she is still feeling better."

And in a flurry of mutual compliments, she took her leave. It was not until she and Leah were almost home that she realized that she had not accomplished any of her goals in the household of Master Vicens. "That nasty little flirt," she muttered. "It's her fault."

"I beg your pardon, mistress," said Leah, startled.

"Nothing, Leah," said Raquel. "I just remembered something I forgot to do. But we must hurry, or we will be late for dinner."

"That's all I've done since I got up this morning," said Leah. "Hurry, hurry, hurry. I'd be better off in the kitchen," she added under her breath, heading straight for Naomi with a morning's harvest of gossip.

SEVENTEEN

Daniel came by before supper that evening, inquiring for Master Isaac.

Judith shook her head. "I'm sorry, Daniel," she said. "My husband was called out most urgently to go to someone in the city."

"When do you expect his return?" said Daniel.

"It was hours ago when he left," she said. "He should be back any moment," she added, looking over at the gate. "Do sit down with us and take something."

"Thank you, Mistress Judith," he said. "You are very kind, but what I wanted to speak to him about is probably very unimportant, and I have other errands to run for my aunt. The lad is sick and it seems that he left many things undone today. I was astonished to hear it," he added lightly, "since I would have sworn he didn't do a stroke of work from one week to the next. It shows how wrong you can be. My best wishes to Master Isaac. And to Mistress Raquel." And he was gone.

"Who was that, Mama?" asked Raquel, coming down a few minutes later.

"Daniel," said her mother. "He wanted to speak to your father and would not stay. I wonder what he wanted?"

"I really don't know," said Raquel, picking up an olive from a dish on the table and nibbling on it.

"And how was your visit with young Master Martí, Yusuf?" asked Isaac. They were seated in the courtyard in the quiet of the late evening. The warm flower-scented night was pitch-black, and Raquel made sporadic attempts to work at her needle by the light of a pair of candles, in the absence of the moon. The board had been cleared of supper dishes, the servants were nowhere in evidence, and Judith was occupied with the twins.

"It wasn't very successful, lord," said Yusuf. "Master Martí is very impetuous," he added, "and very stubborn, and he does not listen with great care. It makes him difficult to talk to."

"What are you trying to say, Yusuf? It sounds most alarming," said Isaac in amused tones. "I already know how impetuous the young man is, and how impossible to reason with. He is, in fact, the very picture of his father. Good-hearted, affectionate, loyal, and impossible to deal with. That was why they quarreled so bitterly." He poured himself a small amount of wine, diluted it with water, and drank. "Now that we have listened to and accepted your excuses—tell us about it."

"By the time I found him," said Yusuf, "he had already had overmuch wine."

"Where did you find him?"

"At Mother Benedicta's," said the lad. "It was quiet there, and so I thought that would be a good place to talk. I should have chosen more discreetly, lord."

"Don't worry about that now," said Isaac, "tell me
what happened."

"Well, he started off by saying that if you had sent
me, lord, to tell him that Master Astruch was innocent
of his father's death, he already realized that. I said that
I was glad of it. And I started to talk about His Excellency, and Master Martí said that His Excellency didn't
care what happened to anyone's father and so he didn't
want to talk about him—only he said it in rather more
intemperate terms, lord—"

"I understand that you are softening this conversation
so that you do not shock my delicate ears, Yusuf," said
the physician.

"Or mine," said Raquel, laughing.

"Then unfortunately two men at the other table, lord,
began to listen—Master Martí's voice was rather loud—
and they said you couldn't expect the Bishop to do anything, being so ill, and had Master Martí heard about the
blood in the courtyard, and how everyone was afraid to
accuse Master Vicens because he was rich and important
but it was obvious that he had killed Master Gualter.
Because he had killed that Baptista, and the knife he
used was from his house, one of a pair, and Master Gualter was killed in exactly the same manner with an iden-
tical knife that was the other of the pair."

"Is that true, Papa?"

"No," said Isaac. "Gualter was killed with a long dagger blade under the rib cage and into the heart. A clean
blow. Baptista was caught from behind and his throat
was slit. With a very sharp blade, says the captain, who
has some experience in these matters. And the blood in
Master Vicens's courtyard came from a rat. But the fact
that these rumors are not true does not make them less
dangerous." He stopped to consider what he had heard.

"And was Master Martí listening to all this nonsense?" he asked finally.

"Yes, lord," said Yusuf. "First he asked how they knew this, and they said everyone knew it. Then he called for more wine for all—but Mother Benedicta said she wanted to feel the weight of his coin before she put more wine on the table. So he left, calling down the vengeance of the heavens on Master Vicens and Mother Benedicta. I followed him as long as I could."

"Did he go home?"

"Yes, he did, lord, finally."

"And that is why you almost missed your supper," said Raquel.

Wednesday, June 11

"I promised Mistress Laura that I would return to see her this morning," said Raquel stiffly. "And so I should."

"Take Yusuf and Leah," said her father. "They can storm the kitchen while you are pampering the daughters of the rich."

"I didn't say I was pampering her, Papa."

"You didn't have to, my dear."

And so Raquel set out with her entourage, determined that this time she would get people to talk about something other than Mistress Laura's passion for gloves. And glovers.

The kitchen maid opened the gate for her. "Thank you," she said, giving her a farthing, "but surely you are not expected to take care of the kitchen and the court-yard, too. Does Master Vicens have such a small household?"

"Oh, it's not that, mistress," said the kitchen maid,

tucking the coin into a pocket she kept tied under her apron. "But the cook's niece, who was the maid who went to the council and told everyone about the blood in the courtyard, she's been sent off. The mistress was that angry about it. And so the porter is doing his work and most of hers, and I'm doing the rest as well as looking after the gate because the porter doesn't have any time for it. And the mistress's maid, she has enough to do with fussing over the mistress."

"I see. Well, I'll just go up and knock on the door."

"But, mistress, I'm afraid you may not want to go in—there's a terrible row going on. That young man—Master Martí—is shouting at the master—but now I think of it maybe Mistress Laura will be very pleased to go up to her chamber and get away from him. And because of what you said, mistress, I'm to learn to rub her back, and I'll get an extra penny every month, she says. But Mistress doesn't know about the extra penny," she added in alarm.

"I won't say a word," said Raquel.

While the kitchen maid was giving Raquel the family history as she knew it, they were crossing the courtyard, and the noise from inside the house was growing louder and louder. The voice was unmistakably that of Martí Gutiérrez. Just as Raquel approached the door, it was flung open, as if in some kind of bizarre welcome, and the young man's figure appeared in the doorway. He was standing sideways, half in and half out of the door, and still shouting. "And when I finish with you, Master Vicens, I'll use the same knife to cut the throats of your elegant wife and pretty daughter as well. And then perhaps you'll know what it is to suffer, too."

"No," said a reasoned voice behind him. "I don't think I will. According to you, I'll be dead, won't I?"

Martí turned away from the house and found himself

face-to-face with Raquel. "I should have known I'd find the witch here with the assassin, all in the same house." He raised an accusing finger and pointed at her face. "You're in this as well, aren't you, Mistress Raquel, you and your father, creeping from house to house, listening to people's secrets, spying, and worming confidences out of helpless widows."

"My father does not creep, Master Martí," said Raquel with great dignity, her voice cold with rage. "And your mother is far from being a helpless widow. She is, in truth, much less helpless than you are. You are drunk, Master Martí. And it's not even mid-morning."

"I have a right to be drunk," he said. "After all that has been done to me, by God in heaven, I have a right. And you—you sorceress bitch, you sound like your friend the Bishop. Preaching at me. Where did you learn the noble art of preaching, mistress? In his bed?"

A roar interrupted him from behind Raquel, and Daniel, who had come in the gate in time to hear Raquel's comment and Martí's response, erupted into the scene. "You are a foul, lying wretch, Martí Gutiérrez," he shouted, and stalked across the courtyard. Grasping Raquel by the shoulders, he set her to one side, took a long stride forward, and struck Martí across the face.

"Stop all this," said a voice from the hall, and Master Vicens appeared. He caught hold of Martí's upraised arm. "Take his other arm, Daniel," he said, and the two of them held him in a tight grip. "Pere," he roared, and the porter appeared at once, as by magic. "Shove this noisy puppy headfirst in the fountain until he sobers up and then take him home to his mother. Send for Enric if you need help."

"I shouldn't think I would," said Pere. He grasped the struggling Martí by the top and bottom of his tightly fitted tunic and pushed him over to the fountain.

"Mistress Raquel, welcome," said Vicens. "And Master Daniel. You are most welcome, both of you. I apologize for your dramatic reception to my house."

He ushered them into a sitting room, where his wife sat, composed and beautifully coiffed, apparently placidly sewing. He invited them to sit and called for a glass of wine. "I know that we have just witnessed the deplorable effects of too much wine at an early hour, but this was a most distressing incident," he said. "I think Mistress Raquel is in need of a little wine."

"I'm not upset, Master Vicens," said Raquel, although her veil had come away from her face and her words were belied by the pallor of her cheeks. "I realize that Master Martí takes his father's death very hard, and feels that there must be someone he can blame." Suddenly she remembered what she was there for. "After all," she added, "the whole city is talking of nothing but this terrible business, so one must forgive—"

"But he must learn discretion in his accusations," said Master Vicens, handing her a cup of wine into which he had splashed some water. "At least we all know that they are nonsensical."

"Everyone knows one cannot take a drunken man's words at their face value," said Raquel, thinking of the accusations of murder.

"You are a wise woman, Mistress Raquel, for one so young."

She realized from his glance in her direction that he thought she was referring to Martí's comments on her virtue and her cheeks flamed scarlet. "But not so young as Master Martí. It is his youth, I think, that makes him so impetuous and thoughtless—"

"Indeed. And speaking of youth, did I not see your

father's apprentice in the courtyard? Surely he was not frightened away by that performance?"

"I think not, Master Vicens," said Raquel. "I suspect that you will find him in the kitchen. He has a deplorable habit of finding his way into people's kitchens, and into the affections of the most hard-hearted cooks."

"He is most welcome to whatever hospitality the kitchen can afford," said Mistress Alicia suddenly. "Although he need not feel he has to stay there. Is he not His Majesty's own ward?"

"He is," said Raquel. "But he enjoys savoring the freedom of the kitchen as well as the amenities of the great hall."

"He is still a boy," she said, and lapsed into silence once more.

"I'm afraid your household has been terribly disrupted by this unfortunate incident this morning," said Raquel.

"It was," said Vicens, "but we have become accustomed to such things these days, have we not, my love?"

"I'm afraid so," said Mistress Alicia placidly.

"But I have business with Master Daniel over a pair of gloves, and you, I believe, have called to see my daughter. You will find her much improved, I hope."

Near the palace, a tall figure in a long cloak and a Franciscan friar of medium height and slender build, deep in conversation, paced slowly around the Bishop's palace. They took the pathway that led past the door to the kitchen, and entered through a narrow doorway without being remarked.

"His Excellency will be very glad to see you, Master Isaac," remarked the friar as soon as he had closed the door behind them.

"Is he better this morning, Father Bernat?" asked Isaac.

"Irritable and restless," said the Bishop's secretary. "Much better, I would say. I hope you have time for a game of chess." And he led the way up the narrow winding stairs that led into His Excellency's bedchamber.

Meanwhile, in the rest of the palace, little work was being accomplished. Those who pretended to keep busy attended to their tasks in a desultory manner, dropping what they were doing whenever they heard footsteps coming by, ears keen to be the first to hear the news of His Excellency's demise.

Raquel left Master Vicens's house in a state of high irritation. Halfway across the courtyard, she realized that neither had she summoned Leah, nor had she told Yusuf she was going. She followed her nose around the house to the kitchen, opened the door, and glared at them. They were sitting, as she knew they would be, around a table, cozily eating, drinking, and gossiping. Forgetting why her father wanted them along, she snapped at them that she was leaving, and they scrambled after her.

Daniel came out of the house as they were crossing the courtyard. "I hope you have quite recovered, Raquel," he said solicitously.

"From what?"

"He said some unforgivable things about you," said Daniel, looking surprised. "I was upset as well."

"Oh, that. He was drunk," she said. "And he's stupid to boot. I don't see how anyone can take him seriously."

The kitchen maid, in the absence of the porter, let them out the gate, and they turned toward the *call*.

"Did you find Mistress Laura worse than you expected?" asked Daniel, with a puzzled frown.

"There's nothing wrong with her," said Raquel. "Women's troubles. A great fuss over nothing. Don't worry—the next time you come by she'll be all smiles.

As she would have been today," she added venomously, "except that she had to see me and her mother's maid forced her to stay in her chamber until I got there." She turned away abruptly. "I must go. It's getting late," she murmured. "I hadn't planned to spend so much time at Master Vicens's house." And she set off at a pace so rapid that she left Leah panting far behind.

Daniel stopped and watched her go. "Now what was all that about?" he said.

"I think I could tell you, Master Daniel," said Yusuf, "but I am not sure. And I might be wrong."

"Tell your master there is something I would like to talk to him about," said Daniel.

"What is it?" asked Yusuf.

"Curious, aren't you?" he asked. "It's about Joaquim. The monk. Now, that surprised you, didn't it?" And he strolled slowly home.

EIGHTEEN

The Feast of Corpus Christi

Thursday, June 12

Corpus Christi was a brilliant, sunny day, with a cool breeze to moderate the heat of the sun. A perfect day for a holiday, and a crowd of townspeople flocked toward the cathedral for Mass, decked out in their summer best.

Many were curious to see who would celebrate Mass, and even more curious to discover who would preach in His Excellency's place. If it was Father Francesc, then basically the sermon and the orders were still coming from the Bishop himself. If it was someone else—especially someone not usually identified as part of Berenguer's following—it would give interesting indications of what they were in for in coming years.

To no one's surprise, Father Francesc said Mass, with considerable assistance as befitted the solemnity of the occasion. When the time came for him to preach, however, he slipped unobtrusively into his chair among the canons. The small door nearest the pulpit opened, someone emerged and mounted the staircase into the pulpit.

It came as a considerable shock to many—although not to Francesc Monterranes or to Bernat—to see Berenguer de Cruilles looking down on his congregation.

Someone remarked later, with amusement in his voice, that the Bishop looked reasonably fit for a dying man. Others felt that he was a trifle pale. But everyone agreed that when he spoke, it was in his old, firm, resonant voice—a voice that filled the farthest reaches of the cathedral.

"Beatus vir qui non abiit in consilio impiorum," he said, and his voice rang with sorrow. "And that means, my children, blessed is the man who walks not in the counsel of the ungodly." He looked down at his congregation, and his eyes seemed to look into each person's eyes, and straight into their souls. "My children," he said, "listen to me, most carefully, I beg of you, and heed what I have to say. Malice stalks us, as deadly as pestilence, and its prey already numbers two. Two men in the full vigor of life. One was known to us all, a respected citizen; the other was a stranger among us, who, sinner though he may have been, deserved our help and protection.

"Their deaths happened because too many of us— you, who stand there before this altar—have listened to the wicked counsels of the ungodly—of evil or foolish men and women—instead of stopping your ears and listening to your own God-given blessed common sense.

"Today we celebrate the most mystical sacrifice of the body of our Lord. I had originally intended to speak of this holiest of sacrifices, but the words have been snatched out of my mouth by the actions of other powers." The congregation moved uneasily.

"Some say that it is here," he continued in a voice

that, although it carried to the west door, was conversational in tone. "Today, in our very city," he added, his voice rising. "The cup itself, the Holy Chalice, the Grail in which our Lord offered himself as a sacrifice before his disciples. There are those who say that this holiest of all relics is here. And that it is exacting revenge and wreaking evil all around it. And they have said other things. Rest assured, children, I have heard all those things that the wicked and foolish say. That the Grail can bring power and untold riches, that it can disguise itself to stay out of unworthy hands, that it can kill.

"What they tell you is false—all false. Think a moment. Am I to believe that the cup that held the sacrifice of our Lord is an alchemist's stone? Is it a wizard's rod? Is it a fairground charlatan's fire? Or is it a heathen idol? If it is, then it has truly fallen into the hands of Satan, and that I cannot believe.

"It is enough that you should know that the holy cup is safe. It dwells amongst the high and distant mountains; it is guarded by a zealous and careful band of monks. It was carried there during the invasions of the infidels, to protect it. And there it remains, guarded by stout walls and fervent prayers.

"There is no terrifying holy relic here in the city, threatening your life and safety or holding out the promise of endless wealth or power. I assure you, my children, such beliefs are anathema! I will not countenance them in my diocese."

He turned to altar, murmuring, *"In nomine Patris, et filii et Spiritus Sancti. Amen,"* and quickly left by the door he had entered through.

The majority of the congregation found it an interesting sermon, even if they didn't believe a word of it. What engaged their tongues for most of the day, however, was that Berenguer himself had delivered it.

NINETEEN

The afternoon of that same day, quiet reigned at the physician's house. The dinner table had been cleared away and the twins were playing one of their more peaceful games. Yusuf had slipped away unnoticed and Raquel had retreated abruptly to her chamber during dinner, leaving her parents alone in the courtyard. Even the cat was asleep, curled up on the bench beside Isaac.

"Isaac," said his wife, "you must do something about Raquel."

"What must be done about her?" asked her father.

"She is in a foul temper these days," said her mother. "If I happen to chide her, she snaps at me like a stray dog. And she ate nothing at dinner. Naomi was most upset."

"No doubt she has a reason for it," said Isaac calmly. "It may even be a good reason. I would ignore it for now if I were you, Judith."

"It is so unlike her. Do you think she is ill?" said Judith.

"She moves at a lively pace for one who is not well, my dear," said her husband. "Leave her be and see if she regains her usual temper."

The subject of this discussion was stretched out on her bed, staring up at the heavy beams of her ceiling and wondering how long she would be left alone. Halfway through the meal, desperate for solitude, she had murmured some excuse and fled from the table, but now that she had achieved her goal, she was not sure she wanted to be left alone with her thoughts.

She had been staring at the beautifully presented baked fish on her plate—one of Naomi's most prized dishes, with its savory stuffing and sweet-sour sauce—and trying to convince herself that nothing had happened that morning of any importance at all. A man she had no interest in, who had been pursuing her, had shifted his attentions to a cloth merchant's daughter with big cow eyes and no discretion, a woman with two thoughts in her head on her best days—how to dress her hair without her mother's maid to help, and which gown to wear.

Raquel had spooned up a piece of fish swimming in sauce, brought it to her mouth, and then set it down again, untasted. How could he? An empty-headed creature—a Christian—who could no more look after herself than a baby can. At that thought, she had realized to her horror that tears were filling her eyes and she had fled from the table.

Being alone in her chamber was no help. The humiliating truth was that she did care that Daniel had transferred his attentions elsewhere. She cared a great deal. And that, in her arrogance, it had never occurred to her that she might lose him to someone more forthcoming in her smiles and attention. All this time she had assumed that if no one more interesting came along, she would marry Daniel, and he would be intensely grateful that she condescended to do so.

Watching her unmarried friends and acquaintances eyeing him with interest had gratified and amused her. What a fool she had been. Anyone else would have taken it as a warning. Never had she been so angry and embarrassed as when she had dutifully treated little Mistress Laura and been forced to listen patiently as she had prattled on about how enchanting Daniel was. Maliciously, without a doubt. In a town where a simple kitchen maid couldn't have a follower without everyone commenting on it, Laura knew as well as anyone that Daniel was attached to Raquel.

Or was he? What if he had never much cared for her? If he had allowed himself to be pushed in her direction by his aunt and uncle, who would be pleased with the match, since it united families who were already friends and would bring their nephew a handsome dowry as well. Her cheeks burned scarlet, she rolled over, burying her face in the bedclothes, and wept.

A caller at the gate interrupted the peace in the courtyard.

"Who could be calling at this hour?" asked Judith crossly.

"A friend, I would say," replied Isaac. "If one may judge from the placid reaction of the cat." That creature had indeed opened one golden eye, flicked an ear in the direction of the gate, and settled back into her slumbers.

"It's Daniel," said Judith, getting up and heading for the gate. "I'll let him in. He could ring half the day before Ibrahim noticed him. Daniel. Come in. I trust everyone is well?"

"Very well, Mistress Judith," said Daniel. "Please excuse me for breaking in on the peace of your afternoon, but I have come to see Master Isaac over a small matter of business."

"Of course," said Judith, who was too well schooled to remain in the courtyard after such a broad hint. "I beg you to excuse me. I have much work to attend to. Perhaps we can talk later," she murmured, and whisked herself up the stairs to sit where she could hear the rest of the conversation.

From the door of her chamber, Raquel called out, "Mama? Who called?"

"Just Daniel, my love," said Judith. "To see your papa on business of some kind."

"Oh," said Raquel. She closed the door and flung herself down on the bed once again.

"Master Isaac, I bring my apologies," said Daniel. If he had hoped to see Raquel sitting with her family, he gave no sign of it at all. "It is days since I visited the abbey. I had intended to tell you at once what I learned there, but whenever I came by it was impossible for us to have a private conversation. You are a busy man, Master Isaac," he added ruefully.

"I have not concerned myself with it," said the physician. "Your exploits are well known."

"They are?"

"For example, you spoke to Brother Joaquim at great length, I heard. Don Vidal de Blanes mentioned it to the Bishop."

"Oh, no," said Daniel. "I thought that I had been more discreet than that."

"I am astonished, Daniel," said Isaac wryly. "You, of all people, must know the speed with which news and rumor passes through a small community. I suspect a brother cannot sneeze without it being known to all within the hour."

"But they seem scarcely to speak to each other!" said Daniel. "Well—I am sorry if I caused trouble. Let me tell you about the visit anyway."

"Certainly."

"After I transacted my business with the abbot—and it only took him a moment, Master Isaac, to try the gloves and declare himself pleased with them—I asked the brother who had brought me to his study how young Joaquim was. I explained that I had met him once at Master Gualter's and said that everyone would like to know how he fared. I tried to make the question casual—like an inquiry arising from common courtesy rather than out of curiosity. Obviously, I failed badly at that," he added.

"And were you told?" asked Isaac.

"In a manner of speaking," said Daniel. "We were walking along the cloisters, and the brother pointed out a monk working in the small, ornamental garden in the center. 'That's him,' he said. 'His foot has healed well enough, but he's still an odd one. He's good with flowers.' Then he took his leave of me, saying that the porter would let me out, and disappeared. At first I thought that very odd, until it occurred to me that he was tactfully allowing me to speak to Brother Joaquim if I wished. So I went over."

"Were you able to talk to him?"

"Yes," he said. "I suppose I was. It was a very strange conversation, though." He stopped.

"Daniel," said Isaac, after waiting an appreciable length of time, "are you going to tell me what he said?"

"Certainly, Master Isaac," he said hastily. "But it was a very odd conversation," he repeated.

"Tell me anyway, Daniel."

"He seemed completely uninterested in his health. When I asked him about his foot he looked at it and shook his head. Not as if it troubled him, but as if he hadn't thought of his feet in years. As I might look if you asked me how my eyebrows were feeling."

"Interesting," said Isaac.

"And then I asked him if he was thinking of going back to his monastery in the mountains. Well—actually, first I asked him where his monastery was. The one in the mountains. He didn't seem to know, Master Isaac," said Daniel in a puzzled voice. "He shook his head and said that he had planted flowers when I asked about his monastery. When I asked him again where it was, then he suddenly started speaking. 'I must go back to the mountains,' he said, 'for that is the only place where it will be safe from wicked men. I must take it back to the mountains. It is unhappy here.' I was startled, as you can imagine, and I asked him who he was talking about. He just looked at me. Finally he said, 'The cup.' And then I asked him if he had it with him."

"You were alone and not overheard?" asked Isaac.

"We were in the center of the garden, speaking in very low voices," said Daniel. "Joaquim has a very quiet voice. On a busy street, you wouldn't be able to hear him at all. So even if there were brothers lurking in the cloisters, I don't think they could have overheard us."

"I would not be completely sure of that," said Isaac.

"Perhaps not, Master Isaac," said Daniel, looking somewhat abashed. "Anyway, after a long time—you have to be patient talking to Joaquim—he said, 'I don't have it. They took everything when I was sick but I didn't have it.' Then he looked at me very earnestly and said, 'I know where it is. I always know where it is.' He spoke so gently, and so simply, Master Isaac, that I almost believed him."

"Was that all?"

"No," said Daniel. "Having gone this far, I decided I

might as well ask him about the thing. So I asked him if it was true that it was dangerous in a sinner's hand. He told me that it was holy, and good, and would not hurt anyone, but that he had to take it back to the mountains where it would be safe. After that, anything I asked him, I got that same answer and so I gave up."

"That was all?" asked Isaac.

"That was all of any interest, Master Isaac."

"Tell me everything you can remember, Daniel. I would to like to hear the unimportant things as well."

"If you wish, Master Isaac. He seems very confused sometimes, but I'll do my best. I wished him a good journey. He said he was almost ready to go, but that he could not leave while the moon was so bright in the sky. He must be quite mad, Master Isaac, for at that moment, it was the mid-morning sun that was shining merrily down on us. I agreed that it would be difficult—what else could I say?—and took my leave, because I could see several brothers had come out to the cloisters, and I thought they might begin to wonder what we were talking about."

"They did wonder," said Isaac. "But not nearly as much as I do. I would like to speak to the young man." He stood and began slowing pacing the courtyard. "But I am afraid it soon might be too late for that now."

Behind them, there was a clang of the gate closing, and then light footsteps moving quickly over the stones of the courtyard. "It is Yusuf," said Daniel, "back with us again."

"Yes, lord," he said. "Did you need me? You told me that you intended to rest—"

"And I did, Yusuf. I have not needed you."

"I returned so hastily because I was given a message for you," said the boy, handing him a square of folded paper.

Isaac felt it carefully. It had been sealed with wax that had been pressed down, but not with an identifiable signet. "Someone wishes to contact me," he said, "and in such secrecy that he seals the missive as firmly as he can. And who does he believe will read it?"

"I must not intrude on your affairs any longer," said Daniel, rising to his feet.

"Thank you, Daniel," said the physician. "I was most interested in what you had to say."

"Until later, Master Isaac," said the young man, and left.

Isaac broke the seal, ran his fingers over the surface, and handed it to Yusuf.

"The paper has writing on it, lord," said the lad.

"Can you read it?"

"Yes," he said slowly. "I think. But it is not easy to make out."

"Then fetch Raquel," he said. "And the two of you can puzzle it out together."

"It's not easy to read, Papa," said a more composed Raquel. She had bathed her face and eyes, but was grateful that she did not have to face her mother's scrutiny. "The ink is pale, the pen is abominable, and the hand is terrible. Fortunately, the letter is not long."

"Can you read it?" asked Isaac. "I confess I am impatient to hear what this missive contains besides a difficult hand."

"Excuse me, Papa. It starts out, 'My dear Master Isaac. Forgive these hasty summons, but if—' " She paused to puzzle out the next word. " 'If possible, come to my house between sunset and moonrise, with as much—' " She stopped again. "This looks like 'discretion as possible. The Grail has been found and I need your good counsel. If you were to present it to His Excellency as an indication of your goodwill, it might go far toward healing the breach between you.' And then it is signed, 'Vicens,' " she said, giving the paper back to her father.

"Vicens," said Yusuf. "That is not possible."

"Why do you say that?" asked Isaac.

"I cannot believe that Master Vicens would do something so evil," said Yusuf.

"What evil thing do you speak of?" asked Isaac.

"Why—that he would steal the Grail, of course," said Yusuf. "And perhaps the money. As well as kill Master Gualter. Doesn't he say that is what he did?"

"Not here, he doesn't," said Raquel, pointing down at the open page in front of her. "You're not going, are you, Papa?"

"My love, I would not miss that meeting for all the gold in Aragon. Of course we are going."

"We?" said Raquel.

"Not you, my dear. Yusuf and I. But first I have a visit to make. Come, Yusuf. We have much to do before sunset."

"Two witnesses have come my way in the last hour, Your Excellency," said Isaac. "The report of a conversation and a letter. The letter I have with me; I received it right after dinner. I thought you would like to look at it."

Berenguer took it from the physician, looked at it, held it a little farther from his face, and looked at it again. "It is abominably badly written, Isaac," he said, "and in a hand too small for my eyes. Bernat!" he roared, and the secretary opened the door from the study.

"Your Excellency," he asked.

"Read this for me," he said, closing his eyes and leaning back on his bed cushions.

"It is very badly—"

"We know that, Bernat. Read it."

"Certainly, Your Excellency," he said, and rattled it off with the ease of one used to reading the most difficult of hands.

"Is it written by Vicens?" asked Berenguer.

"I don't know," said Bernat. "I don't recognize the writing."

"I doubt it. Vicens isn't fool enough to believe that I could be bought off with a false Grail," said the Bishop.

"I, too, doubt very much that it is from him," said Isaac.

"Why do you say that?"

"Simply because it is signed with Vicens's name, and yet the man who sent it seemed to have gone to some trouble to disguise who he was. Why be so furtive in your messengers if you were handing someone a signed missive?"

"Who gave it to you, Yusuf?" asked Berenguer.

"Some country lout, Your Excellency," said Yusuf. "A peasant."

"What does he look like, this country lout?" asked the Bishop.

"He's tall, and broad in the chest and shoulders, Your Excellency. His hair is a ruddy brown and thin at the crown."

"Anything else?" said Berenguer.

"He was clean-shaven several days ago, Your Excellency, but his beard is growing in again. His nose is large, and twisted—as if it had been broken at some time. His eyes are brown, dark brown. He has sunken cheeks and a cleft in his chin. He was wearing a brown tunic, worn and dirty, and rope sandals. His face, arms, and hands are brown from the sun, and he's dirty. He smells."

"Of what, Yusuf?" asked Isaac.

"A farmyard, lord," answered the boy. "Of pigs and chickens. And he has a long white scar on his left arm. No—it was on his left side facing me—on his right arm."

"I feel as if I know him better than my own beloved mother," said Berenguer. "Although you do not make him sound very attractive, Yusuf."

"He sounds like an ordinary farm laborer, Your Excellency," said Bernat. "No doubt an honest enough type. Someone will have given him a penny to carry a letter."

"You're probably right, Bernat. But I think we might look for him discreetly. A cleft in the chin and a scar on his right arm should be easy enough to find."

"Certainly, Your Excellency," said Bernat. Almost soundlessly, he left the room. Before the conversation had a chance to resume, he had returned. "I have sent for the captain of the guard, Your Excellency," he said.

"I have a morsel of news that might interest you, Isaac," said Berenguer while they waited for the guard to arrive.

"And what is that, Your Excellency?" said the physician.

"It concerns one of your patients. The one that Gualter found and brought here to the city. Joaquim. He has disappeared."

"Disappeared, Your Excellency?"

"He slipped out this morning, having told one of the brothers that he was going to the market—which is odd, since he had no money for marketing. He didn't come back."

"I was afraid that this would happen," said Isaac.

"That he would leave for the market?" asked Berenguer.

"No, Your Excellency. That he might leave today. I should have made an effort to speak to him while I could."

"I don't see why," said Berenguer.

"He might have had something of interest to say. Is Don Vidal upset?"

"Don Vidal is relieved," said the Bishop. "Although somewhat annoyed still. I think I told you that he wrote to the monks at Sant Llorenç to ask if they had lost a Brother Joaquim. It seems that they have never heard of such a brother. He certainly isn't one of theirs."

"Then who is he?" said Isaac. "For I, too, received some interesting information about Brother Joaquim today, Your Excellency. Young Daniel finally took a moment to give me the substance of their conversation." And with great care and accuracy, he repeated what Daniel had told him. "I would judge that he plans to travel by night."

"Then he'll have a dark time of it," said Berenguer. "The moon is on the wane and rises very late tonight."

"Between matins and laud, Your Excellency," said Bernat.

"Where is he now?" asked the Bishop. "He has no friends in the city who will take him in. Gualter is dead and his wife had no great affection for the lad."

"Hiding somewhere, I expect," said Bernat.

"I am beginning to regret that I mentioned him," said Berenguer. "Let us play a game of chess, Isaac, while we wait for the guard to return."

Isaac sent Yusuf home with instructions to inform his mistress that they would be going out that night, and settled down to a game of chess with the Bishop.

A short while after they started their search, the guards found the laborer who had delivered the message enjoying a pitcher of wine nearby. He had little to tell them. "I know the man," said the sergeant of the guard when he returned to report to the Bishop. "I would swear to his honesty. He told me that a girl, someone's housemaid, gave him the paper all sealed up and fivepence with it to find young Yusuf and give it to him. Finding Yusuf was simple enough, since he was standing on the other side of the square. But when the lad asked who had given him the message, he started to worry. It was too much money for such a small errand, and he began to think that he had done something wrong. I asked about the housemaid, but he couldn't describe her any more than that she was young—just a child—wore an apron, and that her hair curls and is dark. She ran off before he could question her."

"Did he go after her?" asked Berenguer.

"Unfortunately, no," said the sergeant dryly. "He went to Mother Benedicta's to recover from his fright, since he was well supplied with coins. He had already spent two on wine and a bite of something to eat. I gave him another and told him to take it home to his wife. But I didn't stay to make sure he did."

"Excellent work, Sergeant," said Berenguer dismissively, and turned to the captain. "And now it is time for us to consider what is in this letter."

"And the question of Brother Joaquim and the dark of the night," added Isaac. "For I believe that it is connected to everything else that has happened here since the young monk's arrival. Whether he is a monk or not is an unimportant detail."

The captain looked from one to the other of the two men. "Certainly, Your Excellency. Master Isaac. Let us by all means consider the dark of the night."

TWENTY

The bells began to ring for vespers as Isaac reached the gate of his house. In the courtyard, Judith was sitting with her work in her lap and her needle idle in her hand; she tossed both onto the table beside her and hurried over to meet him. "Where have you been?" she asked, her voice tight with worry.

"At the palace, my dear," he said. "You knew I would be there. Surely I am not so late, Judith, that you are worried."

"No," she said, her voice oddly flat. "Of course not. But everyone is out and it felt strange here. It was foolish of me."

"What are you talking about?" asked her husband. "Everyone is out? Where?"

"Master Sebastià sent a servant over for that herbal mixture for his digestion—his cook dressed a duck with apricots for their dinner. A foolish meal for such a hot day," she added. "I asked if Sebastià wanted you to visit, but it seems he trusted the herbal mixture to relieve him. Raquel's taken it over there."

"Thank the Lord," said Isaac. "I weary of his digestion. But why did you not give the mixture to Master Sebastià's servant?"

"Raquel had to grind up a new batch, and offered to deliver it when she was done. I told her to leave it at the door with the maid," said Judith firmly. "She should not be in the same room with Master Sebastià, Isaac. He is not to be trusted in these matters."

"You should have sent Yusuf," said her husband. "He does not attract unwelcome attentions from Master Sebastià. I do not like Raquel being at that house—even in the doorway—on her own."

"She is not alone. Leah is with her," said Judith. "And Yusuf hasn't come back yet from that errand."

"What errand?" said Isaac.

"You would know better than I what the errand is."

"What are you talking about, Judith? I told him to come home with a message for you."

"Isaac—you can't have forgotten," said Judith. "You sent Yusuf out of the city to deliver a message an hour or two ago. And Yusuf sent a friend to tell me that he would be back before sunset."

"What friend?" asked Isaac sharply.

"How can one tell, Isaac? It was just a boy. Younger than Yusuf and poor. But Yusuf has friends everywhere, as you well know. I did ask where Yusuf said he was going, and the child said he didn't know. Yusuf hadn't told him." She paused, looking at her husband. "Did you really not send him on an errand?" she asked in a changed voice.

"I told you, Judith. I sent him home with a message. It was to tell you that we would be going out at sunset."

"Then where is he?" she asked sharply.

"He did not come home? Not even for a moment or two?"

"No," said Judith. "And I've been here in the court-yard all afternoon."

"But you must have gone in from time to time."

"I did," said Judith. "But not for long. I would have noticed if he had come home."

"Perhaps he had something he wanted to do outside the city," said Isaac. "After all, he knew he was not needed until sunset."

"He may have taken the mare out," said Judith.

"Yes," said Isaac slowly. "Although it is a warm afternoon for riding. It is not like him to go without delivering my message. Perhaps he gave it to one of the servants. Where is Ibrahim? And get Naomi and the boy," he added. "They may have forgotten to tell you about it."

"Perhaps," said Judith. Her shoulders drooped with weariness, and she seemed to sink into the bench like a neglected cloth toy. Then she raised her head and called the servants.

But none of them admitted to having seen Yusuf since dinner. As they were leaving, Judith murmured to her husband, "We should check with Jacob at the gate. To find out if he saw him come in."

"And at the other gates," said Isaac. "Including the city gates. Tell Ibrahim—"

"The boy is faster," said Judith. "And less likely to confuse the messages."

And so the kitchen boy was sent off to find out if Yusuf had been seen coming in or out of the *call* or leaving the city any time after dinner.

"You must let His Excellency know," said Judith, sitting up abruptly. "Why does that wretched boy keep disappearing!" she added, jumping to her feet and dabbing at her eyes with the housewife's apron she had put on earlier to help Naomi.

"I don't think it is his fault this time," said Isaac.

"But *what* has he done?" asked Judith, furious with exasperation and worry.

"Either he has gone off on a fool's errand, thinking the instructions came from me, or—"

"Or someone has seized him," she said grimly. "To sell or for ransom."

"Where is Raquel?" said Isaac suddenly.

"I told you. At Sebastià's."

"Alone?"

"Certainly not. I told you that I sent Leah with her."

"That's not much better," he said sharply. "We must find her."

"One moment," said Judith. She snatched up her lightweight cloak, pulled the hood down to conceal her face, and headed for the gate.

Just as they rounded the corner Raquel and Leah appeared, chatting animatedly. "Mama! Papa!" called Raquel. "Over here!"

"Come here," said Isaac, waving them over and beginning to explain the situation. Attracted by the sound of their voices, Daniel came up the steps from the glover's shop and joined them, hearing enough to convince him that something was very wrong.

Leah was sent to help Naomi with supper. "I'll just go and find out if there's something I can do," said Raquel.

"Nonsense, dear," said Judith. "If those two can't prepare a simple supper on their own, then we need new servants. I've already spent an hour in the kitchen today, helping. You stay here with us. Your papa might need you."

Raquel, miserably uncomfortable, sat down as close as possible to her parents and stared at her feet. Silence fell over the group.

A leaf fluttered past Daniel. He plucked it out of the

air as he stood there and tore it into little shreds, waiting for a cue. When none came, he bowed. "I have come with my unimportant message at a bad time, Mistress Judith," he said. "If I cannot help you in any way, I will take my leave."

"This is not a private trouble, I think," said Isaac. "Or will not be for long, I fear."

"Yusuf has not come home?" said Daniel.

And as briefly as he could, Isaac sketched out what they knew. "It sounds very unimportant, I know," he said, "but it is not like the boy."

"He wanders off into the city by himself a great deal, does he not, Master Isaac? Everyone in the house complains about it."

"No," said Raquel and her father at the same time.

"Never when he knows that he's wanted," said the physician. "Nor if his tutor is expected. If there is nothing to do—"

"He disappears," said Judith. "Vanishes, like a shadow when the sun goes behind a cloud. You turn to look for him and he's gone."

"Yusuf can be careless, Daniel," said Raquel, looking desperately worried. "He doesn't think sometimes. And he's had so many lucky escapes that he thinks he's invulnerable. You know, Papa, if someone asked him to go off into the countryside, he would be sure he could be back here before you needed him. When did you need him?" she added.

"At sunset," said her father. "But who sent him off? I didn't. I told him to go home and deliver a message—brief but important. He would not have ignored that."

"What do you think has happened?" asked Raquel.

"He's let himself be caught, one way or another," said her father.

"Why would someone want to catch him?" asked Daniel.

"To sell," said Judith flatly.

"We mustn't think that. Not yet. Consider, Judith. A trader couldn't sell him in Girona," said Isaac. "He's too well known. And to get him out of the city, he would have to smuggle him past the gates."

"But then we must tell the guard," said Daniel. "As soon as possible. And have them at the gates."

"We sent the boy to ask at all the gates if he had passed through. But you are right, the guard must be told."

"I will do that," said Daniel. "Immediately." He bowed and left.

"If it is not a trader," asked Raquel, "who is it?"

"Perhaps someone wants me to go out alone this evening," said Isaac.

"But how would taking Yusuf help? Does the world think you have no other friends?" asked Raquel. "That if Yusuf is not here, you must go out alone?"

"I used to, often enough," he said. "And not that long ago."

"And, Isaac," said his wife, "the world believes you have quarreled bitterly with the Bishop. They may believe you would have difficulty finding another man." She stopped. "Unless you were to take Ibrahim."

Isaac stood absolutely still for a moment. "Does everyone believe that without the Bishop I am without resources?"

"And why not?" asked Judith tartly. "Except for Ibrahim, we do not keep an army of great strong men around to act as guards when you go out. When there is danger afoot you stay in or the Bishop sends his men for you."

"And Ibrahim couldn't guard a fast mouse from a slow cat," said Raquel.

"My dear, that's unkind," said Isaac.

"Perhaps, but it's also true," she said.

"He's an honest and conscientious servant," said

Isaac. "But you may be right. Not someone to rely on in a moment of danger."

"True," said Judith slowly. "For all that he's a good size. He'd be likely to hit the wrong man over the head." She paused again. "You think the person who wrote you the letter took him," said Judith, "because he wants you alone when you go to Vicens's house. Not because he wanted Yusuf for some reason. I'm not sure of that."

"But, Mama, it makes sense. He assumes Papa will return to his old ways," said Raquel.

"That is clear," said Isaac. "But I could well bring someone else."

"Who? Slow-witted Ibrahim? One of the women servants? Your wife or your daughter? And how far would you trust someone outside of the household," said Judith shrewdly, "unless he had sworn allegiance to the Bishop?"

Isaac stopped. "And so you bring me back to the quarrel with the Bishop. It is satisfactory to discover that our efforts were successful. The world has heard of it," he said wryly. "Except that I did not consider Yusuf's vulnerability. I am greatly to blame for that," he said.

"This is no time to talk of blame, Isaac," said Judith.

"What better time?" said Isaac bitterly. "Not only am I fond of the lad—almost as fond as if he were our own child—but I am responsible to His Majesty for his safety."

No one had an answer to that.

"We have taken the first steps," said Isaac. "The guards will hunt for him more efficiently than we could. What we must do is think where he could be. And why."

"And how do we do that?" asked Judith. "He could be anywhere in the city, doing almost anything."

There seemed little else to say for the moment. The kitchen boy came back, crestfallen. He had been unable to find anyone who had seen Yusuf at the gates or anywhere else in the last few hours. "Except for one lad," he said in a small voice, "who said it might have been Yusuf he saw talking to a big man." But further questions provided no more information.

Hard on his heels came Daniel, with news that the guard had been alerted, and that the captain waited outside their gate for a word with him.

Shortly after, Raquel and Leah, cloaked and veiled, were escorted to the palace to see His Excellency about the disappearance of His Majesty's ward.

Yusuf had been deep in thought as he left the palace. After crossing the plaza at a pace much slower than usual, he paused near the gate before entering the *call*.

"*Hola!*" The voice behind him was peremptory but unfamiliar, and he had paid no attention to it. "You! Boy."

A quick glance around had convinced him that he was the person being summoned, and he had started for the *call* again at a rapid pace, stubbornly refusing to respond. He didn't like being addressed as if he were a servant or a slave.

"Yusuf!" The voice had been bright with anger. "Are you deaf? I have a message for you."

He turned. An unfamiliar man in the familiar uniform of the Bishop's Guard was striding across the plaza, bearing down on him. In deference to the uniform, he suppressed his annoyance and stopped. He even listened attentively to the message. "Of course," he said to the guard. "One moment." He waved at a passing urchin. "Here, Ramon," he said. "Can you remember a message?"

"Why?" the urchin had asked.

"Because if you can, and can deliver it, you'll get a penny," he said. "But if I discover that you didn't deliver that message, I'll find you and squeeze that penny out of your black little heart. So remember that."

"Give me the penny," Ramon had said, unimpressed.

"First I'll give you the message," Yusuf had replied.

And Ramon had trotted off, clutching a penny supplied by the irritated guard, to deliver Yusuf's message.

Daniel accompanied Raquel and Leah to the gate of the *call*, where he left them in the care of the sergeant of the guard. There being little else that he could do, he went home.

In the courtyard of the physician's house, Isaac and Judith waited. "When was the moon at the full, Judith?" asked her husband.

"Last week," said his wife. "Monday. Not this last Monday—it was the week before. The night Master Gualter was murdered. The moon was full that night and I slept badly. I heard you go out and come in. That was the day young Mistress Delia gave birth—you know it always happens at the full of the moon."

"I thought it was then," said Isaac. "When we walked to the palace Yusuf said the streets were as bright as day."

"But what does that matter, Isaac? None of this gets us any closer to finding Yusuf."

"But it does, my dear. Shortly I shall discover who took him, and if the Lord is willing, he may still be safe."

"Alone? Without help?"

"Never alone, my dear. And not without help." He paused, made up his mind, and turned in her direction. "There is something I need to explain to you. Come and sit by me."

Judith set down her work and moved over until her legs were lightly touching her husband's. He patted her gently on the thigh. "Listen, carefully, and say nothing until I finish."

Judith listened, and her face became blank. "Isaac," she whispered, "you cannot."

"We shall all be safe," he said. "I promise you."

TWENTY-ONE

The first thing Yusuf was aware of when he awoke was the pounding of his head, and then of a terrible thirst. He opened his eyes and saw nothing but darkness. The air was thick with heat and the smell of hay and beasts; the silence was absolute. Panic seized his gut. He reached out a hand to get his bearings. There was nothing above or around him but heat and smell. Then his hand touched hay. He was lying on a pile of dusty hay. For some reason he was in a someone's stable or barn. With great difficulty he suppressed a sneeze. Cautiously, he tried to sit up. To his surprise, he was not fettered by anything but his throbbing head.

Nor was it as dark as he had supposed. Thin slivers of light showed up randomly in the walls that enclosed his prison. He began to crawl over toward the nearest light.

"What was that?" said a voice below him. He froze.

"A rat, probably," said another, sounding bored.

"Do you think he's awake?"

"He won't wake until after sundown," said the bored one. "If at all."

"The master won't like that," said the other, and lapsed into silence. "Why's he so important?" he said at last. "He's just a boy. Lots of them about."

"He knows something, doesn't he?"

"I wonder what?"

The voices fell silent again.

Yusuf was also trying to puzzle out why he was in a stable loft, but the exercise of that much coherent thought made his head ache more fiercely than before. He abandoned the why and wondered instead how he got here. He remembered talking to the strange guard, who had given him a sealed document. He remembered sending little Ramon off to tell the mistress he would be late. He remembered very clearly starting off to deliver the document, and the guard telling him he wasn't to go alone. That His Excellency had insisted that someone go with him to protect him. And he remembered telling the guard that if that were the case, the guard could deliver the message as well as Yusuf could.

"No, no," the guard had said. "The man we are taking the message to is not very trustful. He knows you but he's never seen me before."

Yusuf looked at the man's craggy face and narrow eyes and silently comprehended the man's mistrust.

"I'm a stranger," the guard explained. "A new recruit. There are a couple of us—new recruits—and no one knows us yet."

He remembered all that. And the heat, as they walked quickly through the north gate, following the river for a while. And the guard offering him some water from a leather bottle slung around his waist.

Bastard! He could still taste that water at the back of his throat.

• • •

While the man in the guard's uniform had been handing that water bottle to Yusuf, two genuine newly recruited members of the Bishop's Guard were frowning with worry as they received their first orders from the sergeant. "I think I know where we're supposed to wait for the physician to come by," said the taller of two. "But how do we recognize him, Sergeant? Shouldn't you send someone who knows what he looks like?"

"Well," said the sergeant, in gentle tones that should have warned them what was coming, "I agree that could be a problem. Someone will go with you to point out where you're to wait, but as for knowing Master Isaac, that's more difficult. After all, he is just a man, is he not? Like all men? There are a few little points of difference between him and other men, of course. He is uncommonly tall and broad in the shoulder. But there are many such, I agree. He is a physician, and wears the long tunic of his trade—but so do some others. He carries a tall, stout staff always." His voice began to rise to a crescendo of rage. "And lest you are still confused, remember that he is a Jew, and wears the cape, he has a brown beard, worn longer than most here, and he is blind. Every child in the city knows him. If you fools cannot pick him out from the rest of the citizens of Girona, then you had best go back where you came from." He paused. "Unfortunately, all the other men I have would be recognized instantly by the villains we are looking for. I am forced to use you two."

"Yes, sir."

"Do you know what to do when you see him?"

"Yes, sir."

"Then tell me. I want to make sure you understood it the first three times I explained it."

• • •

In the empty barn where Yusuf fought to stay awake in the loft, the men down below him took out a pair of dice. The rattle of the dice, the movements of their bodies, and their murmurs as the cubes hit and rolled over the floor created a pale wash of sound. If he was careful, he thought, it might cover the rustle of his movements through the dry hay. At least it would be better than lying still.

He crawled very slowly over to the biggest patch of light. It trickled in between two ill-fitting boards and was just wide enough for him to peer out. He saw a tiny slice of meadow and, in the distance, the rock and dark green of the mountains. From the color of the light, he judged that the sun was about to set.

"Six!" The cry was triumphant. "My throw again."

"No, you don't," said the other voice. "That made three."

"Yours. Halfpenny a throw." Rattle, throw, bounce, and then a gasp. Almost instantly, another rattle of the dice. Evidently, the game below was getting more and more engaging. Under the muted noise of his guards' excitement, Yusuf set out boldly to explore his surroundings further.

He soon found the entrance to his little prison. It was a trapdoor in the center of the room. He pried it up very slightly and peered around. There, leaning against the wall, far out of reach, someone had propped a long ladder.

At sunset, the two new members of the Bishop's Guard were down on one knee in a small plaza not far from the Master Vicens's gate, also throwing dice for halfpennies. They had collected a small crowd of admiring children. One of the guards had already piled up a stack of five or six coins when a tall man came by, carrying a stout staff and accompanied by a child. In spite of the warmth of the evening, his hood was up, partially concealing a beard, and he walked with speed and determination.

"There goes Master Isaac," said the smallest boy.

"Is it?" said another boy, without looking up. He found the game more absorbing than the passing of such a familiar figure.

"Look at that," said one of the guards. "Almost sunset. If we don't hurry, we'll be late."

"That we will," said the other. He winked at the children, tossed them his winnings, and the two strolled up the street.

They parted shortly after, one following the tall man and the boy toward the south gate to the city, and the other moving quickly down a narrow street where the sergeant waited with two more guards.

The guard following the tall man was a slow, ponderous fellow. Near the gate, his quarry stopped suddenly. Two steps later the guard stopped, too, narrowly avoiding a collision. The tall man said something to the boy, who scampered off. He watched the boy leave and then turned and headed purposefully through the gate. The guard looked from man to boy in an agony of indecision.

He was sorely tempted to follow the boy. There had been much talk in the barracks of the importance of this lad, and the glory—and gold—that might come to the guard who brought him safely to the Bishop. Then he thought of the sergeant's orders, which were to protect the physician above all else, and then of the gold, and of the sergeant again, and the gold once more, before deciding that following the physician was the safer course. Except that now the physician was so far ahead that he could not see him in the crowds out strolling by the river. But with relentless optimism he resumed his pursuit, trusting to luck to send him after the right man.

• • •

Isaac passed the slow, difficult minutes until it was time to leave the courtyard in listening to his wife and daughter attempt unsuccessfully to make conversation. At last Leah called down from the attics that the sun had dipped below the mountains.

Isaac sought the quiet of his study to say his prayers, and then sat, tranquil in its silence, for a quarter of an hour to clear his mind of distracting emotions and extraneous thoughts.

At last, accompanied by a figure wearing a threadbare and tattered brown cloak, he set out in the direction of Master Vicens's house. The warm evening had brought the citizens of Girona out into the flower-scented dusk, and everywhere around them they heard the murmur of conversation and bursts of laughter. "Not a very discreet moment to have a secret meeting, I think," said Isaac. "The streets seem full of people."

"They are," said his companion. "And a very good thing it is, too."

"Why do you say that?"

"Because, sir, I think this invitation may be a trick to lure you to Vicens's house."

"I know it is. That is why we are here," said the physician calmly as he climbed steadily up the street, his staff in his right hand and his left resting lightly on his companion's shoulder.

When they reached Master Vicens's gate, another cloaked figure, broad of shoulder and more than usually tall, who had been standing a few paces away, walked quickly up to them. "Master Isaac?" he asked.

"I am," said the physician.

"My master wishes me to say that he had not realized the warmth of the night would bring so many out into the streets."

"Then your master lacks a certain amount of ordinary good sense," said Isaac, in amused tones. "It is June. The nights are commonly pleasant."

"Well—he begs you meet him outside the city gates, in the fields by Sant Domenec."

"Where in the fields?"

"I will take you to him," he said.

"Excellent," said Isaac, in cheerful tones. "To the fields by Sant Domenec."

"Shh," said his guide. "You will disturb the household."

"Do they retire so early to their beds on a summer's night at Master Vicens's house?" remarked Isaac, without altering his voice. "Come, sir. Lead and we shall follow."

"Sir," whispered his companion, "I don't think we should go with this man. Not outside the city. What if—"

"Peace, child," said Isaac in normal tones. "The fields outside the gate are not the fabled deserts of the East. Many a man will be strolling out there as well. You cannot expect Master Vicens to conduct private business in the middle of the crowd outside his gate. How goes the night? Is it dark?"

"Not yet, sir. There is still light to the west."

"Good," said Isaac. "Come along, lad."

The heavy gates to the city had been closed and barred since sundown. When Isaac and his companion reached them, their guide had already negotiated his way out and the porter had finished locking the small inner door and hanging up the key. He was about to return to his principal preoccupation of the evening, which was a good-sized skin of wine. It was to celebrate the holy day, he explained, and offered to share it with them. He seemed puzzled by their refusal, and even more by their irrational desire to have him open the narrow pedestrian gate once more so that they could leave the city.

"It is too late, sirs," he said. "Much too late. You had best stay inside now."

"There is someone I must see," said Isaac, "who lives outside the gates."

The porter peered into his face. "Ah," he said. "I know who you are. You're the physician, aren't you? Someone ill, is there?" he asked. "That's different." As an earnest of his good intentions, he plucked his ring of keys from its nail.

"Not at all," said Isaac. "I go merely to enjoy the air."

"You'd pay money to breathe the air outside the gate?" said the porter, bemused. "It's all the same air, isn't it?" This exercise of logical thought required a little wine to lubricate it, and he hastened to apply the required remedy. He stared down at his keys.

"It is, indeed, porter. All the same air," said Isaac, jingling a handful of coins. "It's who happens to be breathing it with you that's important, isn't it?" he added.

"That it is, master," said the porter, now staring at the physician's hand.

"Open the door, good man," said Isaac's companion impatiently. "Our friends up ahead will be missing us."

"Oh," he said. "Indeed," and fumbled with the keys, trying first one, then the other. "There it is," he said, giving the stout boards a push. "Door's open, isn't it?"

Isaac pressed a coin into the porter's open hand, and then another. "For your holy day," he said.

The porter left the gate open to stare after them. "He must be drunk," he muttered, looking down at the money in his hand. "Drunken fool," he said aloud, wrapping his tongue around the words with difficulty. He shook his head, blinked, counted his coins, and tucked them with exaggerated care away in his purse.

His little fortune safe, the porter sat down, his head against the timber of the gate, and soothed by the breezes that came in through the open door, fell peacefully to sleep.

"*Hola*, Señor Mercury," Isaac called out. "Wait a moment."

"What?" said the guide, stopping his furious ascent of the steep hill and looking back.

"Where is the place appointed by Master Vicens for the meeting?"

"I am to escort you to the place, Master Isaac," said the guide. "He will bring you back."

"Yes, I know that," said Isaac. "Where is it?"

"It is still too early for the master to meet you safely. The sky is not yet dark. If you will follow me, I will take you to where you can wait in comfort." He turned and plunged on ahead of them.

"An unsatisfactory informant," whispered Isaac to his companion. "Do you recognize him?"

"It is hard to tell, sir. He is hooded and his face is in the shadow, but he does not seem familiar to me."

"Ah," said Isaac. "His voice is one I have heard before, but not recently. His name is Marc. A big man," he added, "with coarse features and a rough air."

"Then you have seen him? With your eyes?"

"Yes. Long ago, when I still had sight. It was one or two summers before the Black Death struck the city. He left after an unpleasant incident made it unwise for him to stay. I am surprised that he has dared to return."

"What was he? A guard?"

"A servant. To a rich family. A most useful servant," he added wryly. "Where is he now?"

"Higher up. Moving toward a stand of trees near the top of the slope."

"Is there anyone else about?"

"No one that I can see. Did you expect someone to be here?"

"I had hoped there might be," said Isaac.

Darkness invaded the courtyard of Isaac's house sooner than it enveloped the mountainous hillsides around the city. In the fading light of the courtyard Judith sat and thought. She had little taste for contemplation and her busy, well-organized life did not leave her much time for it. She was not one to waste time questioning what was right and what was wrong in this world, nor the wisdom of pursuing, unexamined, a path she had learned in childhood. But now, she felt, it was her clear responsibility to lay aside her work, ignore her husband's instructions, and think long and hard about what should be done next.

Leah and Naomi had finished their tasks for the day; they stood in the passageway in front of the kitchen and looked into the courtyard, observing their mistress with some alarm. She was sitting still, doing nothing. The twins, who should have been in bed by now, were playing over by the shrubbery, and she seemed not to have noticed their presence.

"You had best fetch the children in, Leah," said Naomi. "She's worried. And ask her if she wants anything. That'll wake her up."

But Judith just looked up at the housemaid and said, "Candles, Leah, of course. Or do you expect me to sit in the dark?"

And Leah scurried off for candles. When they were lit, and she had been chased away again, she sat on the courtyard bench closest to the kitchen with Naomi. There they could keep a close eye on their mistress and still while away the warm and pleasant night in soft-voiced gossip.

The candles had burned down some distance before

their mistress stirred again. "I need Ibrahim," she said suddenly.

Leah jumped up and ran off to fetch him.

Ibrahim returned, triumphant, with Daniel, whom he had found prowling restlessly about his uncle's house. "Mistress Judith, I came at once," said Daniel. "What has happened?"

"Nothing, yet," she said tartly. "Or if it has, no one has told me of it. I want to know what is going on, and I need you to find out for me."

On the steep slopes to the east of the city, the long summer dusk faded slowly to dark. The guide moved erratically over the rough meadowland; the path underfoot was becoming more and more difficult. Finally Isaac's companion stopped. "Sir, I can no longer see him."

"Why?" asked the physician with a touch of impatience.

"He's been darting back and forth, moving farther and farther ahead of us. And now he has disappeared into the dark. I don't know if he's hiding behind something, sir, or reached the stand of trees to our left."

Isaac listened to the faint noises of the night. "We, too, will head for the trees."

Armed with a lantern, flint, and steel, as well as the knowledge that his quest started at Vicens's house, Daniel walked rapidly up the curving street leading to Master Vicens's gate. Tucked under his belt was a purse well supplied with small coins, oil for reluctant tongues.

The street was no longer filled with neighbors enjoying the evening air. In their place he saw only four street urchins, playing a complicated game with sticks in the faint light.

"*Hola,*" he said. "Lads. Who wants to earn a half-penny?"

"What do I have to do?" said the biggest suspiciously.

"Tell me if you've seen my friend. I was supposed to meet him but I think I mistook the place."

"What does he look like?" asked one, fairer in hair and complexion than the rest.

"Who is he?" asked the biggest, with the confidence of one who knows everyone of importance.

"Master Isaac the physician."

"But what if we could all tell you?" said the fair-haired one. "Would he still get the money?"

"If you all know, then you'll all get some," said Daniel, jingling his purse.

"We saw him," said the fair-haired one.

"He was here," said the fourth, shyly determined to get in on the action.

"We was watching the Bishop's Guards playing at dice," said the smallest one.

"We were waiting for *his* sister, Ana," said the biggest, pointing at the smallest one. "For the longest time. Ana works in there and she brings him out things for his supper sometimes, and some for us if there's enough. We look out for him," he added, "because he's just a baby."

"He thought he saw Master Isaac," observed the shy one. "He doesn't know much. When he said it, the two guards went running off after the man he saw. But it wasn't Master Isaac."

"That's right," said the fair-haired one. "Master Isaac didn't come by for a long time."

"He came just before Ana brought us some bread," said the smallest one. "She said for everyone to wait because there'd be cheese and sausage. So we're waiting."

"So Master Isaac came by later," said Daniel. "Where'd he go?"

"Out the gate," said biggest one. "With this tall man who works over there now," he added, pointing up the street. "He's new. His name is Marc. And Master Isaac had someone with him, but it weren't Yusuf."

Judging that he had had his money's worth and more, he took four pennies out of his purse and handed them gravely around.

"It's a whole penny," said the biggest, awestruck. "Thank you, Master Daniel. And Master Daniel," he whispered, "they've closed the gates. No one can't get out. If you want out, you'd better go that way." Again he pointed up the street.

"Another penny if you'll show me," murmured Daniel.

The night was black as ink by the time Daniel had crawled through a carelessly blocked-off hole in the wall created by the construction of new and enlarged city defenses. His youthful guide set him on a path and assured him that Master Isaac and his lad had been heading up the steep incline over the meadowlands when he last had seen them.

The captain of the guard looked at his sergeant in disbelief. "What do you mean, you lost him? Is he a penny to be dropped in the straw? My God, man, he is a full-grown man of uncommon height and breadth. How could you lose him?"

"Not that way, Captain," said the sergeant. "I posted the only two men we had who would not be recognized as ours, sir, as you instructed."

"As we decided, Sergeant."

"Yes, sir. As we decided. And it might have been an excellent idea if they themselves hadn't been deceived by someone disguised as Master Isaac."

"What?"

"A tall man, with a staff, walked by them. A street

urchin said, 'There's Master Isaac,' and without looking
at the man, one of those two idiots set out after him.
The other fetched us and we went along, innocent as
babes. And, Captain, we followed our own guard out of
the city and down the Barcelona road, not realizing he
was wandering aimlessly, looking for a tall man. He'd
lost him at the gate," he said bitterly. "It shames me to
think that we were taken in by such an old trick."

"But surely the gatekeeper should have known the
physician hadn't come through," said the captain.

"You'd think so, Captain. We asked him, of course.
But he was so drunk he wouldn't have known his own
mother if he'd had to open up for her. We scoured the
fields west of the river until I was sure we'd been duped,
and then checked at the other gates."

"And?"

"Two of the gatekeepers told us who they had opened
up for, and who they remembered of those who passed
through before they locked up at sunset. The third—"
He paused. "The third is too drunk to make sense right
now."

"We'd better check the names we have," said the captain unhappily. "And then we'll have to take it to His
Excellency. He won't be pleased."

And pleased he wasn't. His roar could be heard throughout the palace. "Not only my physician, Captain," said
Berenguer, "but His Majesty's ward. They are both out
there, somewhere, in danger."

"Yes, Your Excellency."

"Then bring in the sergeant. We must decide what to do."

"Yes, Your Excellency," said the captain, and hastened to the door, beckoning for the sergeant.

"Will Master Isaac return to the city when he realizes
he has no escort?" asked the sergeant, coming directly
to the point.

"Who can say?" said the Bishop gloomily. "But I think he's too worried about the boy to come back."

"Then we must find out which gate they went out," said the captain.

"And if they are still in the city?" asked Berenguer.

"It's not likely, Your Excellency," said the sergeant. "First of all, the gates to the Jewish Quarter were opened for him when he left, and he has not returned through them. Second, I have men waiting here, here, and here," he said, pointing to a chart of the city. "He could not have turned back into the center without someone seeing him. I will admit that a man who has friends and knows the city could escape our vigilance, but Master Isaac is not trying to hide from us, Your Excellency."

"True," said Berenguer.

"He must be outside the city walls. As soon as we find out which gate he left by, we will know where to concentrate our search. Probably one of the south gates. But we're inquiring everywhere."

"Good. Then this is what I suggest," said the Bishop, bending over the chart.

Isaac and his companion walked side by side, picking their way, stumbling from time to time until they reached the trees, guided as much by Isaac's staff as by the other's eyes. "Is he trying to get us lost, sir?"

"I expect he is," said Isaac. "But I only worry about the unexpected. I think this is a good time to get out the lantern."

"Yes, sir. If you will stay where you are, I will find the flint and steel." Isaac's companion set a good-sized bundle on the ground, untied it, and stepped back to allow enough room to spread out its contents.

With an involuntary cry of shock, Isaac's companion stepped back from the earth and twigs and dried leaves of the forest floor into nothing.

TWENTY-TWO

Isaac's companion reached out desperately for a hand-hold, anything to stop her fall. Some leaves brushed against her hand, and she clutched at them, just as she landed on her back. The surface she was on sloped dangerously and she pulled hard on the frail branch in her hand to stop her downward momentum, teetered for a second, and came to a halt. She lay still, shivering with the suddenness of it all. It took her a moment or two to realize that the branch she was clinging to so fiercely had already broken loose from its parent.

"Raquel. My dear. Speak. Are you . . . ?" The voice from up above her was terrified, appalled.

"I'm fine, Papa," said Raquel, somewhat breathlessly. "Startled, that's all. Not hurt. I wasn't expecting to fall. But I don't know where I am," she added. And there was an edge of panic in her voice.

"Not far down, I hope," said her father. "Can you move? But be careful."

Raquel reached out her right arm until she touched

the surface she had tumbled down. It felt like earth, interspersed with rough vegetation and rock. Very cautiously, she rolled toward it, onto her stomach. She waited for a moment, then pulled her knees under her, and began to edge herself up onto her feet. "I'm standing up, Papa," she said at last. "But I'm not sure I can get back up to the top again." A rough lump in her throat cut off the rest of what she had intended to say.

"This is no time to be afraid. To find where you are," said her father, "follow the surface up with your hands. Can you reach the top?"

"I'll try," she said, and began feeling her way up. "Yes. With my fingers. A little high to climb without a foothold," she added with a shaky laugh. "If I had something to hold, I might be able to pull myself up."

"No. Don't try to do that. Just wait." He stopped speaking.

Waiting was difficult. Even perilous action was easier than standing, still and quiet, with her face against a surface of smooth rock, jagged stones, and loose earth. From time to time she heard what sounded like hands stirring dried leaves, as if someone were searching for a lost jewel. "Papa?" she said at last, unable to bear the silence any longer.

"Raquel, are you wearing a sash of some kind around your tunic?"

"Yes, Papa," she said. "Do you want it?"

"Yes. Please, my dear."

She untied it and held it up. "It's here, Papa."

"Good." Another scuffling sound, this one like an animal running through dry leaves, told her he was hard at work doing something. "Now," he said finally. "I have found something I hope you can stand on. I have tied your sash to it and will lower it to a spot next to your feet. Stand on it and it will bring you nearer to the top.

From there we can get you out. Place your hand up here again so I can find it. I need to know where you are."

Soon she felt the reassuring touch of her father's hand. "It's my right hand, Papa."

"I know that, my dear. Unless you have recently grown an extra thumb," he said dryly. "I am starting to lower this piece of tree trunk right now."

"Shall I help you?"

"I think not," he said. "Concentrate on staying where you are."

Raquel felt a rough object scrape against her arm and then her hip. It lurched its way downward, knocking against her leg, and then hitting her anklebone as it landed on the ground beside her.

"There," he said. "I will let go of the sash, and we will see how stable it is. Now."

The chunk of log paused for a brief moment by Raquel's feet, and then, as if invigorated by its little rest, it gave a lurch and went bouncing down the slope.

"It is as well we did that," said Isaac, in a shaken voice. "Wherever you are standing at the moment, the ground beside you to the right will be no help."

"Papa," said Raquel, with more determination and much less fear in her voice than she felt, "there is no difficulty. We need only be patient. We will wait until moonrise and then I will be able to see. I am sure there is some easy way up if I could only see it."

"There will be only a slender moon tonight, my dear," said her father. "Much hidden by all these trees, I suspect."

"Then we will wait for dawn. The nights are short; I can wait till then. Once it is daylight, there will be people to help us."

"Raquel, my dear, I think you will find it more difficult than you anticipate."

"No, Papa. I know how difficult it will be," she said. "But I can do it."

"Let me think about this," said her father.

The captain and the Bishop were seated in a reception room on the ground floor of the palace, flanked by the sergeant, Bernat, and a scribe, while a small group of lesser scribes recorded the information that was being hastily collected. The city had been closed off long since to lessen the difficulty and complications of a search. Everyone who was known to have left the city had been accounted for, one way or another. Those who lived outside had been hauled back inside, and were sitting about, grumbling.

"Have you managed to sober up the porter at the southeast gate?" snapped the captain.

"To some degree, Captain," said the sergeant cautiously. "Do you want to see him? I've already made an attempt to question him."

"What has he had to say?"

"First of all, Captain, that someone—and he's not sure who it was now—gave him a large skin of wine."

"Why?" asked the Bishop. "I mean, did he have a reason for his generosity?"

"No, Your Excellency, he didn't," said the sergeant. "The porter put it down to pure good fellowship," he added. "It was all in good fellowship."

"We'd better have him in."

"Your Excellency might prefer to go to him," suggested the sergeant tactfully. "Rather than have him up here in the palace."

"He's that bad, is he?" said Berenguer. "Then we shall go down to him."

• • •

Daniel angled up the hillside, moving slowly and feeling his way, and then stopped. Somewhere ahead he heard sounds of people—or one person—crashing through underbrush. With misgivings, he headed toward the darker mass of the woodland.

As difficult as traversing the rocky meadowland had been, the woods in that moonless night were infinitely worse. Small rocks seemed to rise up out of nowhere and catch him by the ankle; every second step his toes slid under a fallen branch and he came close to tripping. He must be making enough noise, he thought ruefully, to alert everyone within miles to his presence.

He stopped after a painful encounter with sharp rock, unhooked his lantern from the belt around his tunic, and set it on the ground in front of him. He slung the bundle he was carrying down and took out flint and steel. The lantern had just caught when a sound behind him made him turn. He rose, holding it high in front of him, and lighting up the coarsely rugged features of a big, broad-shouldered man.

"*Hola,*" he said, on the general principle that it was better to assume that this individual was not necessarily hostile.

The stranger raised his arm and took one fast stride toward him. In a fraction of a second, Daniel realized his peril, began to move, and caught a glimpse of a looming black shadow beside his assailant which seemed to be bearing down on them both.

At that, the world went dark.

In the silence of the night, the wood and the meadow were never still. Small things rustled in the dead leaves; in the distance light footsteps padded through the grasses, already dry enough to betray their passage. Suddenly a crashing noise echoed between the hills around them. It was followed by a whole series of subsequent crashes and the squeal of a terrified animal.

"Papa," said Raquel, her heart racing. "What was that?"

"Shh," said her father.

Her breath caught in her throat and she gasped convulsively, trying to control it.

"A rabbit caught by a fox, I would think," he said. "Dislodging a stone that fell down the hill."

"Nothing more than that?"

"Nothing to worry about. Things always sound louder at night."

"Papa," she said, after another endless silent interval. "Do you think you could find the lantern? It's in my bundle."

"I could try," he said. "Lighting it might be a greater problem."

"Oh."

"Are you frightened?"

"No, Papa," she said. "It's not that. But I think my foot is slipping backward. Could you look for the lantern?"

"I am trying to find it."

"Hurry, Papa," she said in a panicky voice. "Please."

"It is not where I can find it," said Isaac. She heard a slight thump. "Reach up your arm."

She stretched up her arm once more. This time the slight shift in body weight caused by the movement made the earth under her foot give with a tiny, sickening lurch. Then something struck her arm; she peered up for the first time and realized two things. Her eyes, now well accustomed to the blackness around her, could see objects in the less profound darkness above her, and one of those objects was the reassuring shape of her father's stout staff.

"Take hold of my staff," he said. "I am holding down the other end back here."

She grasped it—smooth, well handled, and so well known to her—and gave an involuntary sob of relief. "I have it."

"Does that help?"

"Yes, Papa," and realized that tears were trickling uncomfortably down her face, but she dared not change positions or let go of the staff long enough to wipe them away. Nor had she the strength and agility of a tumbler at the fair who might have been able to draw her body up to where her father was. Father and daughter seemed doomed to be frozen to this position until her arms—already tired—gave way.

The porter was lying on a heap of straw near the guards' station down in the episcopal prison. He was asleep, snoring, wet from repeated attempts to sober him up, and had been copiously sick. He was an unlovely sight.

"He's got rid of most of it," said a guard philosophically. "He should be easier to wake up this time. If I had known that Your Excellency was on your way, I would have started in on him again." And with the calm of someone who has done this before, he picked up a bucket of cold well water and trudged over to the already sodden porter.

"Wake up, you fool," he yelled, and dumped the water over his head.

It worked. "Quit that," said the porter, sitting up. He wiped his face with his hand and peered around him. "Give us something to drink, will you?"

The guard handed him a cup of water. "Here," he said.

"Water!" muttered the porter, after taking a mouthful and spitting it out again.

"Drink it, you drunken lout, and pull yourself together. His Excellency wants to talk to you."

"His Excellency! Dear God Almighty," said the porter.

"No," said Berenguer mildly. "Just the Bishop of Girona."

It took a great deal of time and much patience before they could get anything resembling a coherent answer from the porter. Finally he looked up. "The physician. I remember. He came through with his apprentice."

"When?"

He started to sing, grasped his head, and moaned.

"When, man," said the captain, "before I give you something extra to moan about. When did the physician come through?"

"I never did nothing."

"When did he come through?"

"After sunset. I opened the door to him and he gave me—" A sly look crossed his face. "He gave me a pretty thanks along with my fee."

"Are you sure that was his apprentice with him?" asked the captain.

"Who else?" he said. "Who else," he sang, "who else . . ." He fell sideways again into the straw and began to snore.

Yusuf's prison had been plunged in darkness for some time. He had occupied himself—whenever there was enough movement below to cover any noise he might make—in going over every inch of it. The men below had a candle; with the trap raised a sliver he had been able to judge the distance—far, but not impossible—to the floor where they were sitting. He had only to wait until they fell asleep, he thought optimistically, and he could drop down and flee.

And so he waited. From time to time, overcome with drowsiness, he slept lightly, waking again with a start at the slightest noise from below.

Suddenly the sound of a bell ringing filled the air, and he almost laughed. It was the abbey bell, he was sure, and that meant he was not far from home. Midnight, he thought. He must have slept through the bells for compline, because he remembered none at dusk.

As soon as the bell died down, he was aware of movement down below.

"You think he's alive?" said a voice.

"Not our problem," said the other. "We're supposed to make sure he stays up there, that's all."

"If you say so. You dropped your hood."

And somewhere down there a door opened and closed again with a crash.

Yusuf waited, almost without breathing, counting in his own language, and then in the language of the city, up to hundred. When he finished, he grasped the ring on the trapdoor and slowly pulled it up.

They had left the candle burning—foolish, thought Yusuf, with all this hay and straw—but it meant, no doubt, that someone was expected to replace them soon. He set down the trapdoor, grasped the edge of the opening, and dropped down until he was dangling a few feet above the floor.

Suddenly hands grasped him about the waist, very tightly. "Good evening, Yusuf," said a cultured voice. "You have saved me coming up to fetch you. I thank you."

TWENTY-THREE

Raquel listened to the midnight bells with despair. Her hopeless vigil had already lasted what seemed like an eternity—it would be even longer to moonrise, forever until dawn. She could not stand like this, her arm aching and her fingers cramped, for much longer. It would be easier to accept her doom and let go.

Then a completely unexpected sound from above her made her jump; a little more earth trickled away from beneath her feet.

"Mistress Raquel, is that you?" said a soft, gentle voice, male, but higher-pitched than her father's.

"Who's that?" asked Isaac. "Joaquim? Brother Joaquim? Are you there?"

"Aye. Joaquim. I heard you and came over. You'll not tell anyone I'm here?"

"No, Joaquim. I won't. That's your name, isn't it?" he added. "You're not a brother."

"Nay. I've no brothers nor no sisters neither," he said.

"And I don't live locked up in a big building. Is Mistress Raquel hurt?" he asked.

"She fell," said Isaac. "Down there. The ground gave way."

"How far?"

"Not far, Joaquim," said Raquel. "If you can see Papa's staff, I'm holding on to it."

"I'd pull her up," said Isaac, "but the ground isn't firm. As soon as I step close enough to the edge to reach her, it crumbles."

"Aye," said Joaquim. "But's she's just a small thing," he said. "She shouldn't be a problem. We'll have her up in a minute."

There was a agonizing pause. Joaquim did not accompany his actions with words and Raquel strained eyes and ears to no avail. Everything above her seemed to rustle, each in its different way: cloth, and dead leaves, and something else, perhaps the leaves on living saplings. She heard them all and they told her nothing. Up above, she could distinguish patches of starry sky from the leafy canopy, and various shades of black in the wood. But she still could not see her father or Joaquim. Her right arm ached painfully; the hand that clutched the staff was slippery with sweat. Very cautiously she tried to shift hands, but the sensation under her feet stopped her.

She knew now that she was going to fall.

Yusuf struggled long and hard before he was stilled, his arms pinned behind his back, by an adversary who held him facing away from him. "Now, Yusuf," said his opponent in a hoarse whisper, "you might wonder why I went to so much trouble to bring you here." He paused as if he expected Yusuf to answer him.

Yusuf let his muscles go slack for the time being, but kept silent.

"You see," his captor said at last in that same voice, "I know about you and Baptista."

"Me and Baptista?" said Yusuf, startled into speech.

"Don't talk—just listen." He continued to whisper, as if he thought eavesdroppers were hidden behind every bundle of hay, and under every swatch of straw. "Baptista told me, before—" He stopped, as if searching for the apt phrase. "Before he died," he went on, "that you knew where it was, that you and he were the only people who could find it. I've been watching you every minute of every day since then. Why didn't you go and get it for yourself, Yusuf?" His murmur turned almost plaintive. "He promised that he would take me there, up past Sant Domenec, where it is, but he was greedy, Yusuf. He was much too greedy."

"I have no idea—"

"Quiet," whispered his captor. "I'm calling my louts in. If you say a word in front of them, anything that tells them what is happening, I will slit your throat, Yusuf." He stamped one booted foot down and his spurs jangled harshly.

What could he possibly know that he was not to tell them? Yusuf thought desperately. That their master was a madman? If they did not know that already, they, too, were mad.

His captor stamped his boot again and growled, "You out there!"

Yusuf had a shrewd idea what "it" was, the "it" that he was to find, but why had this madman decided that he—Yusuf—knew the secrets of Baptista's heart? A man he had not spoken to more than two or three times in his life. Or was he supposed to lead him to the fifteen thousand *maravedís*? For a moment he was tempted to tell his captor that he was wrong, that he had the wrong person, to say, "I know nothing about Baptista but what everyone knows." He remained silent, partly out of stubborn pride, and partly because he feared this madman would kill him at once if he were to believe him.

The door opened and the two came in, muttering incoherent apologies.

Yusuf turned his head just enough to catch a look and stiffened in horror. Under a capacious hood, his captor was faceless. This was no madman. He had been trapped by a phantom with supernatural strength and nothing but blackness under his enveloping cloak.

He blinked, looked again, and began to breathe. Someone had picked up the candle, and in its light he saw eyes moving restlessly inside that hood and the swell of full lips surrounded by blackness that wrinkled and moved slightly. A mask. The man was wearing a loosely fitting black cloth mask. And, he told himself firmly, there would be strong arms and a stocky body under that cloak if he could rip it off.

"Tie his arms behind his back, and firmly," said his captor in a normal, very human voice. "We'll ride the rest of the way."

"What about us?"

"I won't need you. I have a man waiting at the other end."

"What is the state of things?" asked the captain, who was seated at the table in reception room at the palace once more.

"I've ordered those who were deployed outside the south gate to return here," said the sergeant. "As soon as they have their new orders, we will sweep the area to the east."

The door opened and both men rose to their feet. "Your Excellency," said the captain.

"I'm riding with you," said the Bishop.

"Very good, Your Excellency," said his captain, with a calculating glance at the Bishop. "The sergeant was giving me the latest report. As soon as the others arrive, we will start."

"The patrols have searched the built-up areas," said the sergeant. "They have found nothing of significance. And that's odd," he added, dropping into a more relaxed mode of speech. "The conditions are ideal for a search, Your Excellency. The warm evening brought many people outside who had nothing to do but notice their neighbors. Many of them know the physician and young Yusuf well enough to have recognized either one of them, even at night."

"Where does that leave us?" asked Berenguer.

"With the meadowland and the heights, Your Excellency," said the captain. "They thought it unlikely that they would find much up there and left it to the last."

"Then that is where they must be," said Berenguer.

"I would agree. Do we try to take them by surprise, Your Excellency?" asked the captain.

"And how do we conceal the presence of a troop of men, with horses, on a still night like this?" asked Berenguer, not expecting an answer. "It doesn't matter how slowly and cautiously we move, Captain."

"Very true, Your Excellency."

"I would be inclined to ride in there at speed," said Berenguer, "with torches blazing. Unless you can advance strong reasons for not doing so?"

"Strong reasons? No," he said. "We move in openly, then."

"But not until we are in place, Your Excellency," murmured the sergeant.

"We are agreed?" said Berenguer.

"Agreed," they all murmured.

Falling no longer felt like a desirable solution. Panic twisted Raquel's gut; her legs began to tremble. More earth slipped out from under her feet. To control herself she took a deep breath and tried to think rationally. How far was she going to fall? After all, she might have slipped off into a little gulley—a mere dip in the shoulder of the mountainous landscape. In that case she would already be close to the bottom, and they would laugh about it as her bruises faded. Or the blackness behind and beneath her might hide the river valley; in that case she was doomed. The valley's sides sheered off in precipitous slopes that would challenge the nimblest goat. She began to pray in a soft murmur.

"Now, mistress," said the soft country voice with its strange accent. "I'm lowering a rope to you. It's thick and it's got knots in it, like. Don't leave go that staff yet, but with your other hand feel the rope as it goes by, and when you come to the third knot, grasp it just above with both hands. Wrap your knees around the first knot and we'll pull you up. Hold on tight."

"I've got it," said Raquel. "The third knot."

"Hold it, and when you're ready, say 'now.' "

Raquel grasped the rope with her left hand, let go the staff, and reached for the rope with her right. As she did that, the ground beneath her gave way. She screamed, "Now!" and grabbed the rope with both hands. She fell back down the slope some six or ten inches before her weight took up the slack. The rest of her body dangled helplessly as she scrambled to clamp her knees on the end of the rope.

A shower of earth and pebbles rained down on her. The rope bit deep into the edge until it hit firm rock and then she was scraping and bouncing upward until suddenly she was lying flat on her stomach. She opened her eyes and could see, dimly, right in front of her, two pairs of boots.

"We'd best get away from here," said Joaquim. "Can you walk, mistress?"

"Of course I can walk," said Raquel, and grasping a warm and familiar hand, pulled herself to her feet. She gave an involuntary gasp.

"Are you all right?" asked her father. "Are you sure you can walk?"

"I think I have scrapes and bruises all over my body," she said, "but nothing is sprained or broken. I'm fine, Papa. Truly."

"Very well," said her father. "Then let us carry on."

Joaquim led them quickly out of the band of wood and back into the steep meadowland. In the open, the dark night seemed almost bright to Raquel. Stars carpeted the skies; the pale rocks seemed to catch the starlight and reflect its faint illumination over the hillside. "We'll sit here," he said. "That way we can see them coming."

"But, Joaquim," said Isaac. "Listen. We're looking for someone, not hiding. And he may be the same person you're running from. We must find him. He has my apprentice, Yusuf, and claims that he has the Grail as well."

"Aye," said Joaquim. "He has the boy. I know it."

"The Grail does not concern me," said Isaac, "but I must rescue my apprentice. That is very important."

"How do you know he has them, Joaquim?" asked Raquel softly.

"I have been watching him," he said calmly.

"He has killed already, Joaquim," said Isaac, despairing of ever communicating his sense of urgency to this strange young man. "I fear for Yusuf's life."

"The lad's still alive," said Joaquim. "Or he was when I saw him."

"You saw him, Joaquim?" asked Isaac softly. "When?"

"It was in daylight," he said. "I could do nothing. And he didn't have the cup with him, but he had the boy."

"So long ago?" murmured Isaac. "Lord—I have been arrogant and foolish—all that they have said of me and more."

"Papa, don't say that. You didn't know what would happen."

"Exactly," he said bitterly. "I should have. One moment's rational thought and I would have."

"No harm will come to him, not yet," said Joaquim. "We will wait here. He will come here and bring the boy."

"Why?"

"He has to come here, but perhaps not until after moonrise." He paused to look up the sky, slowly and carefully. "It is very beautiful," he said, still looking up. "As beautiful as my painting. He thinks the boy knows where the Grail is," he added, as if the two statements were part of the same thought.

"And does the boy?" asked Isaac, who would not have been surprised to hear that he did.

"No," said Joaquim. "But he will bring the boy with him. You'll see. Until he does, we must wait here."

Silence fell on the little party—a silence so complete that Raquel stretched out on the long grass and dozed for a moment or two. She awoke with a start and sat up again.

"How did you come to be in Girona dressed as a monk?" asked Isaac.

"I found a dead monk in the snow," said Joaquim with the literal simplicity that characterized his remarks. "The foxes had been at him and all. He was wearing a warm habit and a thick cloak," he added, "so I don't know why he should have died, but he did."

"And you changed clothes with him?"

"I made him a shroud of my cloak and my tunic—a proper shroud, like—and I buried him beneath a pile of stones with a piece of pine branch marking his grave. I took his clothes because I was cold."

"You were running away?"

"No. I was tracking someone."

"But how did you live?" asked Raquel. "In the mountains, in the snow and the cold? It was a terrible winter last year."

"I found a deer that fell—like you, mistress, only you

don't have horns to get caught in rocks. It was hanging there with a broken leg and so I killed it. I lived on its meat for weeks, and even traded some for bread. I was fine."

"Who were you tracking?" asked Raquel.

"I can't say, Mistress Raquel," said Joaquim miserably.

"Why not, Joaquim?" she asked.

"It's not our business," said Isaac. "You tracked him across the mountains and then here. Did you find him? And kill him?"

"No, Master Isaac. I've never killed a man in my life," he said simply. "Except—" He shivered. "Never mind."

"Did he know you were following him?" asked Raquel.

"Oh, no, mistress. I stayed away from paths and roads. Sometimes I traveled by day, like him, and then I followed him high up. Sometimes I traveled by night. It depended on the moon, and how difficult the way was. I never had any trouble until I got where there were too many people."

"What do you mean?" asked Raquel.

"Someone stole my boots," he said. "Off my feet. While I was sleeping."

"How did you know where to go?" said Raquel. "I mean, he could have gone to a lot of places, not just Girona."

"At home," said Joaquim, "he used to talk to me all the time. He was the only person who talked to me. Except Father Xavier, and the baker sometimes. He came to town one day with a pack full of things to sell, and stayed with my mother for a long time. We were friends," he said, and all the sorrow of friendship betrayed lay in his voice.

"You were friends," said Raquel.

"Aye, we were. He was a clever man. I didn't understand all he said, but still he talked to me. He told me over and over that it shouldn't be lying there hidden in that cupboard where no one even knew where it was but me and the sacristan and Father Xavier. He wanted to take it to Girona, where there was a beautiful cathedral, and put it in the cathedral. And then I found out he was going to sell it. So I knew that once he had it, he would go to Girona."

"Did you know where Girona was?" asked Raquel.

"I knew it was to the east. He told me that. So I traveled east. When I got to the road, then I asked people where it was. Everyone knew."

"Were you going to sell it?" asked Isaac.

"No, Master Isaac," said Joaquim doggedly, as if he had had this discussion a hundred times before. "It's not right to sell it. I wanted it to be in the beautiful cathedral, not in the cupboard, but it isn't happy being here."

"How do you know?"

"I know, just like I know where it is, near enough."

"Where is it now?" asked Raquel, desperate to keep the conversation—any conversation—going. She was cold, uncomfortable, and deathly tired, sitting here in the threatening dark and chatting with a madman.

"Close by," he said. "That's why I'm here. He used to keep it by him all the time, and I didn't know how I was going to get it from him."

"All this time it's been at his house?" said Raquel.

"Nay, mistress. The one I give it to, he didn't get here until long after I did. But I knew he would. I only had to wait for him."

"Baptista?" said Isaac.

"Aye, master," said Joaquim. "So you knew him, too? Were you waiting for him?"

"No," said Isaac. "But I knew him a little." There seemed no answer to that.

Once their low-voiced conversation ceased, the silence grew ominously. No one else was moving about on the slope. "Where is the guard?" asked Isaac.

"Who, Papa?" asked Raquel.

"There's no guard up here, Master Isaac," said Joaquim.

"Four guards," said Isaac, "were posted near Vicens's house. When we met that guide, they were to follow us at a discreet distance. Did you not see them?" he asked, turning toward Joaquim.

"Nay," said Joaquim. "And I would have. And if they were down there, I think we both would have heard them."

There seemed nothing more to say. The silence stretched out around them, broken from time to time only by the buzzing and chirping of insects and tiny, menacing sounds from the woods.

Joaquim was lying stretched out on the grassy slope, staring up at the sky, paying no attention to the stray noises or to his new companions. Suddenly, he sat up. "Look," he said softly.

The moon, already in its last quarter, was rising above the hills into the clear night sky.

"It seems so bright for such a tiny sliver of light," murmured Raquel.

Joaquim rose to his feet. He muttered something incoherent, and melted away into a patch of darkness—the faint shadow cast by a tree in the pallid moonlight.

"What did he say, Papa?" asked Raquel.

"I think he said, 'Here,' " said her father.

"He's disappeared," said Raquel. "He walked into a shadow and was gone. As if he'd never been."

"I'm sorry for that," said Isaac. "He has eyes like a hawk and ears like a wild deer. I was glad to have him with us, but he has his own concerns."

"He's not very clever, Papa," said Raquel.

"In his own way," murmured her father, "he is wiser than most men. Now—is the moon bright?"

"It seems bright," said Raquel. "But then the night felt very dark before."

"Then we, too, should disappear into the shadows," said Isaac. "And into silence."

TWENTY-FOUR

Yusuf was pinioned firmly and slung up across the front of his captor's saddle. He traveled for an incalculable distance in this uncomfortable and humiliating position, able to see nothing but the track beneath the horse and an occasional bridge. Mostly they avoided roads, scrambling through rock-strewn grassland and streambeds already dry from the summer heat. Twice the horse stumbled. Yusuf was convinced his neck would be broken long before they reached their destination.

At last the moon rose, and although the way was rougher, both horse and rider could see the ground beneath them more clearly. At a walking pace, they began a long climb up the side of a hill.

His captor finally dismounted, keeping one hand on the boy's back, pressing him against the horse. Then he grabbed him once more around the waist and pulled him down, setting him on his feet like a child. "This is where we begin to walk. There's not much moon," he said, "but it should give you enough light to see where you're going."

"Where am I going?" asked Yusuf.

"Don't try these childish jests on me, Yusuf. I am a very short-tempered man and I have a sharp knife in my hand." A painful jab behind the ear made him go very still.

"I am holding the rope that ties your wrists together. If you shout or call for help, it will be last noise you make. I will search for it myself. The wood is there," he said. "Up ahead of us. Now go."

And firmly trapped in someone else's nightmare, Yusuf started to walk toward the wood.

"I don't feel that we are very safe here," said Raquel, as firmly as she could without raising her voice.

"Out here, in the hills, do you mean?" asked her father. "Or just here, in the wood, where, I trust, it is darker than in the meadowlands?"

"In this wood, Papa," she said. "I cannot see far enough from where I am sitting to know if people are coming."

"But it is easier to hear someone walking through the woods than through the meadow," said Isaac. "And we are not as visible here as we were out there."

"But, Papa, what are we waiting for? Except for someone to find us?"

"If you are frightened, my dear, perhaps we should try to get you away from here. I, at least, must stay. Our only hope of finding Yusuf lies in my being here," said Isaac.

"I don't understand," said Raquel.

"No more do I," said Isaac. "Unless this is a story told by a madman. For some reason he wishes me to be here—he has gone to great trouble to get me to this place—and he has taken Yusuf. If he has not killed him—and I do not think he will—"

"Why not?"

"Because after His Majesty's visit, everyone in the city knows how valuable the boy is."

"Perhaps he hopes to ransom him, Papa," murmured Raquel.

"That is possible," said Isaac. "Or, for some reason that we do not know, to control me. I wish to find out which it is," he said. "I believe it will be easier to recover him if we know why he was taken," said Isaac. "But now I suggest we remain silent, before we attract Wild Marc's attention."

"Wild Marc?"

"The man who brought us here."

"Hasn't he left?" said Raquel in sudden fear.

"I have heard various footsteps in the wood," said Isaac. "Some I can account for; others not. But I have heard no one leave the wood, or go down the hill. And I think I would have. The night is still." He paused. "Listen," he murmured. "Someone is moving around out there— someone who is not concerned with keeping silent."

They sat for a long time without speaking until a long, low whistle broke the silence.

"What's that?" whispered Raquel.

"There's someone here," said Isaac. "Calling for reinforcements, I suspect."

It is surprisingly difficult to walk over rough ground on a dark night with your arms pinioned behind your back, decided Yusuf, concentrating hard on small things to avoid thinking of the larger ones. And somewhere off in the distance—ahead of him and to his left—there were people. He heard a murmur that was not from the occasional light breeze, and a faint scent drifted past his nostrils. He slowed down to listen.

The rope jerked his arms painfully and the point of the knife jabbed the side of his neck. "What are you doing?" whispered the man behind him.

Yusuf stopped completely and said the first thing that came into his head. "I think it's up ahead there," he said.

"You think?" he muttered, jerking the rope. "You'd better do more than just think."

"But, sir," said Yusuf, in his most plaintive voice, "things look different at night."

"So they do," he said very softly. "Go ahead."

"I must look carefully first."

"Don't take all night," he whispered.

But as hard as he strained his ears to listen, the boy could no longer hear the murmurs. Perhaps he had never heard them. Perhaps they were spirits sent to comfort him in his last hours. He shivered. Who else would be up here at this time of night? Except, of course, the confederates of this man behind him. "Not here," he muttered, and stumbled on ahead, through the dead leaves and pine needles of the wood.

The breeze sprang up again, and this time the trace was stronger. Mingled with strong scents of pine, and earth, and woodland animals, he could distinctly smell the scent of jasmine. Jasmine oil in glossy black hair. It must be Raquel and his master. He stopped again.

"Have you found it?"

"Just up there, sir. That's where it is."

And the man behind him whistled, a long, low whistle.

And then Yusuf realized that if he carried on in the same direction, he would bring this madman and his followers straight to his master and Raquel. If they were the ones he had heard. And what could they do against one of his strength? For he was strong, without a doubt.

"Where is it?" said the man behind him, grabbing his upper arm and giving it a shake. "Where?"

"Over there," he said, pointing away from the scent. "Beside that rock, sir. I remember it looked like that rock over there," he added, wondering how long he could stretch out this farce.

"Quiet," he said. "And go on. I'm not letting go of

you yet." He gave him a shove in the direction of the
rock. "Where is that fool?" he added, and whistled again.

For a second or two there was silence, except for faint
echoes of the second whistle. In the quiet of the night, it
had sounded shockingly loud. Even the insects and small
animals whose nocturnal activities provided a muted
backdrop to the quietest scene fell silent. Yusuf's captor
gave him a shake. "Go on," he said. "Find it. My man will
be here in a moment with a lantern and the shovel."

As soon as he heard those words, the strength ebbed
from Yusuf's limbs. He tried to walk on, to lead this
man away from the source of the comforting noise and
human scents, but stumbled in his panic and weakness.
"Somewhere around here, sir," he said, as loudly as he
dared, looked down, and gasped in astonishment.

His captor shoved Yusuf to one side with such ferocity
that he lost his footing and fell—heavily and painfully.

"What is this?" the man screamed. "Who has done
this to me?"

Daniel awoke in a state of confusion. His bed was hard
and uncommonly lumpy, and his head pounded and his
stomach heaved queasily as if he had drunk a full skin
of wine the evening before. Had he? He searched his
memory and found only vague shadows.

His hand was lying on his chest. He moved his fingers
and grasped the cloth of his tunic. He had gone to bed
fully dressed. Cautiously, he wiggled his foot. He had
also left his boots on. Reaching over to the edge of his
bed, he came up with a handful of pine needles and
twigs and memory trickled back. He had been in the
woods. He must have stumbled in the pitch-dark night,
fallen, and hit his head. He reached up to feel it and his
hand touched woolen cloth, thickly folded. Astonish-

ingly, he seemed to have landed with his head softly
pillowed on good wool.

He opened his eyes and blinked. Above him the
moon, reduced to a quarter of her splendor, scattered
light over the woods. The last time he had been con-
scious, the night had been dark—as dark as he had ever
known it. Then the vision of an upraised arm and a
coarse and angry face caught in the light of his lantern
flitted through his mind. He may have hit his head in a
fall; but first, someone else had hit it for him.

Very gingerly, he sat up and felt his head. There was a
distinctly sticky patch above his ear—a very tender sticky
patch. The movement worsened the pounding and the
queasiness; he stared fixedly at the ground to calm his
stomach. Dimly in the pale moonlight he could see his
lantern sitting close to his side, its flame extinguished,
flint and steel neatly arranged next to it. A tidy assassin,
he thought confusedly. And a compassionate one. He
picked up what looked to be a generously cut monk's hood
that had been folded as a cushion for his injured head.

He spent some time trying to hook the lantern on his
belt with clumsy fingers. That accomplished, he draped
the hood over his shoulders and pulled himself to his
feet on the trunk of a medium-sized sapling. He was
hanging on, swaying dizzily back and forth, when he
heard the first faint whistle.

He had not been able to bring himself to move before
the second whistle, with its peremptory tone, summoned
him again. He lurched toward the sound, grasped another
tree, and stopped. Perhaps he ought to rest for a moment,
he thought. Until his head was no longer whirling. He
crumpled down at the foot of tree and ceased to think.

The first whistle had been barely audible among the in-
evitable noise, controlled as it was, of the troops mus-

tering outside the gate. "What is that?" murmured Berenguer.

"Someone whistling, Your Excellency," said the captain.

"Are you sure it was a person? Not a bird or an animal?"

"I wouldn't think so. Sergeant? Did you hear that?"

"Someone whistling, Captain. Up on the heights."

The second whistle was louder, and less equivocal. "I hear it now," said the Bishop. "A man. Summoning his dogs?"

"Perhaps," said the captain. "Or his followers."

"What are we waiting for?" asked Berenguer impatiently.

"The last squad, Your Excellency. Ten men. Do you wish to proceed without them?"

"No," said Berenguer. "We have waited so long now, we might as well wait a few minutes longer for the rest."

Yusuf's captor stood motionless, staring down into a shallow hole in the floor of the wooded area, newly dug.

"Isaac! Thief! Charlatan! Where are you?" he shrieked, and flung himself onto his knees. Frantically, he began to scrape away the earth with his fingers.

On the far side of the clearing, Isaac turned to his daughter. "Do you see him?" he asked. "What is he doing?"

"Digging with his hands, like a dog after a bone," said Raquel.

"Who is he?"

"I cannot see," she said. "Where his face should be is a deep black shadow."

"A mask?"

"I think it might be."

Isaac rose to his feet, and feeling his way cautiously toward the sound of the voice, moved closer.

"You wished to speak to me?" he said.

TWENTY-FIVE

A t the sound of Yusuf's voice and the noise of his fall, a burst of fierce anger drove out Raquel's fear. When her father went straight forward—having firmly rejected her whispered offer to accompany him—she crawled in a wide circle toward the spot where she judged the boy to be.

"Yusuf?" she whispered.

"Over here," he whispered back.

She could just see a dark shape lying passively on the ground. She rose to her feet in a crouch, and moved crab-wise over to him. "What are you doing here?" she whispered, under the covering noise of her father's resonant voice. "Can you get up?"

"It's my arms," he said. "They're tied behind me. I can't move them. It's so hard to get up," he said, "and I'm tired."

"Let's see," she muttered, bending over him and peering closely. More by feel than sight, Raquel found the rope that encircled the boy's wrists and began the task of untying it.

"Hurry," he whispered.

"They were determined you wouldn't get free easily," said Raquel. "I'm doing my best." Finally, with a snort of exasperation, she opened her pocket and drew out her scissors. "I'll have to cut the rope as best I can with these," she said. "Let me know if I hit your skin."

"Wonderful," muttered Yusuf, with something of a return of his old spirit. "Go ahead. But carefully."

The masked man stopped in the midst of his frantic scraping at the earth and looked up at the physician towering above him. The waning moon was high in the southeast quadrant of the heavens, and in its light, Isaac looked to be gigantic in stature, like one of the biblical patriarchs carved in the stone of the cathedral. "What are you doing here?" he asked. "How did you find me?"

"You sent for me," said Isaac. "And I came. Your servant escorted me up here, and here I am. It is very simple."

"You mock me, physician," said the masked man. "Standing there, watching me, laughing."

"I cannot see. And I do not laugh. I have answered your summons—"

"How did you know it was my summons?" he asked suspiciously.

"Who else would be here to meet me? But I came at your request because I require the answers to two questions."

"What are they?"

"The first is to know why you sent for me. What is it that you want from me that is so important it brings us two out in the dark of the night?"

"I want to know where it is," he said, and scrambled to his feet. "That is all. Where is it? You know. Baptista told me that. He told me that he and your lad were the only ones who knew where it was hidden."

"Then why ask me?"

"He said that the lad always knew where it was—and he must have learned that from you—and then he said you could handle it safely. You knew what to do with it. Where have you put it? No one else could have taken it, Master Isaac. No one but you."

"You have been deceived, sir," said Isaac calmly. "Cheated, cozened, defrauded if you paid money for that information. I know nothing of it. Think. What would I know of it or of its powers?" he said, raising his hands. His staff cast a shadow over the ground to the side of him. "I cannot believe it has any powers, and if it does, I cannot believe that they would be destructive."

"You lie," screamed the masked man, and flung himself at the blind man, fastening his hands around his throat. Isaac threw down his staff and clawed at the hands that choked him. He managed to pry one finger off his skin. He yanked it back with sudden force.

His opponent screamed and stepped back, looking frantically down at the ground.

"Where is my apprentice?" said Isaac, feeling the ground with his foot for his staff.

The other saw his knife, scooped it up, and turned to face the physician again. "Somewhere down there on the ground," he answered coolly. "If you feel around long enough, I am sure you will find him."

The sound of shouting penetrated Daniel's slumbers. A flash of panic jolted him awake and he sat up. His head thumped sickeningly; he touched the stiffening sticky patch of hair and remembered. The thumping eased off, died away, and he rose to his feet. Slowly. This time the earth stayed stable beneath him and the forest remained firmly rooted where it was. He was still trying to remember who or what had wakened him so alarmingly, with no success, when he heard Master Isaac's voice saying, "You sent for me," in clear and ringing tones.

Moving slowly, from tree to tree, Daniel followed the trail offered by the voices until at last he caught a glimpse of the physician's face through the trees. A dark shape was standing between him and Raquel's father, a shape that screamed invectives in a high-pitched voice.

Under cover of the shouting, Daniel moved forward until he had a good view of the second man. The ache in his head was still there, but he no longer noticed it, except as a constant, if unimportant outside irritation— like rain, or a chill breeze. His mind felt extraordinarily alert and clear, and his legs felt strong under him. Automatically, he reached for his knife, and did not think it odd to discover that whoever had hit him on the head had not bothered to disarm him.

The man confronting Isaac reached down to pick up a long and wicked-looking dagger from the ground. Then, with a slight grunt signaling his move, he launched himself at the helpless physician.

Daniel yelled, " 'Ware!" headed for the attacker, and the whole world went mad at once around him.

Isaac heard the warning voice, ducked, and jumped backward. He felt something pull at his tunic and took another cautious step back. "Papa," said a voice at his elbow, "get back. Are you all right?"

"Yes," he said grimly.

"Come back," she insisted, dragging him behind some sheltering trees. "I've found Yusuf," she added. "He's fine. But, Papa—"

She was cut off by the sound of loud shouts and the thump of heavy feet.

"What is that noise?" asked the physician.

"Stay there," she said, and ran out of the trees. "It's

the guard, I think, Papa," she said, breathless from her run back. "Coming up the hill with torches blazing. But, Papa, Daniel is here. He's on the ground. I think he's having the worst of it in a fight with that man. He has a dagger." Her voice trembled as she spoke. "Give me your staff."

"No. You cannot handle it against an armed man. That sounds like horses scrambling up the hill," said Isaac.

Daniel was lacking neither in courage nor in basic skills, but he was lacking somewhat in practice when it came to knife fights. An experienced soldier might have protected himself more effectively in a similar state of confusion and weakness—for Daniel was much weaker and more confused than he could possibly believe. Blind rage was the force that drove him against his opponent. Heedless of danger, he closed in, slashing and stabbing recklessly, inflicting numerous cuts, only one of which— a stab wound in the upper arm—hampered his adversary.

That wound, even as it slowed down his adversary, was his own undoing. It bled profusely, and Daniel's hand, wet with blood and sweat, lost the tenacity of its grip. His opponent's knife caught his on the blade and bounced his weapon out of his hand. Daniel reached out to make a desperate grab for his opponent's knife hand. His opponent feinted, got past his hands, and drove his sharp blade straight at Daniel's belly.

Suddenly there was nothing in front of Daniel. His opponent, screaming curses, staggered back, and fell on the ground. With a whoop of triumph, Daniel scooped up his own knife from where it lay and bent over his foe.

Still swearing, his opponent grasped Daniel's bloody forearm and tried to pull him down on the ground with him.

• • •

The wood and the little clearing were ablaze with light. The captain looked down at the melee on the ground. The sergeant dismounted, drew his sword, and set its tip on the throat of the masked man. "Let Master Daniel go," he said.

Daniel rose to his feet rather uncertainly, stepped back, and crumpled to the ground.

"Get the physician," said the captain.

Raquel ran over, dragging her father behind her.

"Who is he?" asked the captain, pointing to the man the sergeant had under control at his feet.

"We'll have that mask off him in a moment, Captain."

"It's Master Sebastià," said Isaac, raising his head from Daniel's chest. "I knew it the moment I heard his voice. It took you gentlemen a while to keep your appointment," he added wryly.

"My apologies, Master Isaac," said the captain. "How is Master Daniel? It *is* Master Daniel, isn't it?"

"Apparently so," said Isaac. "I believe he is coming to his senses again."

"Master Isaac?" said Daniel. He struggled to a sitting position. "I think my head is better now."

"Lie down," said the physician, feeling Daniel's head. "Someone has given you a sound crack on the head."

"No need," said Daniel. "I am quite recovered," he added, and fell back in a swoon.

"Shall we join His Excellency as soon as Master Daniel can be moved?" asked the captain. "He awaits us at the foot of the hill."

"Certainly," said Isaac.

Daniel blinked to bring the world back into focus and looked wildly around him. Yusuf stood beside him, rubbing his painful wrists. Across from him he saw the physician. Behind him in the shadows was a person he did not recognize, a boy with a dirt-blackened face, wearing a rough tunic and hood. Otherwise he could see nothing but soldiers—members of the guard. "Where is Raquel?" he asked. "Master Isaac, what's happened to her?"

"I'm right here, Daniel," said the grubby-looking boy crossly. "You might say hello."

"Raquel?" he said, peering more closely. "But—"

"Clearly you are well disguised, my dear," said her father, "although I would have thought that with her hood down, you would know her."

"It's your face," he said. "All that dark stuff smeared over it. It changes your appearance greatly," he added apologetically.

"Dark stuff?" said Raquel, mystified. "How is your head?" she said in a worried voice.

"A little sore," he admitted, "but now that I see you are safe and well, I'm fine."

"If Master Daniel is well enough to shower flowery compliments upon my daughter," said Isaac, "he is well enough to be transported down the hill."

"Then let us proceed," said the captain.

"How did it happen?" asked Raquel as they were helping Daniel to his feet.

"Never mind that now," said Isaac. "We will examine everything when we have water, light, and clean cloths enough to deal with it. What I wish to know is how you came to be here."

"Mistress Judith sent me. She said I was to find out where you had gone, and then to follow you as closely as I could without being noticed, and to make sure that the guard didn't lose you. I didn't do a very good job," he said. "On any of those things—except that I did find out where you were going."

"And how did you do that?" asked the captain.

"I bribed some children to tell me," he said modestly. "They also showed me how to get out of the city without passing through the gates. It was useful to know, but perhaps tomorrow—"

"It shall be dealt with," said the captain. "And now, Yusuf. Your master must be delighted to have you back. His Excellency will be most pleased as well, and I am glad to see my pupil again."

"If I had been wearing my sword, Captain," said Yusuf, "they might have hesitated before trying to capture me."

"Perhaps," said the captain. "You must come back with us, if you are able to talk to us tonight. Well, Yusuf? Are you fit enough to describe what happened to you?"

"I am famished," said Yusuf.

"What brought you to this place?" asked Isaac as the guards dealt with Sebastià and prepared to depart.

"Someone whistled," said the sergeant.

"Who was that?" asked Daniel. "I heard it, too. That was what brought me."

"He did," said Yusuf, pointing to Sebastià, now pinioned and held securely by two of the guard. "He was whistling for his man—but he never came." He looked around, as if he expected to see him lurking in the trees. "I wonder where he is?"

"I would think that as soon as he saw how the land lay, he melted into the distance," said the sergeant. "I don't expect he'll stop walking until he reaches a town so far away that no one knows his name."

TWENTY-SIX

As the rescue party passed the gate of the *call*, the sergeant and one of his men escorted Raquel to the physician's house. Her mother, sick-hearted with anxiety, was waiting in the courtyard for news. Judith raised the lantern in her hand, allowing its light to fall on her daughter's face and tunic. She gasped. "What has happened to you, Raquel?"

"Nothing, Mama," she said. "We're all fine. We found Yusuf. This is just dirt. I'm well, Mama, and Daniel's head is—" She gulped, burst into tears and fell sobbing on her mother's shoulder.

"Good," said Judith, patting her on the shoulder. "I'm glad everyone is well. Come and have something hot to drink and we'll talk about it in the morning. Thank you, Sergeant," she added. "Can I get you something?"

"No, thank you, Mistress Judith. Unfortunately I am expected back at the palace right away."

"And my husband and the boy?"

"They will be here shortly," he said.

•   •   •

In spite of the sergeant's optimistic words, the rest of the participants in that long night were destined not to see their beds for some time yet. They were gathered together around a table in the episcopal palace, and by whatever magic governs kitchens like those of the Bishop of Girona, food—hot soup, cold meats, fruit, and bread—miraculously appeared in front of them, in spite of the hour. Yusuf, who had not eaten since midday, was doing justice to everything within his reach. Daniel, by now desperately tired and uncomfortable, was attempting to give a coherent account of the night as he had experienced it.

"I'm afraid," said Daniel as he came to the end of his story, "that it was only through sheer chance that I wasn't run through by Sebastià's dagger."

"Why do you say that, Master Daniel?" asked Bernat.

"I could almost feel the point on my skin when the man lost his footing. He gave a shriek and fell, dropping his knife."

"Not precisely chance," said Yusuf, his mouth full of bread. He swallowed. "It wasn't much," he added apologetically, "but I didn't have a weapon, and I couldn't think of anything else to do."

"What do you mean?" asked Daniel groggily.

"Well," said Yusuf, looking annoyed. "He seemed to be about to kill you, and he is too strong for me to wrestle to the ground bare-handed. I threw a fistful of dirt in his face and I think some of it went in his eyes."

"It was enough, Yusuf. I owe you my life," said Daniel.

"That being the case," said Berenguer, "we had better take care of it. Convey the young man to his bed with all care and diligence," he added with a wave of the hand, and turned back to his conference.

And while Daniel was being taken home on a litter to the careful attentions of his aunt Dolsa, and the scribes started to take down the testimony of the rest of the witnesses, Raquel was staring horror-struck into the glass by the light of a single candle at the dirt, tears, and sweat mingled on her face.

"I am not surprised," said Raquel to her only witness, the night, "that he didn't recognize me."

Meanwhile, in the scant light of the dying moon, Joaquim walked with long, confident strides, dividing his attention between the stars that guided him and the ground behind his feet.

Occasionally another human being crossed his path—someone who for reasons of his own was also out in the moonlight. None observed him. Only the creatures of the night saw him pass by, making little more noise than they did as he moved among them.

The Bishop was seated comfortably with his physician in a shady corner of the episcopal garden. "Sebastià," he said. "One would not have expected it of him. He seemed such a feeble man. Greedy enough, and not pleasant, but no cutthroat."

"I believe he was assisted by one of his old servants," said Isaac. "Does Your Excellency remember the man they used to call Wild Marc?"

"I do indeed," said Berenguer grimly. "It was a happy day for everyone when he fled the diocese."

"Unless I am badly mistaken, he came back," said Isaac, pausing while a servant brought them a pitcher of cool drinks. "And his strong arms were no doubt of great use to Master Sebastià. But for all his complaints and his poor digestion, Your Excellency, Sebastià himself is a very powerful man."

"Young Yusuf was quite indignant on that subject," said the Bishop, laughing. "He seemed to feel that it was ungentlemanly of him to be so strong. What puzzles me, my friend, is that someone like Sebastià should get caught up in such crude villainies."

"But Your Excellency knows that birth and breeding are no guarantees of virtue," said his physician. "Not that my suspicions were aroused. I, too, considered him a negligible figure," he added ruefully. "And, of all people, I should have thought of him immediately. A rich man, he complained constantly of how he suffered because of his poverty; one knew his avarice from the way in which he treated his unfortunate servants. Everyone else, in his opinion, had more than he did, and a happier life. But the man spent gold enough for what he wanted."

"He wasted a great deal on seers and astrologers—"

"And physicians, Your Excellency. Do not forget us. Although he would gladly have refused to pay our fees if he had thought it possible."

"You would refuse to visit a sick man who could not pay your fee?" asked the Bishop. "I had not thought that of you."

"If he is a poor man, or even one who has suffered recent reverses, I never worry about my fee. But a rich, miserly fellow like Sebastià? I fear, Your Excellency, that then I am likely to insist on receiving my just fee if he wishes me to visit again," said the physician, laughing.

"And so Sebastià always paid?"

"He did, Your Excellency," said the physician. "Not that I could hope to cure him. Sebastià suffers from an illness that is beyond my skill. He is tormented by lust— for women, for attention, for gold, for power. It is a terrible weakness. And suffering as he does, he believed

Baptista's claims that the cup would bring him untold riches. And he also believed those fearful threats about its deadly powers."

"Spread by one of my canons," said Berenguer. "With, he insists, the best intentions in the world."

"It must have annoyed Sebastià greatly that Baptista expected gold for the cup."

"Do you still think he alone lured Gualter to his death and stole his money? Had Baptista nothing to do with it?"

"I suspect so. Gualter was not a man to stay silent about anything that excited him. Once Sebastià heard that he was willing to pay a fortune for it, it seems likely he set a trap to catch him."

"With Wild Marc's help."

"No doubt, Your Excellency." Isaac paused. "After all, if they had been partners, Baptista would have expected Gualter's death and not rushed out to bury the cup. He knew that someone else had killed Gualter for the cup or the money. The night he died he was planning to leave town in fear of his life. But Sebastià found him first."

"But by that time, he no longer had the cup with him."

"From something Sebastià said, they had a conversation about that before he died—whether earlier the same day, or just before he killed him, I don't know. Sebastià became convinced that I knew where it was, and had the key to reining in its destructive powers. He believed Yusuf to be Baptista's confederate and assumed that the boy had confided what he knew to me, Your Excellency."

"Poor Yusuf," said Berenguer. "He is more interested in horses than magic, I think. But there are those who feel a Moorish lad would be likely to know such secrets. And so Sebastià planned another trap to get both of you up on that mountain."

"Where we would find him the cup," said Isaac.

"And teach him how to handle it safely," said the Bishop. "Then, I presume, you would have been neatly murdered by Marc," he added. "It is fortunate for you that the ruffian decided to take to his heels that night."

A discreet cough interrupted the Bishop's comments.

"Yes, Bernat," said Berenguer in the tones of a patient martyr.

"Your Excellency, may I intrude for a moment on your conversation?" said his secretary, walking briskly toward them under the trees.

"Certainly, Bernat. Why?"

"Sebastià's servant has been found."

"Good. Have him brought to the palace. I would like to ask him a few questions."

"I'm afraid that is no longer possible, Your Excellency," said his secretary. "He was found at the foot of a small cliff. It seems that he stumbled and fell in the night."

"Dead?" asked the Bishop.

"Dead, Your Excellency," said Bernat.

"It is no wonder, then, that he didn't come when Sebastià whistled for him," said the physician. "They told me it was a dark night," he added. "Is it known who he was?"

"He was recognized by the sergeant of the guard as one Marc, a troublesome lout who used to be a servant to Master Sebastià. He left the city some years ago."

"We did hear a loud scuffling sound last night," said Isaac. "Before the bells at midnight. Something fell. I took it for a fox attacking a rabbit, but it could have been a man tripping in the dark and then falling."

"Did the man scream as he fell?" asked the Bishop.

"No, he didn't, Your Excellency."

"That is odd," said Berenguer. "Few men fall silently to their deaths."

"Unless they are dead already, Your Excellency," said Bernat.

"True," said Isaac. "It is rare, isn't it?"

"He was injured on the very top of his head," observed Bernat. "The sergeant wondered if someone had hit him on the top of the head and then tumbled him down the hill. Anyone who did such a deed, in the sergeant's opinion, would be conferring a great benefit on mankind."

"It was not I, I'm afraid, Your Excellency," said Isaac lightly. "Nor Raquel."

"I would not have thought it of either of you," said Berenguer. "And Yusuf was too firmly bound. I saw the marks."

"He was, they tell me. I could feel the abrasions on his wrists this morning."

"And if Master Daniel hit him over the head," said Bernat, "and threw him off the hill, then who hit him on the head?"

"Daniel does seem to have spent a good part of the night on the hilltop knocked senseless," said Isaac.

"Perhaps someone else was up there with you, Master Isaac. Another person," observed the secretary. "Someone who—perhaps—saw Master Daniel being attacked and went to his rescue. Perhaps he hit the attacker over the head, and when he realized the man was dead, disposed of him in the easiest way possible."

"Is that the opinion of the good sergeant?" asked Berenguer.

"He offered it as a possibility," said Bernat. "That is all."

"There could have been another man," said Isaac. "I did hear several sets of footfalls."

"Would that be the man who made a cushion for Master Daniel's head? And rescued his lantern?" asked Berenguer.

No one answered.

"Someone dug that hole and took away whatever was in it," said Bernat.

"Very true, Father," said Isaac. "Someone did. Unless it was an animal. Animals do dig holes."

"That is possible," said the Bishop. "By the way, Master Isaac, how did you find yourself so close to that particular place in the wood?"

"Are you asking if we were led there by some mysterious stranger? No, indeed, Your Excellency," said the physician, and laughed.

"I am quite sure there is a simple explanation, Bernat, if only we knew it. And now I must write to His Majesty," said Berenguer briskly. "Although, the Lord knows well enough, I have no desire to do so."

"Will His Majesty be angry, Your Excellency?" asked Isaac.

"Yes," said the Bishop cheerfully. "Either we must convince the boy to be warier, or equip him with the means of self-defense. Perhaps he needs a guard," he mused.

"He would lead a guard a merry chase, I think," said his secretary.

"You are without a doubt correct, Bernat," said Berenguer. "It's depressing how often you are. But until I am ready to write that letter, you may leave us. We still have much to gossip about."

"Your Excellency sounds remarkably undisturbed by the situation," said Isaac.

"I am, Master Isaac," he said. "And as you pointed out, it is remarkable. I slept soundly for what remained of the night, and arose feeling well. I firmly believe it is because the wretched cup, with all its problems, has disappeared. It has gone somewhere else, away from my diocese, to torment someone else."

"I imagine it is a good distance away by now," said Isaac. "As is its keeper."

"Its keeper?" said Berenguer. "Ah—you refer to Joaquim. I suppose he does feel he is its keeper. He is an odd man in many ways. Did you know he was afraid of the moon?"

"Was he?"

"The first time he left the abbey without permission, he told the brothers who had been sent to fetch him that he was happy to see them, because he was hungry, and was afraid of being out in the full moon. I thought it odd for a lad from the mountains to be afraid of the moon."

"I suspect that men have been unkind to him," said Isaac. "He might prefer to travel under the cloak of dark, when the moon is not full. No doubt for him the night sky is filled with signposts and milestones, and I can assure you that he seems able to see the villains of the night before they see them. He is a very innocent man, Your Excellency. The very soul of innocence."

"Innocent, Master Isaac? Too innocent to kill a man?"

Isaac stopped to consider that question. "Yes," he said at last. "Unless it were to protect another."

"The sergeant is a very experienced and wise officer," said Berenguer at last. "Young Daniel is a good man, and Wild Marc was not. If one had to choose between them . . ."

"And the Lord spared us, Your Excellency, from having to make the choice," said Isaac.

"It suits us ill to judge those whose lot it was to choose," said Berenguer. "For which I give Him my thanks." The Bishop paused, as if in thought. "If I send for the board, will you join me in a game of chess?"

"It would give me great pleasure, Your Excellency."

• • •

And in Isaac's courtyard, Raquel also wondered about the events of the night as she gently applied salve to Yusuf's wrists and bound them up in soft cloths. "It was a fortunate thing that you chanced to be so close to us last night," she said.

"I did my best to lead Master Sebastià close enough to where you were that you could see us," he said. "Or hear us."

"How did you know where we were?" asked Raquel. "We tried to be as quiet as possible. Or at least, Papa succeeded and I was trying."

"I heard nothing," said Yusuf, "but a faint murmur that could have been voices. It was not that. I smelled your hair. The jasmine in your hair."

"I'm not the only woman to wear jasmine, you know," she said. "What if it had been someone else?" Her voice died away.

"I would have gone away," he said. "But I had to take him somewhere. He seemed to think I knew where to go."

During the same morning, a contingent of guards arrived to search Master Sebastià's house. The servants, who had decided on first hearing the news of their master's capture that their best interests lay in casting aside any tattered remnants of loyalty to him they might have had, joined in with enthusiasm. The cook and the kitchen maid whispered of a locked room hidden in the eaves—a room so well locked that over the years none of the housekeeper's keys had ever given them a way into it, no matter how often they had tried them.

Snatching the opportunity to gain fame and even fortune, the little kitchen maid took a firm hold of the sleeve of the best looking of the guards and dragged him—followed by everyone else in the house—up to the attics to show him. Behind a tapestry, in a narrow space between the eaves and a broad chimney, someone had recently built a wall. In it there was a stout, low, firmly locked door.

It took the sergeant, armed with Master Sebastià's keys, a few moments to open the door. And there, in that dark, cramped space, they found what the whole city had been searching for since Master Gualter's death. Along with chests containing money amassed from Sebastià's own business ventures, there sat two more, sturdy and very heavy, bound with thick bands of metal, and securely locked. Inside them were fifteen thousand *maravedís* of gold, neatly stored in leather bags of five hundred each.

Master Astruch was quietly delighted to receive his money back—all five thousand *maravedís*.

As was Gualter's widow. And instead of closing herself and her ten thousand *maravedís* away in a convent, Mistress Sibilla, thirty-six, still handsome and as clever as always, suddenly became an object of intense interest to a number of widowers and bachelors of various ages. For not only were the family fortunes once more intact, including a substantial sum that would remain in her own hands, but rumors flew about the city that when the estate of Master Sebastià—confiscated on his sudden death at the hands of the public executioner—was settled, the crown would cede a portion of it to the aggrieved woman he had caused to be widowed.

And so Mistress Sibilla, judging her son to be too young and flighty for such responsibility, took on the task of managing Gualter's business. In her unoccupied hours, she amused herself, infuriated her son, and lightened the sorrows of widowhood for a few months by toying catlike with a sucession of suitors, until finally

chosing a hardworking clerk of thirty whom she had
been observing closely at the warehouse. Not only was
he shy, sweet-tempered, and handsome, but he knew a
great deal more than her late husband had about leather.

Long before that momentous event, however, on the
Sunday afternoon after Daniel's ordeal on the mountain,
Raquel and Miriam carried a pot of delicate soup and a
plate of little cakes for the invalid to the glover's house.
As soon as the maid opened the door for them, Mistress
Dolsa rushed up, drowning out their expressions of regard and queries over Daniel's health with a loud torrent
of expressions of gratitude and praise for their neigh-
borly offerings.

"Is all well?" asked Raquel with some concern, as
soon as Mistress Dolsa paused to draw breath.

In the brief pause that ensued a cascade of silvery
laughter—very familiar silvery laughter—issued forth
from the courtyard. Raquel froze in the act of entering
the house. Miriam jostled her elbow in an attempt to get
by and get rid of the plate she was holding and was
sharply chided for her pains. Raquel stepped forward,
smiled at Mistress Dolsa, and thrust the pot of soup at
the maid so abruptly that it splashed onto the unhappy
creature's clean apron.

"We have other errands to run for Mama," said Raquel, lying sweetly. "We will just say hello to Daniel
and wish him well, won't we, Miriam? But I'm afraid
we cannot stay."

"He's in the courtyard," said Dolsa.

"So I thought," said Raquel.

"But, Raquel," protested Miriam, who had come along
because she had expected at least one of the little cakes
on the carefully covered plate she was carrying. "You
said—"

Raquel dropped a sisterly hand on her shoulder and gave it a fierce pinch.

"Ouch!" muttered the twin, and subsided into silence.

Raquel swept into the courtyard, her skirts whirling from her speed, into a galling, but decorous scene. Mistress Laura, accompanied by her mother's very superior-looking maid, was sitting a good two paces away from the couch where Daniel was resting. She was placed so that he would have an excellent view of her and her gown of rose-colored silk, with its surcoat of darker rose embroidered fancifully with silver thread. Under her scanty veil, her pale hair tumbled in curls over her shoulders.

Laura noticed the visitor first. "Mistress Raquel," she cried, as if the entrance of the physician's daughter was the only event she required to turn the day into a jewel of perfection.

"Mistress Raquel," said Daniel coolly. "It is kind of you to visit. May I offer you something?"

Raquel curtsied to Laura; she turned to Daniel, dropping another slight curtsy. "We won't be able to intrude upon your pleasant afternoon for more than a moment, I'm afraid," she said. "We have several more calls to make. I hope you are feeling better, Master Daniel?"

"Much better," said Daniel. "My friends have been very attentive these last few days. As has your kind father."

"I'm so glad," said Raquel. "And I bid you good evening. Come along, Miriam," she snapped, and turned on her heel. Out of the corner of her eye she saw a look of glee flash across the placid, perfect features of Mistress Laura.

"Raquel!" called Daniel as she stepped into the cool darkness of the hall.

"Wait, Raquel," said Miriam, grabbing her surcoat and pulling. "Daniel wants to talk to us."

"I don't want to talk to Daniel, Miriam. Let go of me and come here." She whipped around to reach for her little sister's hand and there was an ominous sound of cloth parting company from thread. "Now look what you've done," said Raquel, tears of anger and frustration welling up in her eyes. The surcoat that went with her best summer gown was torn apart at the right shoulder. "That was all I needed right now," she said.

"What was all you needed?" asked Miriam nervously.

"You, you wretched child. Now everything's ruined," said her sister.

A wail arose from the unhappy child, almost drowning out the voice from the courtyard. "Raquel, wait."

She looked up and saw Daniel. He had crossed the courtyard after her, and was leaning on one of the pillars that supported the floor above. His face was dead white.

"Daniel!" she said, and forgetting the ruin of her clothing, ran over to him, grasped him around the waist, and placed his hand firmly on her shoulder. "Lean on me," she said, and walked him slowly over to a chair in the hall.

"Stop crying, Miriam, and find Mistress Dolsa or one of the servants. Ask for cool water or mint tisane for Daniel. Quickly." She knelt on the flagstones of the hall floor and chafed his icy hands. "What happened?"

"My foolishness," he said weakly. "Nothing else. Don't concern yourself."

"Tell me what happened, Daniel," said Raquel, "or *I'll* hit you on the head this time."

He attempted a smile. "I called you and you paid no attention. Laura started going on about something—the color of your gown, I think—and I realized that by the time she finished, you would be gone. And so I jumped up a little too quickly—"

"What has happened?" Daniel's aunt came hastily in from the kitchen, following by a maid carrying a jug. "Miriam—"

"You should be lying down," said Raquel. "Mistress Dolsa—Daniel gallantly but foolishly rose to his feet to bid us farewell and had a dizzy attack. He should lie down somewhere quiet and cool until he recovers a little."

"Certainly. I'll put him in my sitting room."

"I believe he still has visitors in the courtyard," added Raquel casually.

"I'll soon get rid of them," said Mistress Dolsa.

And in a moment Daniel was lying on a comfortable couch in his aunt's sitting room and Raquel was seated on a low stool near his head. She had sent the servants for cloths and cold water to bathe his aching forehead, and a cup to drink from. Miriam, with a cake in her hand, had followed Mistress Dolsa, intensely curious to find out how one got rid of visitors. Unfortunately for her, it took a long time and was accomplished much more politely than she had hoped for. She was disappointed.

Daniel looked around. "A fine family I have," he said. "At the first sign of weakness, they've all abandoned me."

Raquel's cheeks reddened. "Shall I ring for a servant?"

"Certainly not," said Daniel. "Why would I need a servant?"

"I'm sorry if I ruined your afternoon, Daniel," said Raquel stiffly.

"For heaven's sake, Raquel, stop talking like that. I can't bear it," he said, in sudden anger. "Where have you been? I've been going mad in here. I'm told to rest quietly until my head is better and the whole world has tramped through the house—everyone except you."

"Why should I—"

"Why? I've been lying here thinking you were sick, or injured, or worse, and no one wanted to tell me what was wrong."

"Are you finished?" asked Raquel.

"No—I'm not finished," said Daniel. "Why wouldn't you visit me?"

"Do I owe you a visit?"

"Only as a friend," he said. "We are friends, aren't we? And you know how I feel about you."

"Do I? You have an odd way of showing it," said Raquel.

"That is truly unjust," said Daniel. "How—"

"Every time I've seen you for weeks now you've been hanging over that creature out there, while she smiles, and giggles, and simpers, and tells you how handsome you are—"

"No," he said, a sudden grin spreading across his face. "She's never done that. Did she tell you how handsome I am?" Raquel could feel her cheeks growing hotter. "I can tell she did," he said, with satisfaction. "And I hope you paid good attention to it."

"I can't imagine paying attention to anything she says," said Raquel loftily.

"Well," said Daniel, "she succeeded in making you jealous, at any rate, and that's probably more use to the world than she's been for a while. Why won't you marry me, Raquel?" he said.

"I thought you were going to marry Mistress Laura," said Raquel.

"What? Marry her? Leave my family? Become a *converso*? Just to follow her into a miserable little business in the cloth trade?" Then a fleeting grin touched his lips. "Of course," he said, "if her father were truly wealthy and in a more interesting line of business, one might be able to endure her empty head and endless conversation—"

"Daniel, that's disgusting."

"Raquel," he said seriously, "you know I'm teasing you. But I do want to know why you won't marry me. Tell me and I'll stop bothering you. But I can't stand living halfway between your yes and your no."

"Why haven't I married you? I don't know," said Raquel. "Probably because you haven't asked me yet, and I'd be too embarrassed to ask you."

And when the servant finally arrived with the cold water and cloths, he looked in the sitting room and decided they were no longer required. He set them down on a table outside the room and returned to his other tasks.

"It was Mistress Laura's honey-colored curls that made you change your mind, wasn't it, Raquel?" asked Daniel, a little later.

"She may have reminded me that there were sharp-toothed hunters out there waiting to snatch you up—and everyone knows how foolish a man can be at times."

"And a woman," he said. "I challenge your assumption that men have a natural right to all the foolishness in the world. But I'm sure I've asked you to marry me. You've simply forgotten."

"I don't think so," said Raquel demurely. "You talked about it, but you never stated it simply and clearly. You still haven't."

"You've spent too much time in the study of logic, Raquel. But since you make the request, I obey. Raquel, daughter of Isaac, will you do me the honor of becoming my wife?" he said, clearly and loudly, to the amazement of his aunt Dolsa, who at that moment walked into the room.

She stared at the two of them, and finally said, in an odd tone of voice, "Your gown, Raquel. It seems to be—" Words failed her.

In the time between sunset and darkness, when it is too dark to see, yet too light to wish for a candle, Isaac and Judith sat in the courtyard, finally alone.

"Are you pleased with Raquel's betrothal, Isaac?" asked Judith.

"I think it more important to ask if Raquel is pleased," said her father.

"She is," said Judith. "She looks happy. More than that, she looks excited, like Miriam when something nice happens. She was growing too serious, Isaac. The world's cares seemed to have settled on her shoulders."

"What does he look like?" asked Isaac. "I've wondered that for some time."

"He's handsome. Like you, Isaac. Almost as tall as you, and strong looking. With a smile to catch anyone's eye. If looks mean anything, our Raquel is likely to be burdened with many children." She laughed. "Not that I know. I haven't investigated him *that* well," she said.

"I hope not," said her husband, encircling her waist with his arm. "That would carry the task of a careful mother too far for my taste. But if their children resemble their grandmother, they will be as strong as lions and as beautiful as the greatest queens of the world."

"Much more of this, Isaac," said Judith playfully, "and you will be in danger of having a child and a grandchild to dandle on your knee together."

EPILOGUE

Joaquim's long strides carried him farther and farther from the city of Girona. He followed the road north to Figueres and somewhat beyond as rapidly as possible, and then struck out to the west through the mountains. He was not returning home, as pleasant as that sometimes seemed to him, nor was he seeking any other village. If you had asked him where he was going, he would have looked confused and said that he would know when he arrived.

No one bothered him. Under cover of dusk and dark, he passed through villages and by other solitary walkers like a wind, disruptive but invisible. Only birds and beasts seemed able to see him, and perhaps, the spirits of the air. Those who watched through the night felt his passage, opened their shutters, and looked out, but saw nothing; those who slept stirred and turned over uneasily. When he stopped to rest, the hardy, suspicious people of the mountains gave him food and drink. They recognized him as one of theirs, but they were troubled

by his presence and glad to send him on his way with
an extra loaf or a piece of dried meat to sustain him.

He settled somewhere, for his troubling presence was
no longer felt in the mountains, nor were his bones
found anywhere along the route he followed.

In the years that followed the summer of 1354, men did
speak from time to time of a holy man who lived in a
small hut built into the mouth of a cave. This hermit's
dwelling was happily situated on the edge of a sunny
meadow where a few goats grazed, protected from the
howling winds that come down from the north in winter.
They said that if you could find him, and if you were a
genuine penitent, a visit to the hermit's dwelling place
would bring you grace, and perhaps even health. Those
who came to receive his blessing always left a small gift
of food—a loaf, perhaps, or a handful of grain. He
would accept nothing more.

Someone who claimed to have been to the mountain
fastness said that when he had asked him who and what
he was, the hermit replied that his name was Joaquim,
and that he was a guardian. But more than that he could
or would not say.

HISTORICAL NOTE

Few religious symbols have captured the imagination of the Western world as completely as the Holy Grail, the cup from which Christ and His disciples drank at the Last Supper—their last Passover together.

Among the many places whose people believe they guard the Holy Grail, the claim that it has been and still is in the Iberian peninsula has one of the strongest traditions behind it. According to various accounts, the Grail, a simple cup, was brought there long ago. When the Islamic invasions, which began early in the eighth century along the southeastern coasts of Spain, raised fears for the safety of the holy relic, it was moved farther north, to Huesca, in Aragon.

The battle for control of the peninsula continued for several centuries, moving northward into the Pyrenness before the tide turned in favor of the Christians. Huesca became vulnerable, and the Grail was transferred with great secrecy to the monastery of San Juan de la Peña, in the mountains northwest of Huesca. At San Juan, it was well protected both by its keepers and by its rugged surroundings.

There it stayed, in safety, until the reign of Martin, second son of Pedro IV, and King of Aragon from 1395 to 1410. He had the Grail conveyed to Barcelona and kept there until it could be transferred to the fortified Chapel of the Holy Chalice in the cathedral in Valencia, where it remains to this very day. This chapel had been constructed by order of the Archbishop of Valencia, Vidal de Blanes, who had been abbot of Sant Feliu, just outside the city of Girona, during Bishop Berenguer's time.

During this long period of time, various elaborate and costly additions, as suited the status of the Grail, were added to the simple original.

Among claims and counterclaims, it is not a simple matter to sort out the truth. But legends and tales about the Grail usually place it in a stronghold surrounded by inaccessible mountains; the wall painting, originally in the sanctuary of the church of San Clement in Taüll, high in the Pyrenees, strongly suggests that the Grail was an object of particular veneration during the high Middle Ages in those same mountainous areas. The painting— a work of great skill, delicacy, and force—depicts the Virgin, holding in her cloaked hand a simple cup. Tongues of fire shoot upward from its surface.

The original painting is no longer in the little church. It was rescued from the art thieves who early in this century carefully removed it, piece by piece, for eventual sale in the United States. The wall painting was restored to its original magnificence and now resides in the Museu Nacional d'Art de Catalunya in Barcelona. A faithful replica has been placed in the church of San Clement.

Although, in 1353, the claim of the monastery of San Juan de la Peña to gaurd the true Grail was undoubtedly the strongest, the belief that the holy cup was safely hidden near them seems to have existed in some of the rugged small communities high in the mountains of northeastern Spain. It seems to have been this area that poets had in mind when telling brave tales of noble and virtuous knights, dedicated to knightly ideals and the quest for the Holy Grail. The thought that such men might exist somewhere was no doubt a welcome contrast to reality. At the time, knights—unemployed fighting men, without lords to control them—roamed the countryside raping, pillaging, and committing other acts of random violence. The noble knights of poetry, such as Parsifal and Galahad, on the other hand, sought, found, and even were allowed to become guardians of the Holy Grail itself, a vessel whose holy fire dazzled those who saw it.

About the Author

LUANNE RICE is the author of twenty-five novels, most recently *Last Kiss, What Matters Most, The Edge of Winter, Sandcastles, Summer of Roses, Summer's Child, Silver Bells,* and *Beach Girls.* She lives in New York City and Old Lyme, Connecticut.

Visit the author's website at www.luanne rice.com.

THE GEOMETRY OF SISTERS
BY
LUANNE RICE

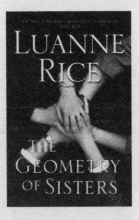

What is one sister without the other?
Is it even possible to imagine?

New York Times bestselling author Luanne Rice
explores the complex emotional equations of
love and loyalty that hold together three pairs
of remarkable sisters. Here in the halls of
Newport Academy, a unique private school
that has attracted generations of rebels, outcasts,
and visionaries, an unforgettable lesson in the
eternal truths of sisterhood is about to begin....